NEXT STOP LOVE

Rachel Stockbridge

♥

This is a work of fiction. All of the characters, organizations, publications, and events portrayed in this novel are either products of the author's imagination or are used fictitiously.

www.rachelstockbridge.com

ISBN (paperback): 978-1-7352494-0-7
ISBN (ebook): 978-1-7352494-1-4

For information on bulk purchases for educational, business, or promotional use, please contact your local bookseller or write to hello@rachelstockbridge.com.

First Edition: September 2020

In loving memory of Doug;
furry writing buddy, purr machine,
and sweetest damn cat in the world.

And for my mom,
who always believed I could do this
"writing" thing, even when I didn't.

NEXT
STOP
LOVE

ONE

The moment Julian stepped off the subway, the low-level nerves that had been plaguing him all day ratcheted up into something much closer to panic.

It was mid-afternoon, and the platform was bustling with the standard combination of tourists, shoppers, and students. Somewhere, a violinist was busking, the high melody competing for auditory space with the screech of brakes and the wash of overlapping conversations and footsteps. The familiarity of it should have made Julian feel more grounded, but the crush of people and the unceasing noise made his stomach clench.

He shouldn't have come back. New York City had never felt like home to him. He'd never quite gotten used to the inescapable packed-in feeling of living in a sardine tin.

And New York didn't seem to care much for Julian, either.

Someone jostled Julian from behind, and he shot the guy a glare, his shoulders tensing.

He still wasn't entirely sure why he'd come all the way down here today. Desperation, probably. Desperation and one final, stubborn seed of hope that refused to fucking die.

Blowing out a breath, he jerked the hood of his sweatshirt over his face and started up the stairs. By the time he reached the sidewalk, he at least had a little room to breathe. The ever-present sounds of traffic and distant construction didn't crawl up his spine the way subway brakes did, and the sight of wispy clouds sailing across the open, blue sky reminded him that he wasn't trapped in some claustrophobic, '80s-era dystopia. Just good old Greenwich Village. Brick buildings, leafy trees, and—thanks to New York University, a couple blocks away—plenty of bars, cafes, and cheap food.

Not so bad when it came to Manhattan neighborhoods.

Julian shrugged off as much of that panicked feeling as he could and headed into the brisk October wind.

It was proving near-impossible to find a job in the small town south of Poughkeepsie where he'd landed after the gig in Philly fell apart. People there seemed to have a hard time seeing past the tattoo that climbed up his shoulder into curling tendrils of smoke on one side of his neck. The hiring manager at a local warehouse had written him off as a dangerous Triad gangbanger. It didn't matter that the Triad was a Chinese organization and Julian was third-generation Korean. Or that the closest thing the town ever got to gang activity was when the local teens got stoned and tagged abandoned buildings. Julian was Asian, and he had a visible tattoo, and apparently, that meant he was Triad.

Finding a job in the city would probably be easier, but it definitely wasn't smarter. There had been an excellent reason for Julian to move out of state three years ago. Several, in fact. All of whom would be quite happy to kill him on sight. If he had any sense of self-preservation at all, he would forget the entire ill-conceived impulse to return and take the next train home.

But that tiny, idiot seed of hope propelled his feet forward anyway.

A jolt of homesickness hit him when he laid eyes on the art center. The posters in the windows were different, and they'd updated the sign that hung above the front door, but everything else was exactly the same as he remembered. The uneven discoloration of the resolutely square brick facade, the wrought iron gate at the base of the front steps, the cheerful lavender of the door. Even the smell was the same when he walked inside—paper, and pencil shavings, and paint, and the mellow scent of crayons.

Julian pushed his hood down and went to speak with the young Latina woman behind the front desk. Her hair was bubblegum pink, and she appeared to have an entire sleeve of floral tattoos blooming up her right arm, under the pushed-up sleeve of her cardigan. That was a good sign, right? At least the Greenwich Village Center for the Arts was unlikely to have a problem with Julian's ink.

"Hi," Julian said. "I've got an interview with Harold Fisk in a couple minutes?"

She didn't look up from scribbling on a sticky note beside her keyboard. "Name?"

"Julian Moon."

"Okay . . ." She shifted the sticky notes aside and tapped something into her computer. She was surrounded by pamphlets for classes and upcoming art exhibits and MOMA and the Met. More pastel sticky notes were lined up in rows all along the edge of her desk, covered in pencil sketches. They looked like frames for an animation. "Yep. Last guy hasn't come out yet, so I think they're still talking. He should be done soon."

She had Julian sign in and then directed him to a small, deserted classroom where he could wait.

Julian dropped his backpack on one of the seats scattered around the room, but he was too antsy to sit down. He started poking around the edges of the classroom.

Flyers pinned up on the walls promoted various showcases and competitions, the occasional yoga class, and the weeks-over

Comic Con. Tacked up in any remaining space was what seemed to be the students' work from the past week or so. Based on the subject matter, this room was dedicated to life-drawing classes for high school students and adults.

Julian's hand twitched as he looked over the sketches, itching to find a pencil and paper somewhere and . . .

And what?

Drawing had never paid the bills. Art never put food on the table, or kept a roof over his head, or made him safe. It was just a distraction. He'd only come here so he could get rid of the nagging hope trying to take root in his soul. Take the interview, fail miserably, and maybe he'd finally get it through his head: Hope was a privilege he couldn't afford.

Julian scrubbed a hand through his hair, turning toward the easels crowding the middle of the room. He shouldn't have come here at all. What was he thinking? That he could find some stable ground again? That he could do more with his life than just scrape by and survive?

He had to snap himself out of this—this fit of nostalgia, or whatever it was, that had overtaken his good sense.

Grabbing his backpack, Julian strode to the door. He couldn't do this. He couldn't do the interview. He had to get out of here before—

The door snapped open as Julian reached it. He startled back a step with a quick, automatic apology.

"Oh, excuse me," said the man who had opened the door. He was holding a clipboard and had the slightly distracted, not-quite-walking-the-earth quality stereotypical of many art teachers. He even had a paint stain on one sleeve of his ill-fitting sports jacket. "Are you Julian Moon?"

"Yes, but—"

"You're the one who went to Dalton, isn't that right?" the man asked, consulting his clipboard. He was an inch or two shorter than Julian, and looked to be in his forties. White guy with thinning, nondescript brownish hair. "Class of '15?"

"Well . . . yes. But I—"

"Ah, yes, I see it here. But you didn't mention anything about being in Tyrell's class."

"Mr. Knowles?" Julian asked before he could think to feign ignorance.

The man with the clipboard smiled. "So you do know him. Why didn't you say so on your application? He's on the board here, you know."

"I didn't think it was relevant," Julian said. "Most custodian jobs don't require you to have taken art in high school."

The other man laughed and shook Julian's hand warmly. "Harold Fisk. Glad to meet you, Julian. Come on back."

Julian sighed and followed Mr. Fisk into his office. It was okay, he told himself. He still had time to blow this interview. He wouldn't even have to try. He'd gotten really good at failing over the years.

Harold Fisk's office was one of the most intensely art-teacher offices Julian had ever seen. Several dirty coffee mugs littered the desk, all of them about an arm's reach from the big graphics tablet set up next to the computer monitor. The shelves around the room were packed with graphic novels, comic volumes, manga, and art books for an assortment of animated movies. Whatever shelf space wasn't loaded down with books was crammed with paper, inks, and paints. Opposite the desk, taking up most of the other half of the small room, was an ink-stained drafting table with more pens, pencils, and brushes sticking out like porcupine spikes from the organizational tray on one side. The office smelled like old takeout, stale coffee, and paper. And crayons, of course. There was no escaping the crayons in this building.

"Take a seat," Mr. Fisk said, gesturing to the chair crammed into a narrow space between the desk and the drafting table.

Julian sat, half convinced the chair had been brought in specifically for conducting these interviews. It was the only piece of furniture in the room that didn't have a random assortment of items flung over it. Even the stool under the drafting table had a half-used pad of Bristol board resting on the seat.

"Tyrell's going to throw a fit when he finds out it's really you," Mr. Fisk said, sliding into the chair behind his desk, which had a sweatshirt draped haphazardly over one arm. He pushed his wire glasses up his nose and grinned at Julian. "When I saw you'd gone to Dalton, I took the liberty of asking Tyrell if he knew you. He had nothing but good things to say."

"That's . . . uh. That's very nice of him, but the praise is unwarranted."

"Really? I haven't known Tyrell to be prone to fits of unwarranted praise. He said you were quite the talented artist. And dedicated. Had your pick of undergrad programs, as I understand it."

"Maybe outdated would be a better word," Julian said, shifting in his seat. "I don't draw anymore. I didn't even graduate high school."

Mr. Fisk frowned. "Oh, I'm sorry. Do you mind if I ask you why that was?"

"I, um . . . had an accident," Julian said, trying to keep his tone even. He didn't like the bitterness that colored his voice when he poked that particular memory. Almost three years and he still wanted to knock things over whenever he thought about it. "After that, everything just . . . spiraled."

Mr. Fisk nodded thoughtfully, peering at Julian through his glasses. "Well, let me ask you this, then: If you don't draw anymore, why did you apply to work here?"

Because I'm an idiot.

"I used to love this place when I was a kid," Julian said. "I would come by every day after school, even if it was just to sit on a bench in the gallery and draw the people coming through . . ." He caught himself and shrugged to make it seem like he didn't care about such impractical, childish pleasures. What did it matter if he'd made his first local friends here? Or if some days—especially those last two years of high school—he'd felt more at home scrunched up in front of an easel in the back corner of a classroom than he did in his family's apartment? Or if this was the place where he'd realized that art wasn't just a casual pastime but a passion he couldn't shake?

Fuck's sake. Julian was supposed to be blowing the interview, not getting all weird and sappy. "I must have had a fit of nostalgia or something."

"Hmm," Mr. Fisk said, far too shrewd for Julian's liking. "You really don't draw anymore?"

"No," Julian said firmly. "I don't see what that has to do with mopping floors."

Mr. Fisk sat back in his chair and scratched his ear, heaving a sigh. "All right. Here's the deal. Far as I'm concerned, the custodial job is yours."

It took a second for this to sink in. "Wait, really? You've only been talking to me for two minutes."

Mr. Fisk shrugged, apparently amused by Julian's reaction. "I like you. Tyrell seems to like you. Provided you pass a background check, I don't see any reason not to offer you the job."

Open your mouth and say, 'Thank you, but no,' Julian told himself sternly. *Tell him, 'No.'*

"Oh," he said.

So close. Just one more little letter and it would have been right. Half a syllable.

"It might put a wrench in the cogs of the other opportunity I wanted to present to you, however," Mr. Fisk said, squinting at the ceiling.

This wasn't how this interview was supposed to go. Julian was supposed to show up, be a huge disappointment to everyone in every respect, and be sent on his way with a dubious promise that someone would contact him later. He wasn't supposed to be getting immediate job offers based on the glowing reference of a teacher he hadn't spoken to in three years.

He was supposed to be killing that little sprout of hope in his chest, not letting its roots dig deeper.

"What do you mean, 'other opportunity?'" Julian asked.

"Well, I don't know if you noticed when you were applying for the custodial position, but we recently had one of our teachers leave, and we're hoping to replace her. So I thought, since you had a background in art . . ."

"You're kidding." Julian had seen the teaching gig listed right next to the opening for the custodian job, but had dismissed it outright. The hope in his chest might not be entirely rational, but it wasn't delusional. The post had required a portfolio of recent art as part of the application. Julian didn't even have any of the things he'd worked on in high school, much less anything new. Besides, Dalton might have a great art program, but it was still just a high school. Which Julian hadn't even successfully graduated from.

Mr. Fisk shook his head. "Dead serious. We're having a heck of a time finding someone to take the position. It's part-time—one or two classes a day—and it's for the younger kids. Usually, we try to hire one of the undergrads from NYU's Art Education program. But with it being mid-semester, and with the kids' classes meeting early in the afternoon, we've been running into a lot of scheduling conflicts.

"Tyrell told us particularly that you might do a good job of it," Mr. Fisk continued, as though Julian wasn't gaping at him in disbelief. "As long as you wouldn't mind changing hats, as it were, over the course of the day. You'd get paid for both jobs, of course."

Julian wasn't sure if he wanted to smash something or burst out laughing. He had been running after jobs to no avail for nearly six weeks now, and here he was being told that Mr. Fisk—and Tyrell Knowles, who shouldn't have even remembered him—wanted to give him *two*. For a place he *liked*.

And he couldn't take either one because this one place he liked was in the city. Along with several people who wanted him dead.

"Mr. Fisk—"

"How much time did you have left when you dropped out?" Mr. Fisk asked him, still frowning thoughtfully into space. "A year, was it?"

"Couple of months," Julian said.

"Hmm . . ."

"Mr. Fisk," Julian tried.

"I gather you don't have a portfolio."

"No. I—"

"What about a sketchbook? Or an Instagram? Something of that nature?"

"I don't draw," Julian blurted, the words coming out angrier than he anticipated. "I'm not an artist. I'm a high school dropout trying to get my life together. And not doing a very good job at it, to be honest."

Mr. Fisk regarded Julian from across the desk. No scatter-brained art teacher should be allowed to look so canny.

Julian dropped his gaze to his lap, resisting the impulse to apologize for the sharp outburst. He *was* supposed to be blowing this interview, after all.

"All right," Mr. Fisk said at last.

"I understand if you want to withdraw the original offer," Julian said tightly.

"No need," Mr. Fisk said, with an amicable shrug. "If you want the custodial job, it's yours. And if you change your mind about pursuing the other one, you let me know. Tyrell thought you had a real gift."

"Like I said—" Julian began.

"Outdated," Mr. Fisk finished for him, smiling. "I heard you. I'm just an over-eager art teacher. We tend to assume all our students have the same bone-deep need to create as we do. But if you are happy only mopping our floors, Julian, I am the last person to stand in your way."

Julian should have declined that job, too. But somehow he found himself taking it on. It was the only offer he'd been able to get since his last gig fell apart. It was the smart thing to do, right? To take whatever job was available before he ran out of money and ended up on the street again? Nothing was preventing him from continuing his search elsewhere, while he was waiting for the background check to go through.

Mr. Fisk had Julian fill out all the initial paperwork before he left the room, and then shook his hand again and welcomed him aboard. Julian staggered down the steps onto the sidewalk when he was released, feeling dazed.

He checked his hood was up as he walked back to the subway. By the time he turned the corner onto Sixth Avenue, he was already regretting accepting the custodial job. The offer of the teaching gig kept nagging him. He was itching to find a way into the art world, and here was an opportunity to do just that. Hell, he was already forming lesson plans in his head.

"Fucking idiot," Julian muttered to himself, trying to shake the thoughts loose as he started down the subway steps. He wove through the small crowd of people going the other way with practiced ease.

It probably wasn't as bad as he was making it out to be in his head. Right? It wasn't like any of the people who hated Julian's guts hung around the Greenwich Village Center for the Arts. Manhattan was a big place, and the likelihood of Julian running into Vito, or any of the others, was pretty slim. As long as he stayed away from where he knew they hung out, he should be fine.

He'd only gone maybe half a dozen steps when a spike of adrenaline shot through him.

He didn't understand why, at first. His body reacted to the information before his brain realized there was any information to be had. Then it registered: Down at the base of the stairs, a man in a plain black sweatshirt with close-cropped brown hair was trailing after the rest of the lately disembarked crowd. In his right pocket, Julian knew without having to see it, was a wicked-looking switchblade.

As soon as Julian glanced at him, the other man looked up. Recognition flashed in his eyes, followed very closely by naked, all-consuming hate.

"Shit." Julian spun, shouldered through a tight gaggle of students, and booked it the hell out of there.

TWO

Standing in an empty study room trying to read by the fluorescent light filtering through the interior window by the door was turning out to be a less convenient way to finish the last three chapters of *Jane Eyre* than Beatrice had hoped.

The obvious fix—extend a hand and switch on the study room lights—was not an option. Because turning on the lights meant drawing attention to the fact that she'd switched them off. Which meant Beatrice might find herself trying to explain to a half dozen of her new boyfriend's hot, rich friends how she'd ended up in a study room in the dark in the first place. She didn't have a good lie to offer them, and the truth was mortifying. She'd been on the library's second-floor mezzanine, looking for a place to camp out with her book, when Greyson and some of his posse strolled into the lobby below. In a panic, Beatrice had dodged into the first empty study room she came to and slapped the lights off.

Not her smoothest move.

It wasn't that Greyson Sayer-Crewe—oft lauded the Best Catch on Campus—was a terrible boyfriend. Frankly, it would have been a lot easier on Beatrice if he was. He was just so . . . *attentive*. There was no way to just sit quietly in the same room and study together. He always wanted to talk to her, draw her out. It was exhausting.

She hadn't *really* meant to start going out with him. She couldn't understand what it was about her that caught his attention. Up until a few weeks ago, Beatrice had only seen him with tall, feminine, skinny girls with shiny hair, who never appeared in public without perfectly winged eyeliner and glossy lips. The types of girls who wouldn't be caught dead in last season's yoga pants, and took any opportunity to drop references to their most recent summer trip abroad.

Beatrice was about as opposite to that as any person could get. She was short and pear-shaped, with the all-over freckles of a wild farm child, and an untamable mane of walnut-brown hair. Her fashion sense was probably best described as 'this is comfortable and doesn't have too many holes in it,' with a dash of 'I found this on consignment for three dollars' thrown in to add some interest. Bonus points if it came in a color that would make any stylist in the United States faint dead away from its garishness.

Today, for example, she was wearing a pair of acid-wash jeans, her favorite floral hiking boots, and a sweater that was a bit too big on her. The sweater was striped with the ugliest shades of yellow, green, and brown that had ever assaulted the eyes of decent human beings.

Beatrice happened to think the ugliness was part of the charm, but she was pretty sure people like Greyson "Über-Rich" Sayer-Crewe didn't think ratty and old was the sexy, new look of the season. She hadn't yet been able to work out why he was suddenly willing to see past her wardrobe.

She was probably overthinking it. On paper, Greyson was the kind of guy any straight girl in her right mind would be tripping over herself to go out with. The fact that he was interested in

Beatrice should be flattering. She ought to be over the moon that a rich, handsome, charismatic guy like Greyson had decided that she was worth his time and effort.

And yet . . .

It was just that he had never shown a modicum of interest in her before, even though—because they were both marketing majors—they had been in the same classes multiple times over the past few years. If anything, he seemed to dislike her. She'd made more than one presentation pretending not to notice Greyson laughing at her with two or three of his friends. Heck, Beatrice still suspected that he had tried to convince one of her professors to flunk her out of their marketing research class during her first semester at NYU.

Then, three weeks ago, they were paired up on a group project, and by the end of the week—out of nowhere—Greyson was bugging her to let him buy her dinner.

She thought it must be some kind of joke, at first. It was weird, and she felt flustered, and it was impossible to give a simple, 'no thanks.' He always wanted to know *why*. Before long, Beatrice had run out of excuses.

So about a week ago, thinking he'd give up the joke if she called his bluff, she agreed.

It hadn't been a joke.

Somehow, by the end of that first dinner, she found herself in a *relationship*. And she couldn't seem to find the polite-person exit ramp. Every time she wanted to step back, Greyson prodded her into rhetorical corners until she felt like all her excuses were flimsy and inadequate.

It wasn't like he was a bad guy. At least, not now that he'd decided he liked her. He didn't even seem to mind that she was a little weird and skittish about the whole *relationship* thing.

Whatever friction that may or may not have been between them in the past had vanished, as far as Greyson was concerned. A case of mutual misunderstandings of each other's character.

Beatrice had never been great at confrontation. And she wasn't sure she could screw up the courage to break things off when she still had zero good reasons *why*. At least, not beyond the small, quiet voice in the back of her head that kept asking, *Are you really sure about this?*

Beatrice blew out a breath, making herself focus back on the dimly-lit pages of *Jane Eyre*.

She didn't have the time to figure the whole Greyson thing out. She didn't have time for much of anything, really. She'd already pushed her graduation date back a semester because she hadn't had the money to pay for classes last year. She was trying to catch up by taking sixteen credits this semester and next, and another twelve credits in the summer. She was starting to think she'd have to drop one of her classes this semester because she was struggling to keep up. If her grades slipped too much, she would lose her partial scholarship, and she needed her week-ends-and-holidays job at the coffee shop near her apartment because her parents were already struggling financially . . .

Beatrice rubbed her eyes to stave off her developing headache. If she finished *Jane Eyre* early, that would give her time to start on the presentation she had due in her marketing class tomorrow morning, which meant she could work on her English paper on the train home, which meant tomorrow afternoon she could focus on memorizing terms for her evening Spanish class.

Greyson and his friends must have settled into some out-of-the-way corner by now. She could probably turn the lights back on. She might even be able to risk slipping down to the coffee shop next door. She was trying to figure out whether a coffee run would put her at more or less risk of running into Greyson again when the study room door burst open. A person-shaped shadow barreled into the room and slammed the door.

"Hey!" Beatrice squeaked, nearly dropping her book. Annoyed at her default high-pitched squawk of surprise, she made an effort to lower her voice to something more threatening-sounding. "I have this room reserved, buddy," she lied, ignoring the fact that the intruder would've been hard-pressed to realize anyone was in here with the lights off. "You can't just—"

The intruder slapped a hand over Beatrice's mouth and pinned her against the wall.

Jane Eyre hit the floor with a thud.

Beatrice's stomach jumped, and her mind went blank except for a long progression of question marks. She only came up to his chin. All she could see was the neck of his hoodie. The scent of soap and something peppery she couldn't place washed over her. She could feel the imprint of his sweatshirt's zipper through her sweater every time he took a breath.

"Shut up," the intruder hissed, his face so close she could see herself reflected in his dark eyes.

Oh my God, I'm being assaulted in a library. Beatrice got her hands against his chest and shoved him away, sucking in a huge breath in preparation for a scream if he came at her again. Instead, he glanced at the window, swore, and dropped into a crouch, pressing himself against the wall under the window.

The question marks intensified.

"I'm not here," he said, glaring up at her. "Got it?"

Beatrice let out the pent-up scream in a silent puff of air. *It's okay,* she told her racing heart. *You're not being assaulted. Chill out.*

Now that he didn't have her trapped against the wall, he didn't seem so scary. Beatrice's step-dad would've probably called him a punk, due to the hoodie-jeans-sneakers combo, and what looked like the edge of a tattoo coiling up his neck from beneath his collar. But the tough-guy aesthetic was somewhat softened by the loose black curls falling over his eyes. His hair was short on the sides, too, which made him seem less like a mugger and more like an art student. The tattoo wasn't even the harsh, blocky ink you'd expect on a gangbanger. It looked like soft tendrils of smoke. All he needed was one of those portfolio things the kids in the art department carted around—and maybe a beanie—and she'd have pegged him for a visual arts major.

Heart rate returning to normal, Beatrice peeked out the study room window for a clue as to what the intruder was running from. There were a lot of students milling around, none of them particularly shifty-looking. But before she could do much more than note the absence of Greyson and his posse, *Jane Eyre* hit her in the shin.

"Ow!" Beatrice said, returning the intruder's glare and rubbing her leg with vigor.

"Would you cut that out?" he demanded in a harsh whisper.

"What, I'm not allowed to look out the window?" she returned, lowering her volume to match his.

"*No.*"

Beatrice deepened her scowl. She had developed a pretty good one over the years. It was useful in keeping her younger brother in line without resorting to violence. "What's your problem?" she asked. This was *her* study room, after all. Well, maybe not technically, but she *had* been here first.

"What's *your* problem?" the intruder shot back with perfect logic.

"I'm not the one barging into other people's study rooms and accosting strangers."

"But standing in the dark reading a massive book is par for the course," he said, picking the book off the floor and waving it at her.

"It's my life," Beatrice pointed out, snatching the book from his hand as her cheeks warmed. "I can read in the dark if I want to."

He rolled his eyes and started to say something else, but his attention snapped to the window. His whole demeanor shifted from exasperation to fear. "*Shit.*"

Beatrice turned to follow his gaze, but he grabbed her arm— poor, abused *Jane Eyre* slipped from her fingers and fell to the floor again, pages down—and pulled her around to the far side of the conference table.

"Ow!" Beatrice said again, as he yanked her to the ground with him. "Would you *stop*—"

He slapped his hand over her mouth. "For the love of God," he hissed, his eyes boring into hers. "Shut. Up."

She didn't even think about screaming this time. Even in the dark, she could see genuine fear in his eyes. He was in trouble. Real trouble.

Beatrice nodded, agreeing to his terms.

That was the precise moment the door to the study room banged open.

Julian flinched at the harsh sound, his hand still pressed firmly over the lurker's mouth. The table Julian had pulled them both behind wasn't ideal cover, but the room was designed for small groups of students to study. It was long, with blocky padded chairs crammed around it. And unless Julian wanted to try his hand at blending in with the wall, he was out of options.

Julian kept his head low, watching Vito's feet in the slivers of space between the padded chairs and legs of the conference table. Vito paused inside the door, silent except for the sound of heavy breathing.

Julian's mind raced ahead. If he timed it right, he might be able to tip the table over on Vito and buy himself a little time. Or, if that didn't work, maybe he could throw a chair. Having a second person to deal with wasn't making this easier.

Beside him, the lurker's hands curled into fists against her knees.

Vito's weight shifted. His hand appeared as he reached down and picked up the damn book from the floor.

Shit.

Julian shot a quick glare at the weird girl next to him, hoping she knew that if Vito found and killed them both, it was her fault.

She wrinkled her nose at him, apparently not impressed by the silent blame-shifting. She looked a little like a lion with all that hair. But not a terribly threatening one. The Tawny Scrawny Lion, or maybe Simba. "Hakuna Matata" Simba, though—all hair, no bite.

"Who's in here?" Vito barked, breaking into Julian's fear-induced nonsense-thoughts.

Simba grabbed Julian's wrist and pushed his hand off her face. He panicked for a moment, thinking she was going to scream, but she didn't make a sound. She didn't move except to turn her head in Vito's direction. Not even to let go of his wrist.

The *smack* of the book hitting the table made both Julian and Simba jump. Vito slapped the switch on the wall, throwing the room into fluorescent brightness. His shoes hit threadbare carpet as he came around the table.

Julian yanked his hand out of Simba's grip and went for his pocket. He used to carry a knife with him everywhere. Now all he had in his pocket was a ballpoint pen, which was not great, but it was better than nothing. Vito was always more of a knife guy than a gun guy, so at the very least, Julian might be able to defend himself long enough for Simba to get out and scream for help.

But before he could even get a good grip on the pen, Simba

popped to her feet. Julian grabbed at her sleeve, but he wasn't quick enough.

"Excuse me," she said, planting her fists on her hips like a diminutive Wonder Woman. "I have this room reserved. You can't be in here."

"Fucking—Where the fuck did you come from?"

"I was *trying* to take a nap," Simba said. Like this was the most natural thing in the world. Like she wasn't talking to a dangerous gangbanger with a switchblade in his pocket. "You got a problem with that?"

"You were taking a nap?" Vito repeated. "In *here*?"

"Don't judge me," she said, drawing herself up. "I live two hours away by train, and I'm taking a crap ton of credits, and there are only so many places that are any good for napping on campus. And I guarantee you all the couches in the student lounge already have smelly dudes sleeping on them. I think I'm allowed to use the room that I reserved to take a freaking nap in. Now, are you going to get out of here, or do I have to call in Ms. Newton so she can kick you out?"

"Fine. Jesus," Vito said, retreating a step.

Julian was astounded. He had never known anyone to get Vito to back down so fast.

"I thought I saw someone I know come in here, was all."

"Well, clearly you were wrong. Now if you don't mind . . . ?" She stared at Vito, five foot three—plus another two inches or so of hair—of impatient exasperation.

Amazingly, Vito seemed to buy it all. He tossed out a grudging apology and left, slamming the door behind him. Simba stayed where she was, glaring at the window for a long moment.

Julian gaped at her, equal parts impressed and appalled. If she had *any idea* what she had just done—

She let out a puff of air and sagged into the nearest chair. "Oh my God," she muttered, pressing her hands to her face. She appeared to be trembling.

Inexplicable anger slammed into Julian. "Are you insane?" he demanded, keeping his voice low, in case the walls were thin. "What the hell did you do that for? He could've killed you."

"I have no idea," she said, turning wide gray eyes on him. "It seemed better than getting caught hiding back here. I didn't realize he'd be so . . . I mean, this is a *library*."

"Fat lot of difference that would have made." Julian glanced at the window, but the only people walking past now were students, their attention on their phones or each other. He got to his feet and walked around the table to get a better look. He spotted Vito near the end of the hall, seemingly undecided about whether to keep searching for Julian in the massive library. Julian pressed his back against the study room door. He was going to have to wait him out.

"What did you do to set him off, anyway?" Simba asked, sliding her book across the table and tucking it against her stomach.

"What do you care?"

Her eyes narrowed. "I don't think it's too much to ask for an explanation after I stuck my neck out for you."

"I didn't ask you to do that."

"Well, what were *you* going to do?" she said, motioning to the pen still gripped in his left hand. "Embarrass him into leaving by drawing a mustache on him?"

Julian shoved the pen back in his pocket, anger rising in him again. "It doesn't matter what I would've done. What matters is that what *you* did was stupid and dangerous, and you should have your head checked before you get yourself killed." He cut himself off, realizing that it wasn't her he was so angry at. He was yelling at himself.

Simba frowned at him. "*I* don't usually go around getting on murderers' bad sides."

"No, you just help random strangers like some kind of idiot," Julian snapped before he could stop himself. "What if *I* was a murderer?"

She rolled her eyes at that, some of her earlier confidence returning. "You're not a murderer."

"You don't know that."

"I'm pretty sure if you were a murderer, you wouldn't be telling me about it." She stood and retrieved a messenger bag and jacket from one of the chairs. "I'm also pretty sure you wouldn't have been planning on defending yourself with writing implements."

Julian scowled. "You're not taking this seriously. Trust me: Vito isn't someone you want to mess with."

"What do you care?" Simba asked, throwing his own words back at him. "I'm just some random girl whose study room you appropriated for your murder drama. You're welcome, by the way. For saving your butt."

Shit, this girl was weird. He couldn't seem to stop staring at her. She wasn't even that pretty, judging by conventional beauty standards. Her hair was ridiculous, she had freckles which looked like they'd been placed by an overenthusiastic Georges Seurat wannabe, and she was wearing the most hideous sweater he'd ever seen outside of a '70s sitcom. Yet she was . . . strangely compelling.

He opened his mouth, determined to say something clever, or at least sarcastic, in response to her quip, but not a single coherent word came into his head.

She shook her head, sighing. "I gotta find an actual quiet place to finish reading," she said, shoving her book in her bag. "If that guy comes back, shout for help or something, okay? I'm pretty sure most of the librarians here know how to dial 911."

The concern on her face threw him. Why did it matter what he did? He was nobody to her.

Anyway, the concern was irrelevant. There was no way he

could keep coming back into the city for work every day. Not after Vito had spotted him. If Julian was smart, he'd put himself on the next Greyhound to California and stay there. And stop letting some shadow of a childhood dream persuade him that he could find a way to get on his feet for once.

"Don't worry," Julian said, stepping away from the door so she could leave. "I'm not going to run into him again."

Something in his tone made Simba pause, her hand on the doorknob, and look at him. He had the strangest feeling, for a single moment, that her eyes had pierced something inside him and laid his soul bare. That she knew everything about him—every secret, every shame—and was weighing what to do with him.

And then she smiled, somewhat sardonically, and the feeling was gone. She was just a tiny, freckled stranger again. "All right. Well. Take care, fugitive."

Despite everything, he found himself returning the smile. "You too, lurker."

She snorted, her eyes dancing, and then she slipped through the door and was gone.

THREE

Beatrice was still distracted and tense by the time English Lit let out. And ravenously hungry. She filed into the hallway with the rest of the students, half her brain occupied with whether she should get something to eat before she headed home. She'd been good at staying on budget this week, so grabbing something at the food court wouldn't set her back. But the food court was also loud and crowded, and Beatrice's nerves were already frayed after the incident in the library.

The part of her brain that wasn't calculating whether peace of mind was more important than an empty stomach was busy trying to convince her that Not-an-Art-Student and his ballpoint pen shiv had gotten home safely. He'd seemed so sure the other guy—Vito, she thought it was—wanted to kill him. And after facing him down, Beatrice believed it, too. Though who the heck knew why. Not-an-Art-Student didn't strike Beatrice as the kind of guy who'd hang out with scary guys like Vito.

Because *clearly*, Beatrice was an authority on the habits of strange men whom she barely knew.

She shook her head as she trailed after some of her classmates down the stairs to the ground floor. It was a good thing she didn't have any more classes today. Between fretting about the library confrontation and her growing hunger, she hadn't paid as much attention in class as she should have. Thankfully, the hardest thing about English Lit was keeping up with the reading. She'd managed to cobble together a couple of semi-intelligent answers during the discussion, and everything else she could get from the official class notes the professor uploaded every week.

Beatrice hopped off the last step, adjusting the strap of her bag. She might as well stop somewhere nearby for dinner. She rarely wanted to fight the press of people in Grand Central for food, which meant if she didn't eat here, she wouldn't eat until she got home, in another two hours or—

Arms wrapped around her waist from behind, jerking her back. Beatrice squawked in a particularly unladylike fashion and twisted out of the hold, her fist raised, heart in her throat.

Greyson laughed and put his hands up in mock surrender. "Please don't shoot," he said. "I'm unarmed."

Beatrice dropped her fist, flushing. "Don't *do* that."

"Sorry," Greyson said, grinning.

She didn't much appreciate how funny he seemed to find the whole thing, either. Her heart was pounding, and she couldn't get the defensive, bristling feeling in her shoulders to settle back down. "I'm serious, Greyson. You scared me."

He made a brief attempt at an apologetic expression that couldn't take the humor out of his pale blue eyes. "I said I'm sorry." He had the kind of voice that you heard in the soles of your feet. The kind of voice that invaded your chest and settled there like heavy velvet. The kind of voice that made Beatrice feel small and squeaky in comparison.

He ducked his head and stole a kiss. "In my defense, I did try to call your name like five times first."

The kind of voice that she completely tuned out when distracted by food.

God. She had to be the worst girlfriend in all of New York State. "You did? I didn't even notice."

"Must have been some class, to have you so distracted." Greyson tugged at a lock of her hair.

"Riveting," Beatrice muttered, pushing her hair back over her shoulder, out of his reach.

"Careful, you'll make me jealous." He turned her chin up with his fingers and kissed her again.

Beatrice pulled back, her face warming. You heard people talking about butterflies in their stomachs when they were around people they liked a lot. Beatrice's stomach seemed to be inhabited by suffocating trout on a dock when she was around Greyson. Less flutter, more flop. Maybe that's what it was like for everyone, and butterflies were simply more romantic-sounding than dying fish. Or maybe there was something seriously wrong with her.

She suspected it was the latter, since she also enjoyed wearing clothes in the most hideous colors she could find. And she had spent most of her lit class worrying about a scowling stranger with gentle eyes.

Gentle eyes? Good God. Guilt washed over her, giving new life to the trout in her stomach. *Don't mention that to Greyson.*

She pointed vaguely towards the front doors. "I should, um—"

"You hungry?" Greyson asked.

Beatrice's stomach took a quick break from flopping to growl, but she shook her head. Food with Greyson meant being on a *date.* She didn't have that kind of energy right now. "I can't. I have a paper I need to start tonight, and I still haven't finished that presentation for marketing tomorrow—"

"So we'll get something quick and I'll drive you home," Greyson said. "How does pizza sound?"

"I was going to write the paper on the train."

"But you can't write it in the car?"

"Not if you're talking to me the whole time," Beatrice said. It took her another split second to realize it had come out more of a grumble than anything. Why was everything she said to Greyson the exact wrong thing today? "Wait, no," she backpedaled, "that came out wrong—"

"Beatrice," Greyson said, resting his hands on her shoulders and trapping her gaze with his inscrutable, ice blue eyes. "It's okay. I can refrain from talking for an hour if you need to write a paper. Let me drive you home."

"But—" Beatrice began, floundering for a good excuse. "I—I don't want to put you out. It's a long drive. And you have to come all the way back. And it's already getting dark—"

"I don't mind." Greyson squeezed her shoulder, offering one of his perfect smiles. He had the chiseled jawline and razor-sharp cheekbones of an A-list movie star. Sometimes he didn't seem quite real. "Listen," he said, lowering his voice so the few students still milling around the lobby area couldn't hear, "I know you think I've got some secret agenda, wanting to date you. But I don't. I really like you. And I think we'd be good together. I just need you to give me a chance to convince you."

"I don't—"

"Plus," he said, "you'll get home faster if I drive you. And it's safer than taking the train, right? It's win-win-win for you."

"I guess." Beatrice sighed. He was trying to help. And she *was* hungry. She just didn't like feeling as though she was indebted to him. But she didn't want to make him think she didn't appreciate the offer, either. She didn't have the emotional wherewithal to force another confrontation today. "Okay," she relented. "But I'm paying for the pizza."

♡

Julian's sister was perched on a suitcase outside his apartment when he returned home that evening. She had her arms crossed and was giving the darkened window of the out-of-business tobacco and liquor store across the street her worst death glare.

For one uncharitable moment, Julian thought about turning around and hiding out in the 24-hour laundromat around the corner until she gave up waiting for him and went away. When Fabiana turned up without warning, it was always because something terrible had happened that she expected him to fix. And Julian had already had one hell of a bad day. He wasn't sure he had any fix-it powers left.

He took a deep breath and went to meet her, certain he was going to end up sleeping on the floor tonight.

Fabiana looked up as he approached. Her shoulders tensed, and her expression turned guarded. Yep. She was definitely in trouble again.

"What happened, Fab?" Julian asked, stopping beside her, hands in pockets, his tone flat.

Her bottom lip stuck out as her frown deepened. "I need money."

No surprise there. "I don't have any money."

"Bullshit. You have an apartment." She eyed his hoodie and frayed jeans. "You do have an apartment, right?"

"I have the shittiest apartment in the shittiest building on the shittiest street in town," Julian said in the same expressionless tone. "I have thirty bucks and a Metro Card in my wallet, and less than a hundred in the bank. I'm not going to be able to pay rent next month, and then I *won't* have an apartment. I don't have any money. Now, will you tell me what happened?"

She glared at a trio of teenagers down the street who were

sharing a bottle in a brown paper bag and talking over each other in loud voices. Julian didn't know how long Fabiana had been sitting here in front of his apartment, but he was surprised she hadn't been mugged. She was in stilettos, for Chrissakes, and an expensive, strappy clubbing dress under a fitted leather jacket. In a neighborhood like this, that kind of ensemble just screamed *Take my money! I have lots!*

She did have a pretty impressive glare, though, and despite the expensive getup, she could switch into alley-cat mode in a blink. She would be more than willing to use her manicured nails to defend herself if it came down to it. Which it probably wouldn't, because Julian suspected she had Mace or a Taser inside the tiny black bag tucked under her arm. And she did look forbidding, leaning on her suitcase on the street.

"Fabiana," Julian prompted when she didn't seem to want to answer his question.

She huffed. "Walter cut me off again. And Arthur's being a dick about it. That puts you next on the list. Congratulations."

Translation: Their step-dad had kicked Fabiana out—again—and her latest boyfriend wasn't willing to help out. Julian couldn't remember if Arthur had been the name of the boyfriend from six weeks ago, which was the last time he'd spoken to Fabiana, but it didn't matter. If Fabiana had ever had a boyfriend who wasn't a first-class dickbag, Julian hadn't met him. Mostly Fabiana went for rich, middle-aged white guys, a good third of whom were already married. Not one of them had ever lasted longer than a few months.

Not like Julian could judge. He didn't have a great track record with romantic relationships, either. He was usually the one responsible for blowing them up. Fabiana just had a knack for picking terrible partners.

Julian took another breath, resigning himself to his twin-saving fate, and dug his keys out of his pocket.

"Come on," he said, making for the door.

"What about my suitcase?" Fabiana demanded. "Aren't you going to help me?"

"I could," Julian replied. "But if you make me carry that up the stairs, I'm going to make you sleep on the floor. I've only got the one mattress."

Fabiana gave him a withering look, but when it became clear he wasn't going to give in and carry the suitcase for her, she grabbed the handle with a huff and marched after Julian, stilettos clicking on the pavement, swearing in his direction under her breath.

FOUR

Julian didn't have much in the way of food in the apartment. Just peanut butter, macaroni, crackers, and a few packets of ramen in the pantry. Butter, eggs, and a half-eaten bag of grapes were all he had left in the fridge. Fabiana turned her nose up at all of it and tried to talk him into ordering Chinese. Julian ignored her and put on water for ramen. Then he went to the narrow coat closet and took out a clean set of sheets and a sleeping bag.

He ought to tell her to change the sheets herself, but he couldn't bring himself to ask. The poor-me pout might not have any effect on him, but he knew beneath the crusty exterior she was probably hurting more than she wanted to let on.

Julian had made his peace with being adrift a long time ago, but Fabiana fought tooth and nail for stability. It always seemed to elude her, and she still turned around and tried to grab it again. He sympathized with her, but he wasn't sure how to tell her as much without making the situation worse. The least he could do was make sure she had a place to sleep until she convinced their step-father to take her back, or spun off to her next sugar daddy scheme.

"Did the wise and generous Walter give a reason for cutting

you off this time?" he asked, dropping the linens on a chair and stripping the bed.

"Same old Walter reasons, I guess," Fabiana said, her eyes traveling around the scant furnishings of the studio apartment. "Something about disapproving of Arthur or my shopping or . . . something. I don't know." She wrinkled her nose at a small pile of laundry on the floor and prodded them with the toe of her shoe. "Don't you ever pick up after yourself?"

"Never," Julian said, deciding not to point out that Fabiana had always been worse about leaving her things strewn around than he was. The quick deflection made him think she was lying about why she got cut off, but he let it go. It didn't matter why. He'd try to help her regardless. He threw the old sheets at the laundry basket he kept against the wall near the bathroom. "You're welcome to tidy up if you don't like it."

"Screw you," Fabiana replied, and crossed to the single window. She pushed aside the old tablecloth that served as a makeshift curtain and scowled at the street below. "Your apartment is shit."

Julian couldn't argue with her. It *was* shit. The whole thing was one room plus a closet-sized bathroom. The walls were paper thin. The power had a tendency to short out for no reason. He was fighting a losing battle with a colony of ants in the bathroom, and a steady parade of cockroaches everywhere else. It always smelled of grease and fish and cigarettes. Sometimes the smell of weed smoke crept through the vents, to change things up. He'd taken to wearing headphones at night to drown out the baby down the hall who never stopped wailing, and the upstairs neighbors having loud, drunken arguments every other night, and he was still sometimes woken by the slamming of doors shaking the walls.

His table—a tiny chipped kitchen nook thing—he'd gotten out of a dumpster, and the two chairs were thrift store finds with uneven legs. Even the sheets were from a thrift store. Not that he was going to tell Fabiana about that. He didn't have a couch or a TV. He had a phone with crappy service and a nearby library he frequented for their computers and Wi-Fi. He didn't spend much time here, really. He mostly came back to crash at night, or to grab a quick bite to eat.

Once he finished making the bed, he checked on the ramen, ignoring Fabiana's continued bitching about his subpar living situation. The last time she'd had to crash with him had been over a year ago. He'd been staying in a one-bedroom that wasn't so bad except for the mold in the carpet. Fabiana's then-boyfriend had kicked her out of his place while Walter was out of the country. She'd gotten ahold of Walter the next day, and he set her back up in the apartment he kept for her in Brooklyn when she wasn't living with boyfriends. Julian had been at work when it happened, and the only thing his sister had communicated to him was a text saying she was going home. And then she hadn't spoken to him for months.

He hadn't exactly tried to talk to her, either. They always ended up fighting, when neither of them were mid-crisis. He thought she was still angry at him for leaving Walter's penthouse without her, after the incident with his hand. He was still angry at her for staying. But they never talked about it. They just fought about every other thing they could think of.

Apparently, shared trauma didn't always bring people together. Sometimes it pushed them apart.

Fabiana leaned against the pantry as Julian cooked, her arms crossed, scowling at the dingy paint. He left her alone. She'd talk if she wanted to. More likely, she'd keep on trying to pick a fight. Like she thought if she didn't ever say how hurt she was, then it wouldn't be true.

"You know, you could always ask Walter to find you a job," Fabiana said as Julian got a couple of hard-boiled eggs out of the fridge.

"I don't need his help," Julian said, mirroring her clipped tone.

"Don't try to tell me you *like* living in this hellhole."

"I'm sorry it's not up to your standards of living."

"It's not up to a rat's standard of living," Fabiana replied, wrinkling her nose in disgust. "I could talk to him for you if you wanted."

Julian looked up from peeling eggs to glare at her. "Drop it, Fab."

"Whatever." She pushed off the pantry door, going to examine the stack of library books and other random crap Julian had thrown on the shelves of the built-in bookcase across the room.

Julian went back to ignoring her, pouring the ramen out into his one bowl and a chipped coffee mug. He added the eggs and a handful of chopped chives to finish it up. Not the most elaborate ramen he'd ever made, but at least it was food.

"Still not drawing?" Fabiana asked.

He turned and found her flipping through a sketchbook she'd given him on their birthday last year. He should have thrown it out, instead of sticking it in the bottom of his backpack when he moved.

"Jesus," Fabiana went on, thumbing through the final pages. "There's nothing in here. At all."

Julian abandoned the ramen and strode over, snatching the sketchbook out of her hands. "Stop looking through my things."

"Is it your hand? Does it still bother you? You know Walter would still probably—"

"Butt out, Fabiana."

She scowled at him. "I'm just trying to make conversation."

"Could you make conversation about something other than *me*?"

"So I'm worried about you. Is that a crime now?"

"You're not worried about me," Julian snapped, "you're trying to avoid talking about how you got cut off again. You think that if you keep prodding into my life, you won't have to stop and examine your own. You won't have to think about why it is you always end up needing *me* to bail you out of shit you get *yourself* into."

Dead silence. Fabiana only looked at him, her expression dark and guarded.

Half an hour in and he'd already crossed a line. Yeah. Sounded about right.

Mentally cursing himself, Julian attempted a halfhearted backpedal. "I didn't—"

"Whatever," she snipped, storming past him. She snatched the bowl and some silverware off the counter. And then she swept towards the bathroom, the only place inside the apartment with a real door.

"Fab," Julian began, knowing he should apologize. Knowing he didn't have the patience to do it properly.

"Screw you." Fabiana slammed the bathroom door behind her.

Julian shut his eyes and rubbed his temples. Why was today the Day to Bother Julian About His Failed Art Career? He had almost pushed that particular failure out of his mind over the past months. He'd gotten to a place where he didn't think about it much at all. And then, today, the world seemed determined to remind him of his past hopes and how they'd all gone up in flames.

And anyway, who told Fabiana to be so damn nosy? It wasn't like she cared what he did. She wasn't any more forthcoming about her own shit.

He looked down at the sketchbook, squeezing the cover until his knuckles turned white. He'd had good doctors after he broke his hand. A narrow scar at the base of his palm and a slight inward crick in his small finger were the only visible indications that it had ever been in bad shape. It didn't even hurt much anymore, except for the ache and stiffness he felt when it was damp and cold.

Julian cursed under his breath, shoving the empty sketchbook in his backpack, where Fabiana couldn't easily find it again. Trying not to be bothered that his sister was locked in his bathroom and unlikely to come out anytime soon, he crossed to the kitchen and dug into his mug of ramen.

Beatrice's parents were arguing again. She could hear them through the front door as she walked up to the apartment. Which meant the neighbors could probably hear them, too.

She hesitated on the third-floor balcony, a chilly breeze stirring her hair as it rushed through the branches of the foliage below. Her parents had been doing a lot of arguing lately. If it was about finances, as it often was, Beatrice could sneak past them to her room and drown them out with headphones while she finished her homework. But if it was about her, or—even worse— her younger brother's disaster of a freshman year at Stanford, she could end up spending the next hour or so trying to referee the fight.

And she still had so much homework left to do.

Fortunately for Beatrice's sanity, it sounded like her parents were arguing about her step-dad's spending. Something about him sending money to someone—most likely his aunt in Baltimore—without discussing it with her mom first. From the sound of cabinets slamming, they were arguing in the kitchen. Unless Beatrice was *very* unlucky, she could slip through the foyer, into the living room, without either of them noticing her passing the kitchen archway.

Holding her breath, Beatrice unlocked the door and slid inside. Her step-dad, Mike, was facing away from the foyer, talking to

Beatrice's mom as she unloaded the dishwasher in a rage. Mike was taller and broader than Joyce—who was short, like Beatrice—and he blocked most of the archway. Neither of them turned when Beatrice shut the door behind her, easing it into place so it wouldn't make any noise.

She left her keys and MetroCard on the narrow catch-all table by the door, for when the arguing petered out and it occurred to one of her parents to wonder if she'd ever made it home. She tried to tune out their raised voices as she edged between the TV and the coffee table, with its little piles of junk mail and bills. Neither of them noticed or tried to call her back. A moment later, she was safe in her room.

She stood with her back against the door for a moment and let out a slow breath. She didn't have to play referee. All she had to do was finish her marketing presentation.

She'd wanted to do the bulk of the presentation in Greyson's car, but it was awkward figuring out how to get her laptop set up in a way that didn't hurt her wrist. Then she found the music Greyson was playing—some kind of club music whose sole purpose seemed to be blowing out eardrums—both annoying and distracting. She hadn't wanted to say anything because he was going out of his way to drive her home. And he was going to have to drive all the way back to Manhattan afterward. She wasn't even allowing him to talk to her.

So she'd suffered through the music. But she'd only managed to write out the very roughest, sparsest bones of her presentation. She was going to have to do the bulk of it tonight, then race to finish on the train tomorrow morning. Which meant that she'd have to find the time to both memorize Spanish terms *and* start on the *Jane Eyre* paper during her long break between classes tomorrow.

Wednesday night, and she was already woefully behind on her study schedule for the week.

Wonderful.

As she settled into her pillows, Sunny, the family cat, crawled out from under her bed, where he seemed to have taken refuge from the yelling. He sprang up next to Beatrice and settled by her hip, fixing his wide, yellow eyes on her imploringly. He was a gray Scottish Fold, with cute folded-over ears, a round face, and a habit of drooling when he got too enthusiastic with the purring. Which was pretty much any time anyone paid him any attention. Beatrice had named him when she was fifteen—*We should call him Sunny because he looks like a fluffy little raincloud. It'll be funny.*

She scratched Sunny's misshapen ears. He started up the high-powered purring at once, kneading the fleece blanket with his claws.

Smiling at her furry study buddy, Beatrice put on her headphones and turned her music up loud, drowning out everything but the bluesy beat and her own thoughts. The knot of tension in her neck started to loosen at the sound of Janice Joplin's voice in her ears. She closed her eyes, stroking Sunny's back, and took a few slow breaths.

She was probably more irritable and tense than usual because of that incident in the library. She didn't know what she would have done if the maybe-murderer—Vito—hadn't bought her crazy 'taking a nap' story. He hadn't looked like the kind of guy you'd want to meet in a dark alley. Or an empty study room, for that matter. Beatrice didn't know what made her do it. Her legs shook the whole time, her heart racing. It just seemed like her options were to make up a wild excuse and hope for the best, or be found hiding behind a table with no way to defend herself. Not-an-Art-Student's ballpoint shiv certainly wasn't going to save them.

She should have screamed for help when she first had the chance. Then at least campus security could have dealt with the problem, instead of Beatrice sticking her neck out for a stranger on a misguided impulse to play high-stakes Good Samaritan.

It had worked out okay in the end, Beatrice reminded herself, taking another slow breath. She wasn't hurt. Not-an-Art-Student wasn't hurt—at least not that she knew of. The bad guy had gone away.

She'd probably never see Not-an-Art-Student again.

All . . . good things.

Shaking her head, Beatrice pushed those thoughts away and clicked back to her presentation.

FIVE

*Y*ou look terrible," Kinsey observed, falling into step beside Beatrice on their way into Statistics. Kinsey was seven-eighths Chinese, and one-eighth who-even-knows, according to her. There was some dispute within the family over whether a particular great-grandfather was French or Bulgarian. She was petite, though not quite as short as Beatrice, and delicate-looking, with a flair for vintage-inspired fashion. The combination of all these things often fooled strangers into thinking she was demure and soft-spoken.

They were usually disillusioned of that misconception within a few seconds of Kinsey opening her mouth.

"What was it?" Kinsey went on. "Rat tried to take up residence in your hair on the train?"

"It's not that bad," Beatrice complained. She wasn't going to win any beauty awards today. Her hair was tied up in a messy knot to disguise the appalling bed head she'd woken up with, and she felt gross and sweaty from missing her chance to shower. But she thought she deserved some credit for getting out the door fully dressed and with the correct homework in her bag within five minutes of waking up.

"It's not great," Sasha said around a mouthful of granola, trailing after them. "How'd you get ink behind your ear?"

"Must have been the rat," Beatrice said, scrubbing the offending spot as they funneled into the classroom.

"What did it do, steal your pen?" Kinsey asked.

"Maybe it was trying to give her its number," Sasha suggested, waggling her pale eyebrows at Beatrice. She had several inches on both Kinsey and Beatrice, being on the taller side of average. Her hair was wheat-colored and straight, always up in a braid or ponytail. She was a striker on the college's women's soccer team, but she was surprisingly laid back for how competitive she got on the field.

"Can we do the joke factory thing *after* class?" Beatrice begged, sliding into her usual desk. She took out her notebook to finish the last two problems in the few minutes remaining before the professor arrived. "I'm behind on everything today."

"Just drop your English class already," Kinsey said. "Who cares if you graduate a semester late?"

"I do," Beatrice said, more sharply than she intended. She felt off-kilter and half a step behind already, and the nagging caffeine headache she'd been fighting all morning wasn't helping. "I'm already behind everyone else, and I know I can catch up if I just stay focused. And I wish you'd stop trying to tell me that I can't."

"We don't think you *can't*," Sasha said, leaning against the desk right behind Kinsey's. She popped the last bit of granola bar into her mouth. "We're just worried you might be overworking yourself. And I, for one, don't have any wish to witness first-hand what someone looks like when they literally work themselves to death."

"I'm not working myself to death," Beatrice snapped, bending over her notebook. She didn't like the use of 'we,' implying Sasha and Kinsey had discussed this already.

Sasha put up her hands in mock surrender. "No, you're right. You seem completely relaxed. I don't know what I was thinking."

"Where's your coffee?" Kinsey asked, unperturbed by Beatrice's increasing frustration.

Beatrice didn't look up from her homework. "I left it on the counter at home."

"Uh-oh," Kinsey said. Out of the corner of her eye, Beatrice saw her throw Sasha an alarmed look.

"This isn't helping," Beatrice complained in distress. "I only have a few minutes to finish these problems—"

Sasha rocked off her desk. "Do you want coffee or an energy drink?"

Beatrice shook her head. "Sasha, you don't have to—"

"Coffee or Red Bull? Five seconds to decide."

"I'd prefer coffee, but you don't—"

"I'll be right back," Sasha said. She grabbed her wallet, leaving the backpack on her desk. "Don't let anyone take my stuff," she told Kinsey, pointing at her in a mock threat.

Kinsey did a two-finger salute in acknowledgment of this directive, and Sasha took off, breaking into a jog as she left the classroom.

"She doesn't have to do that," Beatrice said, turning to Kinsey. "She shouldn't do that. I was just really mean to her."

Kinsey plucked a loose thread from the shoulder of her citrus-print blouse and rolled it between her fingers before flicking it away. "Honey, being slightly irritable with your talkative friends pre-coffee doesn't exactly qualify as being 'really mean.'"

"But—"

Kinsey reached across the aisle and patted Beatrice's head. "Just finish your homework, dear."

Beatrice meant to glare at Kinsey for the condescending behavior. She really did. But to her utter dismay, she found herself tearing up instead. She pressed her hand to her mouth, trying to push the tears back down. If she had to cry, she should at least try to keep it together until after class.

"Oh no," Kinsey said, her face softening. She got out of her desk and came to wrap her arms around Beatrice's shoulders. "It's okay, sweetie. You're doing fine."

"I have to finish these problems," Beatrice blubbered into Kinsey's elbow. There was no stopping the tears now. They were going to run their course, no matter how many of her classmates were giving her funny looks. Fortunately, Kinsey was shielding her from most of them, creating a circle of reprieve. "I got all behind on things yesterday, and then I fell asleep trying to write a paper, and I overslept because I hadn't set my alarm—"

"Don't worry about the homework, Bee. You've only got a couple problems left, and it's just small beans homework. It won't hurt your grade hardly at all. Just take a breath. You're doing fine."

"I'm not."

"You are. I promise. You're doing great." Kinsey turned and dug in her bag, producing a small pack of tissues. She handed them to Beatrice. "Deep breath, honey. It's Friday. You just have to get through the rest of the day. Then you don't have to come back to the city until Monday."

Beatrice wiped her eyes and tried to follow Kinsey's advice to breathe. By the time Sasha came back, skidding in just seconds before the professor, Beatrice had mostly pulled herself together.

"Caffeine," Sasha announced, setting a tall cup of coffee on Beatrice's desk.

"Thanks, Sasha," Beatrice sniffed, reaching for her wallet.

"Oh my God, don't pay me back," Sasha said. "It was like three dollars."

"Are you sure?"

"Of course. Listen, at some point in the future, you will be nice and buy me something cheap, and we'll be even." She paused, frowning thoughtfully. "We might already be even, actually. I don't think I ever paid you back for your vending machine run last week."

"Thanks," Beatrice said. "I'm sorry I snapped at you."

Sasha waved it off as the professor started calling roll. Beatrice handed in her mostly-completed homework with only the smallest twinge of guilt. By the end of class—between the coffee and Kinsey being aggressively supportive—she felt a little better. Tender, still, but less likely to burst into tears over tiny things. Maybe small-to-moderate things, but that was a step up. And Kinsey was right. It was Friday. She just had to get through the rest of the day.

Beatrice kept digging through her bag as she walked the last half mile from the train station to her home. She was certain that in her cranky, exhausted state, she had forgotten something vital on the train, or back at school. She repeated her Monday/Wednesday/Friday checklist to herself as she felt around for the umpteenth time:

　* keys
　* wallet
　* laptop
　* two textbooks
　* one novel
　* essay folder
　* pencils
　* phone

Check, check, check . . . Crap.

She stopped, moving closer to the stone facade of the bank so she'd be out of the way of any foot traffic, and rummaged in the bottom of her bag for her phone. She was sure she'd had her hands on it two seconds ago.

"Oh come on," she grumbled, flipping the top flap closed and shoving her hands in the outer pockets. "I *know* you're in there."

Her fingers met the cool plastic case of her phone—

"Lost your pet gremlin?" a male voice asked from behind her.

Beatrice jumped back with a squawk, scraping her shoulder against the rough wall. She clutched her school bag to her chest like a shield.

The tattooed intruder from the library stood on the sidewalk next to her, a canvas grocery bag in one hand. He cocked his head to one side, raising both eyebrows at her reaction. "Hey."

Beatrice let out a puff of air, her face heating. She hitched her bag up on her shoulder, trying to regain some of her lost composure. "So you're stalking me now? That's great. Just great."

"Yes," he said sardonically. "I used my extensive network of spies to track down a tiny, weird, crazy girl whose name I don't even know because I've become obsessed after fighting with her for five minutes in a library."

"You could have followed me home the other day," Beatrice pointed out, crossing her arms.

"Give yourself some credit. I think you would have noticed if someone followed you all the way out here." He motioned down the street with the grocery bag—which did indeed seem to be filled with groceries. Some kind of leafy vegetable stuck up from one corner, the end of a box of noodles from another. "I'm not actually stalking you. I live over there."

Beatrice frowned, annoyed at herself for believing him. She hardly knew anything about him. Not even his name. She should be cautious, instead of just trusting whatever he said because he *looked honest.* Plenty of serial killers probably looked honest, too. And it ought to raise a red flag or two that he allegedly lived in the same small town as her.

He shook his head when she didn't reply. "Okay, well. Good luck with that gremlin, Simba." He hit the button for the crosswalk a couple of times. "I hear they can be kind of a handful. Especially when fed after midnight."

"I'm sorry, *what*?"

"You've never watched *Gremlins*?" he asked, turning back to face her.

"Not that. You just called me Simba."

"Oh. Right." He made a motion with his hands like he was fluffing an imaginary wig. The grocery bag slipped to his elbow and swung like a pendulum. "Because of the hair."

Beatrice stared at him.

"Simba is a lion from *The Lion King*?" he added. "Kids' movie. Wildly popular. Also a musical. With puppets. They have ads up for it all over Manhattan, all the time."

"I know who Simba is," Beatrice snapped. "I just don't understand why the heck you would call *me* Simba."

"Lionesses don't have manes," he said, narrowing his eyes at her like *she* was the crazy one. "What did you *want* me to call you?"

"I don't," Beatrice said, bristling. Any other day, the comment wouldn't have bothered her. But Kinsey had already implied her hair looked like a rat's nest this morning, and she didn't need cute strangers reminding her that she could rarely get her hair entirely under control. It wasn't like she never brushed her hair. She just had more of it than she knew what to do with.

His eyebrows drew together. Not like he was angry. Not really. More like he was trying to figure her out. "Okay, then." The light changed for the crosswalk, indicating it was safe to cross. He rolled his shoulders and raised his hand in a kind of wave as he turned away. "Sorry to bother you."

Beatrice stood there and watched him walk away, battling the impulsive, stupid part of her that wanted to jog after him and apologize. It wasn't his fault she was stressed out and irritable.

But she didn't have any proof he wasn't stalking her, either. Except for the small, instinctual part of her that had relaxed when she saw it was him talking to her. Like being around him made her safe.

Which was idiotic, considering how they met. Where was this conviction he wouldn't hurt her even coming from? And why should she care if she'd snapped at him? It was weird that he'd run into her again. Right? It was *weird*. She was allowed to get defensive.

Except—halfway down the next block, he jaywalked across the street and let himself into one of the rundown apartment buildings clustered there.

He did live here.

Mentally kicking herself for being such a jerk for no reason, Beatrice slunk the rest of the way home, where she could fling herself on her bed and berate her life choices until she was too tired to keep her eyes open anymore.

SIX

It didn't bother Julian that the weird lion-girl from the library had been so put out with him when he ran into her last night. Because that would imply he cared what she thought about him. Which he shouldn't. Because she was weird. And dressed like a cross between a '70s family sitcom character and a '90s grunge musician. And stupidly stood up for strangers against knife-wielding criminals.

And who cared what weird, fashion-confused, stupid-brave people thought?

It didn't matter, anyway. He was going to have to take off somewhere else as soon as he got the funds to move again. That run-in with Vito was more than enough proof that coming back here was a terrible, terrible idea. Even if he did see Simba again, there'd be no point trying to build a relationship. Not that he *wanted* a relationship with her. He'd mostly avoided getting involved with anyone since he dropped out of high school. He hated letting people down. Especially people he cared about. It was easier to be on his own.

Plus, Julian was already dealing with plenty of crap without adding any more complications to his life. Living with Fabiana was more of a pain in the ass than he'd anticipated. She *never stopped complaining* about the state of his apartment. He had to suffer through a fifteen-minute tirade yesterday morning after her own hair dryer shorted out the power. Last night, she'd gone into a state of near-hysterics when a cockroach skittered over her bare foot. And this morning, he'd been bullied out of the apartment—again—to fetch her coffee. He didn't have a coffee maker, and Fabiana was apparently going to suffer an aneurysm if deprived of her morning caffeine fix.

If all that wasn't aggravating enough, the floor—big shocker— was murder to sleep on. Julian hadn't slept long or well, and he had the beginnings of a headache because of it.

In fact, as he joined the short line at the coffee shop register, he gave serious thought to getting a coffee for himself, too. He wasn't a fan of the stuff, but if he dumped in enough creamer, it was tolerable.

Julian pulled out his wallet as the guy in front of him finished up his order. He had another 75 cents he could use to pick up a second cup. He just wasn't sure the pick-me-up was worth the potential stomachache. Particularly since Java Mama coffee had a certain . . . *reputation*.

The guy ahead of Julian took his change and coffee and headed for a table, eyeing his beverage with trepidation.

"Thanks," the cashier said, to the sound of coins falling into the register drawer. "I can help the next—" She cut herself off when she locked eyes with Julian.

He froze.

She had wrestled her massive mane into something that would only be termed a ponytail by the most generous of souls, and the brown Java Mama polo shirt and baseball cap made her look more ordinary than the eclectic outfits he'd seen her wear before, but there was no mistaking her.

A look of dismay crossed Simba's features. "Oh God."

"Good grief," Julian said simultaneously, tipping his head back in exasperation.

No wonder she thought he was stalking her. It was like he'd developed a bizarre sixth sense for bumping into her.

"Look, I'm just trying to buy some damn coffee," he said, bracing his hands on the counter and scowling at her. "I'm *not* stalking you."

More than one head in the cafe turned at this proclamation. The two other girls behind the counter, who were lackadaisically filling orders, stopped gossiping to stare.

Simba turned a blotchy shade of pink under her freckles. "I know," she said, pressing her hands to her cheeks. "I know, I just— God. You caught me on a really bad day yesterday. Ugh. Listen, let me get your . . . coffee, was it?"

He blinked at her a few times, thrown. She was . . . what, apologizing, now? That was dumb. He didn't blame her for being freaked out yesterday. He knew better than to approach strange girls on the street at night. It made most of them jumpy. And anyway, he reminded himself, he didn't care what she thought.

Christ. He wasn't awake enough for this. "Yeah, but—"

She frowned. "Are you sure? It's . . . not very good coffee."

"I'm aware of that, yes," Julian said, remembering Fabiana's prolonged complaining about the quality yesterday morning. "That's one of the draws, actually."

Simba's dubious expression became outright incredulous. "You *like* terrible coffee?"

"Never mind," Julian said. He was not about to confess he was harboring fanciful hopes of convincing his sister to move her butt somewhere else by sabotaging her with lousy coffee. He slapped his money down on the counter. "I just want a medium coffee, no sugar, three creams. And a little less judgment on my beverage choices, if you don't mind."

"Keep your money," she said, shoving the quarters and nickels back at him.

"But—"

"Moira, did you get that order?" she called over her shoulder, going to the pastry case and putting a selection in a brown paper bag.

"Got it," said the barista with purple lipstick. She looked about as confused about the exchange as Julian felt. He wasn't sure if this made him feel better or worse.

"The coffee is crap," Simba said, "but we get our muffins and croissants from a woman who runs a bakery over in Newburgh, and they're pretty great. Are you allergic to nuts?"

"No, but—Will you stop trying to give me pastries and let me pay for the damn coffee?"

"No," she said, topping the selection off with a walnut muffin. She folded the top over and plunked the bag on the counter, staring him down with those expressive gray eyes, like she was daring him to take it. "The pastries are symbolic."

She was crazy. Absolutely, completely insane. "*What?*"

"I'm trying to apologize for yesterday."

"By giving me pastries?"

"Yes."

Julian closed his eyes and gave his head a shake. He felt like he'd stepped into an alternate dimension where the rules of logic were null and void. But when he opened his eyes, Simba was still standing there, with her ridiculous hair, in her ugly uniform, watching him. Her expression remained stubborn, but her fingers were playing with the apron strings looped around her waist. Like she was nervous.

For a split second, brought on no doubt by his lack of sleep, Julian wanted to reach across the counter and . . . make contact. Flick the brim of her hat, or tweak the collar of her polo shirt, or wrap his fingers around her hand to still the fidgeting.

Oh. Shit.

He pulled his eyes away from her and glowered at the paper bag on the counter. "I don't follow. Why are you apologizing again?"

"You caught me on a bad day, yesterday, and I was acting like a jerk, and I feel terrible, and can you please for the love of God just take the dang pastries?"

"You won't get in trouble, will you?" he asked, glancing back at the two baristas, who were staring at them with open curiosity.

"We're supposed to get free coffee if we work here, and I wouldn't drink this stuff if they paid me," Simba said. "Which— well, you know what I mean. The point is, I won't get in trouble."

"Here, hon," Moira said, plonking a coffee down on the counter next to the bag of pastries. "No sugar, three creams."

"If you try to pay for that, I'll break your fingers," Simba informed him, leveling him with the same stubborn glare she'd given Vito two days ago.

He was pretty sure she was joking. Sixty percent sure. There was a morbid glint in her eye that made him wonder.

"You're so weird," Julian muttered, sliding the bag of pastries and the coffee off the counter.

"Actually," she said, going pink again, "my name is Beatrice."

He lifted an eyebrow at her. "That's a big name for such a tiny person, isn't it?"

The corner of her mouth twitched. "Just be happy my mom didn't go with her original idea."

"Which was what?"

"Desdemona Amaryllis," she said, in a pitch-perfect deadpan.

Julian let out an undignified snort of laughter. He covered his mouth with his wrist and tried to turn the snort into a cough and save some face.

But Beatrice the pastry-pushing, coffee-proffering lion-girl was trying to hide a very smug-looking smile of her own. "Most people just call me Bee," she said.

He recovered quickly and stuck out a hand to shake hers. "Julian. Most people call me Julian."

She smiled at him—grinned, really—as their hands met. Hers was small and slender, but her grip was decisive. It was a nice hand, and warm. The warmth of that single point of contact spread up his arm and all through him like a bonfire on a cold day. And his stupid, tired brain didn't want to let go. He couldn't help but think how nice it would be to keep on holding her hand indefinitely.

Julian gave himself a thorough mental shake and pulled his hand back. The last thing he needed right now was to start entertaining thoughts of being a normal person doing normal things like flirting with weird girls who weren't even all that pretty.

Not that she *wasn't* pretty. She was certainly interesting-looking. Julian kept trying to work out how he'd draw her hair, or the peculiar quirk of her lips when she was trying not to smile—

Dammit, Julian, pull yourself together.

He had to get out of there. He thanked Beatrice again, nearly ran into the doorjamb trying to shoulder his way out, and all but sprinted back to his apartment.

"Really, Jules? Did you have to go back to that shit-hole today?" Fabiana complained when Julian breathlessly shoved the requested coffee into her hands.

"If you want something different, you're going to have to dish out for it yourself," Julian told her. He set the bag of pastries on the counter and took out a chocolate croissant. "You want?"

"You can't go to a decent cafe, but you can afford a sack full of croissants?" Fabiana asked, snatching the pastry out of his hand.

"They're symbolic," Julian said, digging in the bag again for a muffin.

"What?"

Julian checked his grin at the sight of his sister's scowl. "Never mind."

"Okay, freak," Fabiana muttered, dropping into one of the craptastic kitchen chairs. She took a cautious sip of coffee and made a face. "This is disgusting. It tastes like tar made with sweaty feet."

"Gross," Julian said. He leaned against the counter and took a bite of the walnut muffin. Beatrice was right. It was amazing. Next time he had the cash to spare he should go back and—

"You're doing this on purpose, aren't you?" Fabiana demanded.

"Doing what?"

"If you want me out, just say so. You don't have to be a passive-aggressive jerk about it."

Oh. Oops.

Julian sighed and sat at the table with her. "I'm not going to kick you out," he said. "It's just that I'm running out of money, and I only have one lead on one job. Which I can't take. And *that*"—he tipped his muffin at the coffee cup on the table between them— "is the cheapest coffee in a five-mile radius."

Fabiana's shoulders relaxed a fraction, out of their defensive position. "Would you splurge on an actual coffee maker if I told you I've got an interview for a part-time thing on Tuesday?" she asked. "I think I'll get it, if that makes a difference."

"I didn't know you'd applied for anything," Julian said.

Fabiana picked at the edge of her coffee lid. "I may have suspected the blow-out with Walter was coming."

"Why? What did he—"

"It's just part-time," she continued, speaking over him, "but I thought I could at least try to help out until I can bring Walter around. You've got a fridge that looks like it was stocked by an anorexic bird. You're a guy. You need to eat more protein than eggs and peanut butter."

Julian rubbed the back of his head. She'd never offered to help out before. When she crashed with him, she was usually off again a few days later. "Walter's being a real dick this time, huh?"

Fabiana shrugged, absentmindedly taking another sip of coffee. She winced and made a disgusted sound. "What is this made of? Toxic sludge?"

"Maybe you'll get superpowers," Julian offered.

"If I get toxic sludge powers, I'm going to go full super-villain and kick your ass for causing the problem."

"Okay. Fair."

"Coffee maker?"

Julian groaned, annoyed that the guilt trip was working on him. "Fine. We'll get you the coffee maker. But we're getting the cheapest one at Goodwill, and you'll just have to deal until we get some actual cash coming in."

"I accept your terms," Fabiana said, brightening. She got up—leaving her half-finished croissant and the coffee on the table—and shoved Julian's head affectionately on her way past.

"Ow," Julian complained, more out of a sense of tradition than because it hurt.

"You're buying me another coffee on the way over, though," she called over her shoulder as she slipped into the bathroom.

Julian shot her a glare, but she'd already shut the door. He picked up the coffee from the table and sniffed it. It just smelled like coffee, to him. Although he had to admit there was an odd smell underneath. Vinegar? The Wi-Fi at Java Mama must be incredible. Julian had no idea how they would still be in business, otherwise.

The bathroom door popped open, and Fabiana hung out of it, her long, black hair clipped out of her face, toothbrush in hand, her eyes narrowed suspiciously. "Why can't you take your one job lead?"

He'd been hoping she'd miss that. "It's in the city," he said, pushing the coffee across the table.

She stared at him, expression unchanging. No one could accuse them of having twin telepathy.

"What if I ran into someone?" Julian asked, as though he hadn't run into Vito already.

Julian hadn't divulged too many details when he'd told Fabiana what happened with Vito and the rest of them. He didn't like dwelling on that part of his life too much. Vito's guilty verdict had been overturned shortly after sentencing—some kind of technical issue with the jury—but one of the things that put him in prison was Julian's testimony, after he flipped on Vito's gang to the FBI. That wasn't the kind of thing Vito and his thugs took too kindly to. Fabiana was familiar enough with the gist of the story to understand that Julian taking a job in the city was a significant risk.

"Oh. Them. Yeah, I guess that's a good reason," Fabiana said, though she didn't sound convinced. She shook her head. "Whatever. We'll figure it out."

She didn't give him a chance to respond, shutting herself in the bathroom again. Julian bit off another piece of muffin, touched by the fact that she'd said 'we' and not 'you.' They hadn't been a team for a long time.

The stupid thing was, Julian hadn't told Mr. Fisk he was no longer interested in the position at the art center. He couldn't make himself go through with it. He kept coming up with feeble distractions that prevented him from calling, or talking himself in circles to justify how he might still be able to avoid Vito.

That could have just been a fluke, after all. And if Julian was careful to take the more roundabout subway route to Christopher

St. Station, and kept the hell away from Washington Square Park, the chances of running into Vito again were slim to none. New York City was a big place.

Plus, that custodian gig was also the only job Julian had been offered since moving up here. He'd had two more interviews locally since, and neither one had gone well. One position was already filled by the time Julian got there, and the interviewer at the second place couldn't seem to get past Julian's ink. He couldn't keep running in circles like this forever, while his bank account drained to nothing.

It scared him, how much he wanted that teaching job. He'd been lucky to have great art teachers when he was in high school and middle school, and the idea of fostering creativity in other people held a draw he couldn't quite explain.

Just yesterday, he had spent hours on his phone, researching art-related lesson plans for younger kids. The last few pages of the sketchbook Fabiana had given him were now crammed with ideas. He even had a growing list of books he wanted to dig up at the library next time he went.

Rationally, he knew he was getting ahead of himself. Letting hope grow would only mean he'd end up getting hurt when life cut him down again. But . . .

He wanted an excuse to draw again. And there was still that tiny part of him that wanted to believe things could get better. That his shitty, shitty luck had to turn around eventually.

Would it be so bad just to ask Mr. Fisk what was required to apply for the teaching position? He wouldn't be agreeing to take it on. He'd just be getting the facts. In all likelihood, the standards would be above Julian's abilities, and that would be the end of it. At least he would know.

Julian pulled out his phone as Fabiana switched on her hair dryer. Just asking wouldn't hurt, right?

Taking a deep breath, he dialed Mr. Fisk's number at the art center. It was Saturday, so he expected it to go to voicemail, but Mr. Fisk picked up on the second ring.

"Greenwich Village Center for the Arts, Harold Fisk speaking," he said brightly.

"Mr. Fisk, this is Julian Moon," Julian said in a rush, before he could lose his nerve. "I was wondering—if it's still open—if you could tell me what exactly you'd want from me to apply for that teaching gig?"

SEVEN

After the three days of running into Julian in one week, he was nowhere to be found. Beatrice didn't see him at Java Mama on Sunday during her shift. She never saw him around his apartment building on her way to or from the local train station. He'd gone a whole week without barging into her study rooms with scary-looking guys chasing him.

Not that Beatrice wanted terrifying library confrontations to become part of her day-to-day life. Once had been quite enough for one decade.

It was just strange. To have someone burst into her life so emphatically and then . . .

Nothing.

She wasn't sure why she kept worrying the issue. No matter how explosive that first meeting had been, Julian ought to be fading from her memory by now. Not lodging in a back corner of her mind to irritate her at random moments. It wasn't like she had a lot of extra time on her hands to spare for making new friends.

She just couldn't make sense of it. She had only seen him *once* at Java Mama, in all the time she'd worked there.

Not that there was anything surprising about that. He'd

probably come around to the idea that terrible coffee was not, in fact, good.

Shaking her head, Beatrice pushed that line of thought back into its corner and tried to focus on something productive. Her Friday afternoon lit class had just let out, and she was crossing through the park on her way to the NYU food court to grab something to eat on the train home. The sun was already setting, glinting off the tall buildings around her, and casting the Washington Square Arch in gold. The trees were showing off their fall colors in all shades of yellow and red. At every gust of wind, leaves broke free and drifted, dancing, to the ground.

Beatrice took in a big lungful of crisp autumn air, inhaling the mingling scents of earth and cold and the city grit. She slowed her purposeful stride to more of a stroll, allowing herself to savor her surroundings. Yes, she wanted to get to the subway before dark, but the streets around NYU were well-lit and relatively safe. This was one of Beatrice's favorite times of year. It seemed a shame to waste an opportunity, however brief, to revel in it while it lasted.

Anyway, she could spare the time to amble in the park today. To her great satisfaction, she wasn't behind on any of her homework this week. The backlog was clear. She had routine studying and some minor things due on Monday, but that was it. She wouldn't even have to do any coursework on the train tonight. Which meant she might be able to catch a short nap, if the train wasn't filled with skeevy-looking guys. For the next few hours, she was free.

"Bee!"

Beatrice's head snapped around, a sense of foreboding stealing over her. She hoped to God she had misidentified the voice. That it was only some random student calling out to someone with the same nickname, who happened to sound exactly like her little brother.

Her hopes were dashed the second she set eyes on the gawky figure running up the sidewalk towards her, nearly knocking over a student in headphones when she didn't step out of the way fast enough.

He threw an apology over his shoulder at the girl, then waved frantically at Beatrice. "Hey!"

Beatrice's heart sank. Nathaniel was her half-brother, but they looked so alike most people would never guess. He had the same walnut-brown hair as Beatrice, and the same abundance of freckles. He was three years younger and three inches taller—or he had been the last time they'd measured. Still short, for a boy, but he'd been smug about being the taller sibling since the day he discovered he surpassed her in height by a quarter inch. He was sometimes obnoxious, often grumpy, and always full to bursting with more affection than he seemed to know what to do with.

He was also supposed to be in California.

"Gnat!" Beatrice barked, marching back up the sidewalk towards Nath, all thoughts of enjoying the foliage scrubbed from her mind. "What are you doing in New York?"

"I was looking for you everywhere." Nath stopped, dropping his duffel bag on the sidewalk beside him. He also had a backpack slung over one shoulder. That wasn't good. He wasn't supposed to come home before Thanksgiving, which was still three weeks away. "You weren't answering your phone."

"Did something happen?" Beatrice demanded, seizing his shoulder like she could squeeze the truth out of him. "Are you hurt? You didn't go and do something stupid and get yourself expelled, did you?" She pressed her hands to her face, envisioning all the reasons Nath might have been expelled from Stanford. "Oh my God, they caught you smoking weed, didn't they?"

"No, nothing like that," Nath said, tossing her a grumpy frown. "And smoking weed isn't illegal in California, grandma. I just—"

He sucked his cheek and looked around, as though a convincing lie might present itself from behind the Washington Square Arch. "I decided to come home, is all."

Beatrice pressed the heels of her hands to her eyes. "*Nath*," she groaned.

"You don't know what it's like there," her little brother said defensively. "Everything's weird, and I don't know anybody, and I suck at all my classes—"

"Dad's going to kill you," Beatrice said, dragging her fingers down her face and looking at Nath over the top of them. "And then Mom's going to kill you. And then they'll chop you into tiny pieces and put you down the garbage disposal."

"That's why I wanted to come find you first," Nath said, his eyes widening into his best impression of a puppy in an ASPCA commercial. "They won't kill me if you back me up."

"No, they'll still kill you," said Beatrice. "They'll just kill me, first." She groaned again. "Nath . . ."

"Please, Bee," Nathaniel begged, pressing his hands together. "I don't know how I'm supposed to tell them without you. You're like . . . You're like this calm presence of reason. They never yell as much when you're there."

"You know that's not true. It's just that some of it gets directed at *me*."

"Please, Bee. You have to help me. I can't face them alone."

Beatrice shook her head, but she knew she'd already lost the battle. She should be immune to the puppy-dog look by now. But he looked so sad and helpless. She couldn't have felt guiltier if she'd gone out of her way to kick an actual puppy. "Okay," she relented, trying to sound as put-out as possible. "Fine. I'll do it."

Nath brightened, all traces of the puppy face gone. "Thank you, thank you," he said, wrapping her in a tight hug and rocking her back and forth. "You're the best sister in the world!"

"Yeah, yeah," Beatrice grumbled, detaching herself from the hug and trying to restore some of her dignity. "Did you eat on the plane? Do I need to feed you?"

"I'm starving," Nath confessed. "Can we get pizza? The pizza in California is awful. They serve it with *ranch dressing*."

Beatrice wrinkled her nose. "Ew, why?"

"Because it's a disgusting cardboard monstrosity and the ranch dressing is supposed to distract you from the fact you're eating crap. I need real pizza, stat."

"We're getting dinner from the food court," Beatrice said, in her strictest older-sister voice. He was still in trouble for dropping all this drama on her head without warning. She couldn't give in to *everything* he wanted.

Turning on her heel, she started walking, trusting him to catch up. "I can't believe you dropped out," she grumbled when he fell into step with her.

"California sucks," Nath said. And that was all he had to say on the matter.

The blowout at home had been harder to wrangle under control than usual. Nath hadn't come up with a better excuse for dropping out of college by the time they got home, which didn't help. Beatrice's mom had demanded a better explanation while her step-dad, Mike, refused to negotiate at all. His sole focus had been on forcing Nath to return to California and re-enroll at Stanford.

But Nath stood his ground and refused to either expound on his reasoning or go back. So Mike issued an ultimatum: If Nath didn't go back to Stanford, he'd have to find somewhere else to sleep. Nath had started for the door, threatening to sleep in the park with the raccoons.

Beatrice had put a stop to the yelling before he walked out, but only by resorting to shouting herself. The best she could do was to get everyone to promise not to make any rash decisions until they'd slept on it. Mike's ultimatum—which was only issued in the heat of the moment—had been suspended. Nath was set up on an air mattress for the night. Everyone stopped arguing, at last.

It was a temporary solution. Even when she came up with the compromise, Beatrice had known her whole weekend would be consumed with playing referee. Every free moment had been spent talking to her still-fuming family members, trying to get them all to understand each other.

Unsurprisingly, Beatrice's weekend was terrible. And the arrival of Monday morning did nothing to relieve her mood. She was behind on her schoolwork again. What little coursework she'd managed to complete over the weekend was done on the sly at work. It got so bad, she'd almost called in sick on Sunday. She'd wanted to hole up in the library for a few hours with a challenging list of Spanish words she had to memorize, but she couldn't afford the dent in her paycheck.

Not that there was anything to be done about that now, Beatrice thought as she walked down the narrow, outdoor platform of her hometown's train station, a ceramic travel mug of coffee in her mitten-encased hands. She'd caught up from falling behind on her assignments before. She could do it again. Even while refereeing her family's ridiculously explosive confrontations.

She pushed away the thread of resentment threatening to further sour her mood and tried to put the weekend out of her mind. She could vent to Kinsey and Sasha at lunch. In the meantime, the long school day meant she wouldn't have to deal with her family until this evening.

As she made her way to her usual waiting spot near the end of the platform, her eyes wandered over the other commuters. She recognized a lot of faces after weeks of going back and forth to the city, though she didn't know any names.

Then her eyes snagged on a figure she *did* know.

She didn't realize she'd been looking for Julian until she saw him standing there, not ten feet away, waiting for the southbound train. He had the hood of his sweatshirt up, earbuds in, and was playing a game or something on his phone.

Her spirits sprang from her toes to somewhere over her head like a buoy shooting up out of the water. She bounced over without even thinking about it.

"Hey!" she said brightly, poking his arm.

Julian startled back and yanked one of the earbuds out of his ear. "Jesus Christ," he said, putting a hand on his chest. "You scared the shit out of me."

Beatrice took a mirroring step back, feeling herself flush. Why she couldn't have one normal conversation with this boy was beyond her. "Sorry."

"No, it's—it's fine. Sorry," Julian said, running a hand through his curls and knocking his hood down in the process. Frowning, he jerked it back up. "Beatrice, right?"

"That's me." She adjusted the strap of her bag to distract from how awkward she felt. It didn't help much. "Are you going into the city?"

"Um. Yeah." His eyes stayed on his earbud cord as he wrapped it around the phone. "New job."

"Good job?"

"*I* think so." He stashed his phone in a pocket. "There's this art center in Greenwich Village. I'm mostly cleaning paint off the floors, but they're going to try to get me set up to teach a couple of the younger classes."

"A-*ha!*" Beatrice said, pointing at him in triumph.

He drew back a fraction, staring at her outstretched finger in alarm. "What, 'a-ha?'"

"I *knew* you looked like an artist," she said, grinning. "You just need a beanie and a charcoal smudge on your face and you'd fit the stereotype exactly."

He scoffed, shaking his head. "I'm not an artist. The only reason they have me teaching the younger kids is they can't find someone else to do it, and my high school art teacher is on the board. I haven't really drawn in years."

"Why not?" Beatrice asked, a split second before she realized what an intensely personal question it was. "No, sorry. That's kind of nosy, isn't it?"

"No. Well, yeah. But I don't—" Julian huffed and tried again. "It's not a big secret is what I mean." He held up his left hand and did a sort of half-wave with it. "Broke my hand. Fell out of the habit after that, I guess."

"Oh. I'm sorry."

He shrugged. "You're on your way to school?"

"Yeah." Beatrice sighed. "And I'm going to have to do my statistics homework on the train again because I stupidly went out with my boyfriend on Saturday, even though I was already behind on my assignments for this week."

"Oh. Well—I'm sure he would have understood," Julian said, shoving his hands in his pockets.

"Maybe," Beatrice said. She'd *tried* to explain to Greyson about her busy schedule and her family drama. But *a little break from the stress wouldn't hurt.* And *she had to eat sometime.* And *he'd already driven all the way up to her apartment.*

He wasn't wrong. On paper, a few hours away from her family seemed like a great idea. It wasn't Greyson's fault that his well-meaning attempt to cheer her up had only twisted the source of her stress.

Beatrice shook her head. "He was just trying to help. I wouldn't have been able to get much done at home, anyway. Not with—" She stopped, realizing she was on the verge of venting her whole weekend to some guy who seemed perpetually annoyed by her, and whom she had spoken to for less than an hour altogether.

It was a bad habit she had, throwing her friendship at people who had no intention of catching it. She'd thought it was a habit she'd broken. It hurt when she liked someone a lot and later realized they only tolerated her because they didn't know how to back out without hurting her feelings.

And yet Julian wasn't checking his phone, or looking for the train, or doing anything at all to put any more distance between them. He was looking straight at her, his body squared with hers. He lifted an eyebrow when she cut herself off, as though he was listening and not just being polite.

"Shitty roommates?" he guessed.

She made a *ch* noise that wanted to be a laugh when it grew up. "Do parents count as roommates?"

He considered this for a second. "Depends on how shitty they are."

"They aren't that bad. They're just—" Beatrice huffed. And then, maybe because she desperately needed to get it off her chest, she said, "My little brother showed up Friday and announced he wasn't going to Stanford anymore. My parents didn't take the news well. He didn't take their not taking it well well. I somehow ended up as the complaint receptacle for all sides. It's a whole Thing," she said, splaying her fingers for emphasis.

"That would certainly put a damper on the homework," Julian said.

"You're telling me." She lifted her trusty travel mug, still warm in her be-mittened hand. "At least I remembered coffee today."

He made a face. "I hope that's not the crap you sell at that cafe."

"Lord, no. I made this at home."

"And this is somehow better than when you make it at Java Mama?" he asked, lifting an eyebrow.

"I actually purchase good beans, so yes, it's absolutely better. Taste it if you don't believe me," she said, taking the lid off and shoving the cup under his nose.

"I believe you," Julian said, holding up his hands. He looked like he was trying not to laugh. "I don't think I'd be able to taste the difference, anyway. I don't drink coffee."

"Weirdo." Beatrice replaced the lid and took a sip herself. "But wait, what were you buying coffee for, then? Last week, I mean?"

He sighed a great sigh and shoved his hands back in his pockets. "My sister. She's been crashing with me."

"*She* enjoys bad coffee?"

"Hell, no. I *had* hoped she'd get sick of the coffee and get motivated to figure herself out. It sounds really petty now that I say it out loud."

"I mean," Beatrice said, "if it *worked*—"

"Well, I was strong-armed into buying her a coffee maker. And I'm still sleeping on the floor. So, no. It didn't work. But what am I going to do? She's my sister. I can't not bail her out."

The train rattled in, brakes squealing. People on the platform shuffled towards the edge so they could dash on board.

Beatrice adjusted her bag, nervous. She liked talking to Julian, even if he seemed annoyed most of the time. Maybe it was wishful thinking, but his annoyance didn't seem entirely genuine. She'd gotten him to laugh, once. And she could have sworn the last time he'd called her weird—in the coffee shop when he accepted her pastry peace offering—it had sounded more like an endearment than an insult.

"Do you want to sit together?" she blurted out. "I won't be great company because of the homework, but it's better than sitting next to strangers, right?"

Julian blinked at her. He was going to call her crazy and find a different car to ride in. She felt like an idiot. Of course his annoyance with her was genuine. Why wouldn't it be?

She flushed, and she was about to take back the offer when Julian spoke.

"Okay," he said. "Sure. Why not?"

EIGHT

There were a lot of reasons why Julian shouldn't agree to sit next to Beatrice on the train. Starting with the fact he'd been doing his best to avoid her since their run-in at Java Mama. His fixation on her had gotten worse after that. He'd found himself thinking about her at random times. For no reason at all. Which was a really bad sign.

There was a thrift store down the street from his apartment with two mannequins decked out in the most bizarre outfits, and every time Julian passed it, he couldn't help but think of Beatrice and her terrible-yet-endearing fashion choices. He'd stopped going down Cyprus Street entirely because he kept glancing in the window every time he passed Java Mama to see if she was working.

He couldn't get her face out of his brain. He'd even broken out his sketchbook in a fit of desperation, hoping if he got her features down on paper, he could get them out of his brain and forget about her.

But either he was rustier at drawing than he'd feared, or the idea was complete bullshit. No matter how much he sketched, her image stuck in his mind: The slightly upturned nose. The curve of her lips when she smiled. Those stark, brown freckles scattered over her skin like paint splatters, from her hairline down until they disappeared under her collar . . .

Julian was dangerously close to becoming enamored of her. He'd avoided getting involved with anyone since dropping out of high school. He couldn't justify dragging some innocent girl into the overwhelming chaos of his life. Hell, he barely sustained a halfway healthy relationship with his own sister.

He figured the best cure for this budding interest in Beatrice would be to stay away. She was too kind. Too brave. And he was too lonely. It would be easy to forget all the reasons why dating *anyone* was a bad idea. Especially a girl like Beatrice, who was evidently dealing with her fair share of chaos at home already. She shouldn't have to be concerned about Julian's crap making things worse for her. And Julian's crap always seemed to make things worse for people he cared about. If he didn't nip this thing in the bud immediately, he was only going to let her down. Keeping his distance was the smart thing to do. For both of them.

Which was obviously why he'd arranged to sit next to her for the next hour and a half.

Sure.

Besides, she had a boyfriend. Which meant the only person's feelings Julian would be risking if he kept hanging around her were his own. And he was confident he could deal with those himself.

Like, ninety percent confident.

She had a giant statistics textbook balanced with a notebook in her lap and was frowning as she scratched in equations and muttered to herself. Julian didn't know what had been wrong with him in that study room when he decided she wasn't pretty. He must've been thrown off by her hideous sweater. She did have a knack for showing up in the most appalling colors. Today it was a frayed wool peacoat in what might best be described as a mustard yellow, if the mustard had gone a little moldy. Mauve flowers with pea soup–colored leaves wound around the cuffs and hem. It was a color combo that, realistically, could only be marketed to the colorblind.

And yet here was Beatrice, walking around in it like she was actually fond of the thing. Which was maybe why her whole deal was so captivating.

"Dang it," Beatrice muttered, shifting her books around. "I know I had my pencil here a second ago."

She had, in fact, stashed it behind her ear so she could punch numbers into her calculator. Julian had noticed because he'd been watching her out of the corner of his eye while pretending to play a game on his phone.

Christ. He was hopeless.

Careful not to catch her wild hair between his fingers, Julian plucked the offending pencil from behind her ear. He doodled a tiny smiley face in the margin of her notebook before dropping it in the open seam of her textbook.

"Oh my God," she said, clapping a hand to her forehead. "I'm an idiot."

"Happens to the best of us," Julian said, struggling not to laugh. "I once had a pencil behind my ear, another hooked on the collar of my shirt, and still got a third out of my bag because I'd lost track of the first two."

"It doesn't count if they were all different types of artist-y pencils."

"They weren't. They were cheap mechanical pencils for school."

"I guess that's pretty bad," Beatrice conceded. "I once had four of them stuck in my hair and didn't realize until I asked my friend to borrow one of her pencils and she gave me a Look. That was pretty embarrassing."

"To be fair," Julian said, eyeing her nest of hair, "it seems like it would be pretty easy to lose stuff in there."

"Mmm," Beatrice agreed. "Once, when I was brushing it out after school, a whole family of pigeons fell out."

Julian snorted so loudly a few heads turned in their direction.

"We had a devil of a time getting them out of the apartment," Beatrice said, only the barest crack in her deadpan. "Had to get the neighbors in to help. We were cleaning pigeon droppings off the furniture for weeks."

Julian had doubled over in his seat with laughter, his hood pulled over his face. "Stop," he begged. "Please. I'm dying."

Beatrice giggled and patted him companionably on the shoulder. "You okay there, bud?"

"You're so weird," Julian said, getting himself somewhat under control. He wiped tears from his eyes. "A family of pigeons . . . Good grief . . ."

She straightened her homework, smiling smugly to herself. "Don't worry, I'm more careful about sticking my head into pigeon nests now."

Julian shook his head at her, still grinning like an idiot. He couldn't remember the last time he'd hung out with anyone simply joking around. Before he fell into Beatrice's orbit, he couldn't have said when was the last time anyone had made him laugh this much. Or at all.

Oh man. This was such a bad idea.

No. It was fine. He was perfectly capable of just being friends with strange girls with bizarre senses of fashion. He'd been starved of friends lately. It wouldn't hurt to have just one, right?

"So tell me about this art thing you're working at," Beatrice said, writing out another problem from her book.

"Aren't you busy math-ing?"

She laughed. "I can listen and math at the same time. I already learned the concept from another class, so this is pretty easy, thank God."

"Sure," Julian said, frowning at the columns of numbers and symbols marching down the page. It looked complicated to him, but he'd never paid much attention in math. He'd never understood how anyone could expect him to sit there with a pencil in his hand and paper in front of him and *not* draw. "I'll take your word for it."

"Art place, art place, art place," Beatrice prodded, kicking him gently with her floral hiking books with each repeat.

"Good grief, woman. Fine," Julian said, swinging his leg out of the way as he fought off a grin. "It's not all that special or anything. They do a lot of art classes for kids, and they have a few studios they rent out for local artists, or artists in from out of town who need a place to, you know, art. And they've got a gallery they're always promoting a ton of local artists in. They do a showcase for the kids a few times a year, and they'll drag the older kids out to the Met periodically, which is pretty cool. A lot of the kids come from homes where that wouldn't really be an option for them."

"That sounds *really* cool," said Beatrice.

"I mean, I'm just cleaning shit," Julian said. "But if I have to clean shit for a living, that's the place I'd want to do it."

"Sounds more interesting than selling people terrible coffee," she said, wrinkling her nose. "And didn't you say you'd be teaching a couple classes, too?"

"I don't actually know about that, yet. I'm not really qualified for it. I think the guy who hired me thinks my art skills are better than they are. His point of reference was from before I stopped drawing." He flexed his left hand a few times, proving to himself the pain wasn't as bad as he remembered. "It doesn't matter. I'm happy to work there at all."

She tapped the back of his hand lightly with the eraser of her pencil. Julian's stomach did a weird kind of lurch in response. "Does your hand still bother you?"

"Not most of the time."

"But you never got back into drawing?"

He lifted his gaze to meet hers. She watched him so intently, his stomach lurched again. She had the most incredible eyes. He'd never known anyone who could make him feel like they were so soundly in his corner just by looking at him.

"Sorry." She shook her head, and her gaze snapped back to her homework, severing the connection. "I'm being nosy again. You're allowed to tell me to shut up. It just seems like art is something you're still into."

"I wanted to be a comic artist when I was a kid," Julian said, rubbing his thumb over the pale, inch-long scar at the base of his palm. "Or do graphic novels. I used to do this dumb ongoing strip where my sister and I were a couple of reindeer who were always getting into trouble. I thought I could really do it, too. Make comics for a living. I went to this fancy-ass high school with an intense art program, and I had all these plans to get into a great art school and . . . Well. Then life happened." He shrugged, shoving his hands in his pockets as he brushed memories of that time away. "It . . . didn't work out."

"So then you settle for cleaning floors?" Beatrice's pencil had stopped making figures on the paper. The look she gave him was so sad, he wanted to apologize for bumming her out.

"It's not as tragic as you're making it sound."

"Still," she said. "I'm sorry."

"Don't be sorry." He smiled, hoping it didn't look as bitter as it felt, and tried to make a joke out of it. "Show me an artist in any field who hasn't had to take some shitty job to support their habit."

"It just sucks when life takes a crap on what you want for

yourself," Beatrice said, scribbling a jagged little daisy in the corner of her notebook, close to the smiley face Julian had drawn. "It's not fair."

Julian shrugged, not sure how to respond. She was being too kind again. Too empathetic. He didn't know what to do with that. Fabiana was the only person he had left who gave a damn about him, and she didn't exactly have a nurturing personality. Sympathy wasn't something he was used to.

"You know, you could probably still do it if you really wanted," Beatrice said, looking over at him again. "Comics. You just need a plan. And some patience."

"And a crap-ton of luck," Julian put in.

"Or a crap-ton of hard work and a modicum of luck," Beatrice said, with the finality of someone reciting a mantra.

"Maybe." In his experience, if your luck was shitty enough, it didn't matter how many plans you made, or how patient you were, or how hard you worked. Nothing was going to pan out the way you wanted.

He shook his head. Time to change the subject. "Hey, you never told me what you're majoring in."

She hesitated for a split second, debating, he assumed, whether to let the abrupt change of subject slide. "Marketing," she said, somewhat stiffly. "Nothing so interesting as art."

"Are you a fan of marketing?" Julian asked, lifting an eyebrow.

"It's okay," Beatrice said, frowning as she cut a few sharp numbers into the page. "I do pretty well in the classes. And I know I can get a good job after I graduate. I have a few contacts already, and I think a couple of my professors would be happy to help out if they can. And it's not pouring coffee. That's a real plus for me."

"You don't sound that excited about it."

She made a noise close to a laugh. "I guess . . . I don't really feel like it matters. My dreams are kind of mundane. I want a little house of my own and a steady paycheck. I don't care what I do, job-wise, so long as it gets me to a place where I can . . ." She made an empty gesture with her hand, the pencil cutting a yellow line between her fingers. "Where I can just . . . breathe, I guess. I don't know if that makes any sense."

"I think I know what you mean," Julian said, slumping down in his seat and watching the phone lines loop past the window above the brightly-colored foliage. It wasn't so far off from what he wanted for himself, really. "Your dream is stability."

"Something like that."

Julian smiled ruefully at the power lines. That left him out of the picture, then. Stability and Julian didn't get along. Never had.

Not that it mattered. Because Beatrice had a boyfriend. And they were just going to be pals. End of story. He didn't need to feel a pang of regret at her words. He wasn't going to date her. He didn't *want* to date her.

He didn't.

NINE

Julian stood against a pillar at Grand Central Terminal, tapping his pencil against the cover of his sketchbook. A lot of people were on the platform with him, waiting for their train to pull in, but the pillar Julian leaned against meant he wasn't in too much danger of getting jostled. This time of day, the whole building was packed. At least the platforms themselves didn't attract too many sight-seeing tourists.

Julian chewed on the inside of his cheek, scowling at the cover of his sketchbook. His stomach was tight with the idea of seeing Beatrice again. Even though she probably wouldn't end up taking the same train. She seemed like the type of scholastic fanatic to stay late at the library poring over great tomes by candlelight. He didn't know why candlelight would be illuminating a modern library, but that was the image he rolled around in his mind like a hard caramel.

It wouldn't be a terrible illustration idea, actually.

Not with *Beatrice* at the table, of course. A witch character, maybe. An old one, who didn't look like Beatrice in the least. Or some kind of anthropomorphic bird . . .

He opened the sketchbook to a new page, balked at the blankness of it, and snapped it closed again. He shut his eyes tight and made himself breathe, ignoring the anxious fluttering in his chest. He was putting too much pressure on himself. He knew that. But knowing didn't take the pressure off.

Mr. Fisk had pulled Julian aside almost the second he walked in the art center's door this morning and told him he'd decided to put Julian in as a temporary teacher for a class of preschoolers and two kindergarten classes. Mr. Fisk and two of the other teachers had been swapping teaching duties until they found a permanent replacement, and they thought the kids were getting sick of the parade of teachers. All Julian had to do was make sure the kids didn't eat their crayons, according to Mr. Fisk. He asked Julian to shadow him for the next couple of days to get a handle on how things worked before Julian took over.

If Julian's trial run with the kids went well—and if he could get together a portfolio by the end of the year—Mr. Fisk had said he'd like to make the job permanent.

He even pointed Julian to one of the center's empty studios and told him he was welcome to use any of the art supplies there to execute the pieces he'd need.

Julian had felt equal parts thrilled and overwhelmed all day. And apparently the overwhelmed feeling had decided it was more important, if he couldn't even look at a blank fucking piece of paper.

He took a breath, opened the sketchbook again, and put a big, random scribble at the top right of the page. There. Now he couldn't ruin anything, because the page already looked terrible.

Take *that*, inner critic.

He boxed out a rectangle below the scribble and roughed in a general shape. Sketchy lines formed tall shelves, filling the bulk of the rectangle. Toward the bottom, behind a table stacked with hesitant indications of books and scrolls, he put an indistinct figure wearing an off-kilter triangle on its head. He put lines for candles all over the table, and then lightly scribbled in some shadows at the top of the image. It looked like a scribbly mess, but it was a mess he thought he could do something with.

He'd started working on a character design in the remaining space—his first instinct was to do a wizened old crow and wanted to get it out of his system because it seemed a little on the nose—when Beatrice walked onto the platform.

He shouldn't have been able to tell. His head was down, and he was only aware of people coming and going on the edges of his vision. She didn't even look at him. But the second she stepped through the archway, he knew.

His head snapped up, a jolt of awareness shooting through him.

Her shoulders were drooping, like her bag had grown too heavy—the product of a long day at school, no doubt. Coupled with the long train ride she was facing to get home. Where more stress awaited her, if what she'd told him this morning was any indication.

He wondered if the subway ride down had been as terrible for her as it had been for him. Too many people, pushing through all the other people, packing into cars elbow-to-elbow.

He might have tried to play it cool if he had any sense. Pretend he hadn't seen her the instant she arrived. That he was too absorbed in his *art*—or awkward stick-figure scribbles, as the case may be—to notice. But the thought didn't even cross his mind until it was too late. He tucked his pencil behind his ear and crossed over to her, coming up beside her before he spoke. "Hey, Bee."

She turned her face up to him and smiled. It was like turning a light on in a dark room, that smile. The jolt of awareness sang through his veins, more primal than before. He clamped it down quickly, before it evolved again. *She has a boyfriend, asshole. Back off.*

"Hey," she said. She sounded as tired as she looked. "It's my commute buddy."

"Coincidental commute acquaintance," Julian corrected, needing to remind himself of the distance between them. He shouldn't have made those tentative plans to meet up with her on the way home. But he was on a roll with the bad decisions, apparently. And she was just nice to be around.

"Is that what the committee settled on?" Beatrice asked. "That's unfortunate. 'Coincidental commute acquaintance' doesn't really roll off the tongue, does it?"

"They were fond of the alliteration," Julian said, shrugging.

"And yet 'commute comrade' was shot down immediately," she said, shaking her head ruefully.

"I think there was a fear of encouraging communism. 'Commute companion' was in there for a while, but that just sounds like you're talking about your dog."

Beatrice laughed, her eyes lighting up. "And then, of course, 'commute co-conspirator' brought to mind con artists and spies."

"That one did make it pretty far," Julian said, wanting to make her laugh again. "But it got knocked out in the next-to-last round by 'commute cohorts.'"

She snorted. Which totally counted as a laugh, in Julian's book. "I don't know if I trust this committee. They seem suspiciously fond of fellow-criminal words."

"Yeah, I'd keep an eye on them," Julian said. "They're a shady bunch."

She grinned up at him, and he realized he was smiling too. And he was staring, trying to figure out if her eyes were gray or a desaturated blue. Her irises were rimmed in darker blue, but there were threads of silver spidering out from the pupil. And there was a touch of green if they caught the light just the right way . . .

Yeah. He was doing a great job keeping his distance.

Julian cleared his throat and looked away, pretending he wanted to check the time on his phone. He glanced at the screen, and read the number, but forgot it again the second he slipped it back in his pocket.

"Were you drawing?" Beatrice asked.

He looked at her, confused, and she pointed at his sketchbook. "Oh," he said. "Yeah. Kind of. I was thumbnailing."

Her blank stare mirrored his own. "I'm not an art person. I don't know what that means."

"It's just—It's sort of drawing the thing you want to draw, but really rough and in miniature." He hesitated for a second, then flipped open the sketchbook and pointed at the boxed-in rectangle. He wasn't even sure it translated to anything coherent if you didn't know what was supposed to be there. It was *really* rough, and he was out of practice. "That way you can map out where you want everything to go before you jump in on a big piece."

"Oh. Like the art version of outlining a term paper."

"Pretty much, yeah. It's an easy way to try out different angles and compositions without having to spend hours and hours on it only to realize it's all crap."

"What's that going to be when it grows up, then?" she asked, pressing into Julian's arm to get a better view.

His mind went blank for a moment. Yes, there was probably an inch or so of material separating his skin from hers, what with shirts and coats and various other layers, but he could feel her every curve along the length of his arm. The subtle floral scent of her shampoo mixed with cold wind and the dirt of the city filled his lungs. He wanted to pull her to him and breathe her in. Find her mouth with his and see if she tasted as wonderful as she smelled.

Good grief.

He swallowed hard and sidestepped her, closing the sketchbook and tucking it against his chest. She'd asked him a question. What was it?

"It wants to be an illustration of a witch in a library," he said. "But its dreams might be a little ambitious."

"Hey, you're already working on the plan," Beatrice said, blessedly oblivious to his weird freak-out. "All you need is to put the work in. I'm sure it'll be amazing."

"I hope so," Julian said. "My—my boss said that teaching job is mine if I can get a decent portfolio together by Christmas."

Her face lit up. "Hey, that's great!"

"Yeah," Julian said unenthusiastically, mussing his hair. "Except I'm way out of practice. I haven't used anything but a pencil or a ballpoint pen since I started picking it up again. And I'm going to need at least ten nice, finished pieces ready to go in about two months. As in inked and colored. I'm not even sure I have that many ideas for illustrations in me."

"I could help you with that," Beatrice said. "I'm full of ideas. I'm a *master* of ideas. They're very closely related to plans, you see. And I'm very good at plans."

He smiled at that. "I have no doubt."

"Ten pieces in two months," she said, frowning off into space. "That's, what, one and a bit per week? Ish? How fast are you at art-ing?"

He shrugged. "I don't know anymore. I have to take more breaks than I used to, but I think I'm pretty fast if it's just a character on their own. A few hours maybe? Anything with backgrounds, though—especially when there's a lot of little details like this little witch thing," he said, waving the sketchbook demonstratively, "is going to take longer if I'm going to do it right."

"But you could break it up, right?" she said, digging for something in her bag. "Maybe limit the really detailed ones to, I don't know, five or six? And then keep the rest of them simple so you can just knock them out in between the big ones." She produced a pencil and a notebook and flipped to the last page or two. *Julian's Portfolio*, she scrawled across the top.

"What are you doing?"

"I'm very good at plans," Beatrice said again, still writing as the train pulled in. "You happen to need a plan. You're lucky to have me as your coincidental commute acquaintance."

Beatrice was so focused on her list that she didn't even look up when the doors opened and people started filing onto the train. Julian had to herd her up the steps and guide her to their seats. He stood back to let her in by the window, so their elbows wouldn't bump if he tried to do some more thumbnails. Even then, she didn't look up.

He looked over her shoulder at the notebook page when he dropped in beside her. She'd written out the deadline, and the number of illustrations he needed, plus the number of days on average he had to complete each of the pieces—4.9, according to the math she'd scratched into the top left corner of the page. Below all this were a couple of bullet points:

* Limit complex art to approx. 5 total

* Intersperse simpler art with larger pieces to conserve time

"I can't believe you're taking notes on this," Julian said. "Don't you have homework?"

"Yes. But you're going to distract me if you're panicking over there without a plan," Beatrice said, turning to look at him again.

"I'm not panicking."

"You seem like you're panicking."

He shook his head. It wasn't that he was panicking so much as he couldn't see himself doing anything other than failing miserably. That was just sort of what he did. Fail. And this was one thing he really didn't want to fail at. And the idea had him restless and anxious.

So, yeah, okay. Maybe he was panicking. Just a little.

"It's a lot of art," he said. "I don't think I can do it. Even if I have a plan."

"Okay," Beatrice said, tucking her pencil behind her ear and folding her hands over the notebook. She caught his gaze and held it, her expression somehow both inviting and supportive. "Tell me why you think you can't do it."

If anyone else had asked him, he would have either avoided the question or possibly suggested they piss off. But for some reason, when Beatrice asked him questions, he always seemed to end up spilling his guts. He sighed. "I've only got about an hour at the art center on weekdays to work on them, which is going to make everything a lot harder."

"No art supplies at home?"

"Sketchbook and pencils. That's it. And I'm not going to be able to afford to get anything else until probably next month. And that's if I can convince my sister to stay on budget. Which, with her, is not that easy."

"So no weekend work, aside from whatever you can do in your sketchbook, which means you have about . . . mm . . ."—she frowned, her eyes unfocused as she did some more math under her breath—"three and a half hours to do each piece? Possibly less, if they're closed for Thanksgiving."

"Which they are. I don't even technically have until Christmas. It's due on the 14th. And I—I just haven't been drawing. I feel like I forgot half of what I used to know. I have to relearn all of it, and somehow knock out good illustrations while I do . . . It's not enough time."

"Okay," Beatrice said, her frown deepening. She drew the pencil from her hair, adjusted the deadline, and did the figures again for the average. He was down to 2.7 hours per piece.

Yeah, he was definitely starting to panic.

"You see?" Julian said, gesturing at her math. "There's no way I can work that fast. This is impossible."

"I will grant you it looks a little tight," Beatrice said, angling the notebook away from him so he couldn't see the numbers, "but I think we're still in frantic-but-doable land. You can use your weekends to practice drawing and prep what you're going to work on during the week, and I bet you can convince your bosses to let you come in on the odd weekend to work on things, too. From what you've said, they seem to like you and want you to succeed. It's a long way to go for a few extra hours, but it might make up for some of those holidays when you can't go in." She stopped and frowned at something she saw in his face. "That's not all, though, is it?"

Julian exhaled, slumping in his seat. He had been hoping to avoid this one. Though God knew why. It wasn't like he was trying to impress her. She was just some weird girl who wouldn't leave him alone.

And who he sometimes imagined kissing.

Because he'd been starved of human contact, lately. Not because he was attracted to her. It shouldn't matter if she thought he was a failure.

"I also have to pass a GED exam," he said stiffly, waiting for the moment the statement landed and her face fell in disappointment. "And I honestly don't even want to look at the study books because I'm positive it'll be completely over my head."

To his surprise, Beatrice perked up at this pronouncement. "You have study books?"

"What are you, some kind of textbook fanatic?" Julian asked her, frowning.

"Do you have them with you? Let me see."

"I'm pretty sure you already know everything in here, Miss Collegiate Scholar," Julian said, reluctantly opening his backpack and handing over the study guides he'd acquired this afternoon from a needlessly proud-looking Harold Fisk.

She ignored him, flipping open the first book. "How much high school did you finish?"

"Through to about three-quarters of the way into my senior year. And then I broke my hand and everything went to shit."

Beatrice winced. "Ouch," she said, but thankfully didn't press for details. "They should've just found a way to let you graduate if you were that close. Half the seniors in my school didn't even show up most of the time. *They* all graduated." She shook her head and switched to the other book, checking its table of contents while the train pulled out of the station. "Well, good news is, you probably know most of the stuff in here."

"Maybe three years ago," Julian grumbled. "I've probably forgotten all of it by now."

"You're smart. I bet you remember more than you think." Beatrice opened to a page near the back of the book and handed it over. "Where's your pencil?"

Julian scowled at the page she'd turned to. "You're going to make me take a test?"

"It's just a placement test. So you can figure out which things you have down and which ones you're a little rusty on. It'll help focus your studying energy."

"I'm rusty on everything," Julian said.

"I don't want to hear it from you," she said, reaching across and taking his pencil from behind his ear. Her thumb brushed his temple as she did, and for a split second he had to fight the impulse to catch her wrist and pull her closer. She held the pencil out to him, her eyebrows raised expectantly. "I want to hear it from the test."

"You should have gone into education," he said, plucking his pencil from her fingers, carefully not brushing her skin. This human contact bullshit was getting out of control. "You're way too obsessed with homework for a normal person."

She went a little pink for some reason, but turned away before he could be sure. "Tell me when you're done and I'll check it for you."

Julian stared at the first question while Beatrice resumed making notes on what he needed for his portfolio. Of course the first question had to be a fucking geometry problem.

"You're the worst," he told her.

"I'm sorry, I can't hear you over the sound of my own homework calling out to me," she said brightly, ripping out the page and folding it in half. She stuck it in the back of Julian's other GED book and shoved it into his backpack. "I don't hear pencil noises," she added, pulling out her computer.

"So me speaking at a normal volume you can't hear, but *that* you'd be able to pick up," he said, which only made her laugh. He sighed and started on the test, accompanied by the sounds of the train chugging along, a few people talking on their phones, and Beatrice violently attacking her keyboard.

The questions weren't as bad as he expected. It wasn't SAT prep, after all. It was GED prep. He'd frequented enough libraries in the past few years to think he had a good grip on the English portions. He was pretty sure he'd missed a good third or so of the STEM questions, though. He shut the book when he was sure he wasn't going to come up with any better answers and waited for a pause in the deafening clatter of keystrokes beside him.

"Finished?" Beatrice asked, still typing.

"More or less. Don't hurry. I don't want to interrupt the massacre going on over there."

"The—What?" she asked, pausing to look over at him, a confused frown pinching her eyebrows together adorably.

Julian drummed his fingers on the cover of the GED book, miming typing. "Did the keyboard offend you personally?"

Beatrice wrinkled her nose at him, but he could tell she was trying not to smile. "It's more of a tactical assault."

"Well, don't let me interrupt you."

She shrugged, turning back to her computer. "I wanted to take a break anyway."

"Only a homework fanatic thinks grading other people's homework counts as a break from their own homework," Julian said.

"Hur hur," she fake-laughed. "Just let me finish this sentence . . ." She hit the last key with a vengeance and clapped the laptop closed. "Okay. Let's see it."

"Why *didn't* you go into education?" Julian asked, handing over the book.

"I don't have teaching contacts, I have marketing contacts," Beatrice said, digging in her bag until she found a red pen. Of course she would carry a red pen around with her. "I want a job when I leave college, remember? I can do that with marketing. My dad has a friend who said he'd hire me on as soon as I graduated. For a really good salary. I don't know anyone in education except my own professors, and I don't want to teach at a college level, I want to—I *would* want to teach middle or high school."

"So change your major and do that," Julian said. "I bet you'd be a great teacher."

She shook her head. "I can't change my major."

"Why not? I'm pretty sure people do it all the time."

"Not me. I'm supposed to graduate next spring. There's not a lot of overlap in the marketing and education departments. It'll put me off course, and I'll lose all my marketing scholarships, which means I'll have to either pick up a million more shifts at Java Mama or take out a crap ton of student loans, which—Look, my family—We're just—We're not rich. And we're not thrifty. *I* had to pay for my little brother's flight out to California in August because—Well, never mind. But the idea of taking out all those loans in the hope that I'll actually find a job that might, eventually, sometime in my sixties, allow me to pay those loans off . . ." She huffed, rubbing her forehead like she was staving off a headache.

And no wonder. Feeling responsible for one bratty sister was headache enough for Julian. Beatrice sounded like she was trying to take care of her entire family.

"Okay, look," he said, holding up his hands. "Just put all the stressed-out rambling aside for a minute—"

"I'm not stressed out," Beatrice said, carving a furious little scribble into a corner of the book. "*You're* stressed out."

Julian decided to ignore that brilliant comeback. "I know it's not any of my business, but is marketing really going to be any better than serving coffee if you always wish you were doing something else?"

"I know I can get my little house if I go into marketing," she said, meeting his gaze for the first time since taking his book from him. "I just don't see that happening if I change my major now. Maybe if I'd figured it out sooner . . . But it's too late. So it doesn't matter."

Her knuckles were white around the pen, and there was something in her eyes that made it seem like she was drowning. Julian wanted to take her hands and drag her out of the water, but he didn't know how.

"What happened to that whole speech you gave me this morning about just needing a plan and some hard work?" he tried. "What happened to being the *master* of plans?"

"Master of *ideas*," she corrected, jabbing the end of her red pen in his direction.

"'Which are very closely related to plans.'"

She shook her head again, turning back to the practice test. "It doesn't matter. I'm not going to be a teacher. I'm going to be a marketer. Now hush while I grade this."

Julian shrugged and opened his sketchbook. "Whatever you say, teach."

She shot him a glare, but the corner of her mouth twitched and she wrinkled her nose like she was trying not to laugh.

Julian checked a goofy grin and glued his eyes on his sketchbook. While she was busy, he figured he'd work out the bird-witch design, and maybe try a second thumbnail. Beatrice was so hyper-focused on her own homework, he didn't think she'd try to snoop. And even if she did, she didn't seem the type to judge his every pencil stroke. But the thumbnail never got very far. He kept checking her marks out of the corner of his eye . . . and getting distracted by the way she chewed absently on her lip while she worked. More than once, he found himself fighting the impulse to poke her arm just to get her to look at him.

Christ almighty. This commute buddy thing was going to kill him.

When she finished, she pushed her hair behind one ear—where it stayed for only a second before springing free again—and passed the book back. She pointed out what he had a good grasp on, and what he 'seemed a little shaky on'—mostly the more advanced math questions, which had never been his forte anyway. Then she flipped to the table of contents and circled the chapters she thought he should work through first.

"I can work up some kind of study schedule for you if you want, but I don't know if I'll have the time to do it properly until next week," she said.

"You don't have to work up a study schedule," Julian said.

"I don't mind," Beatrice said, opening her laptop again. "I just need to catch up with my homework first. Meantime, just start with those sections and see how it goes."

He knew he should tell her that this commute buddy thing—or whatever it was—wasn't going to be a permanent arrangement.

There was no guarantee he would meet up with her tomorrow morning. Or next week. Or next month. He should tell her that they couldn't be friends. That it wasn't just a tight schedule and a GED exam standing between him and this job he wanted so badly. That one day he might have to drop off the face of the earth with no warning.

He should tell her he didn't want to get hurt when that happened. And if they kept this up, he was definitely going to get hurt.

But . . . Julian didn't want to believe he was going to have to take off this time. He didn't want to tell her to leave him alone. He liked her, dammit. She was ridiculous and tiny and she made him feel like he really could do anything if he broke it into small enough pieces and didn't give up.

So he said nothing. And when they parted ways later that evening, he told her he'd see her the next morning before he could think better of it. The smug little grin on her face almost made the slip worth it.

He forgot about the plan she'd written out for his portfolio until he got home. She'd updated the math and made a note reminding him to ask if he could either borrow some art supplies or use some of the center's studio space to work on his portfolio on the weekends. And then, the very last bullet point read:

    * Let Beatrice help you study ^w^

She'd written her phone number underneath, along with a small note at the very bottom of the page:

    See you tomorrow, commute cohort!

He couldn't help the warm, cozy feeling spreading through him. He smiled. He was doing a terrible job not being friends with her.

And just for that moment, looking down at the neat handwriting at the bottom of the page, he didn't care.

TEN

A tote bag weighing at *least* twelve pounds slammed into Julian's chest the following Monday morning before he boarded the train. The greeting he'd intended to give Beatrice whooshed out of his lungs as he staggered back a step, catching it instinctively.

"I'm glad I found you before we boarded," Beatrice said, brushing off her hands. "That thing is heavy."

"Then don't carry it around," Julian said, recovering his balance and holding the bag out for her to take. "And don't throw it at unsuspecting bystanders." He wasn't about to start carrying her stuff for her without so much as a *please*. The more reasonable part of his brain was still telling him to run.

A less reasonable part—the part that kept him from breaking off this commuting arrangement—wanted to hold onto her and not let go.

At some point in the last week, Julian had settled on an uneasy compromise with himself; he could keep meeting Beatrice, but only if he set himself some boundaries. No texting about anything other than commutes or study questions. No hanging out on weekends. No needless lingering when they parted ways. No talking about his life prior to about three months ago. Absolutely *no* talking about the elusive boyfriend.

Though Julian's less reasonable side was already looking for ways to bend the rules without breaking them. He couldn't truncate a conversation simply because it evolved from a study question into texting terrible dad jokes back and forth. He wasn't going to be *rude*. And if he happened to redefine a single conversation to include anything said between two people with a gap shorter than twelve hours so he could justify texting her a joke or eight over the weekend . . . well . . .

What his reasonable side didn't know wouldn't hurt it.

"Don't even think about it," Beatrice said, backing away from the bag swinging from his outstretched hand. "That's yours. I'm not carrying it another step."

Talking to Beatrice sometimes felt like trying to keep pace with a giant who didn't realize your shorter stature might contribute to your ability to cover ground at the same speed. "What?"

"I don't know if it's anything you could use," she said, a pale pink blush coloring her cheeks. "It's mostly cheap stuff. I found a set of colored pencils under my bed that I barely used—I could never get into that coloring book trend—and I *think* they're supposed to be a good brand. But everything else is kind of crap stuff. Crayola watercolors from a million years ago, and one pack of cheap, no-one's-ever-heard-of-them markers that are mostly dried out. The paper is all cheap kid's stuff. Nath went on an art kick when he was nine that lasted for two weeks, so it's all really old."

He lifted an eyebrow. "You brought me art supplies?"

"Crap ones," Beatrice clarified. "But . . . yeah. You said you didn't really have any. Oh, also—" She pulled the bag open and rummaged inside, holding his wrist still with one hand.

Julian nearly dropped the bag, his pulse jumping. They weren't even skin to skin. She was wearing purple mittens, and she had him by the sleeve. He held his breath and tried not to move. A second later, she produced a folder from the bag and released him.

She waved the folder in the air, looking pleased with herself. "I wrote up some plans."

"Plans?" Julian repeated, still struggling to keep up. Hell, he would've been happy if he could mark the small dot that was Beatrice in the cloud of conversational dust she'd left in her wake.

Beatrice went a deeper shade of pink as her triumphant expression wilted into embarrassment. "Oh. Well—" She pressed the folder against her chest and feigned interest in the post on the platform beside them. "I just thought . . . I thought . . . Never mind. It was dumb." She pulled open her own bag like she was going to shove the folder out of sight.

Julian slung the heavy tote over his shoulder and plucked the folder out of her hand before she succeeded.

She adjusted her bag nervously and muttered something about butting in where she wasn't wanted. Julian only half heard her as he flicked through the folder, distracted. Beatrice's clear, chubby handwriting, interspersed with several printouts of bullet-point lists, filled the folder. They seemed to be sorted into sections— *General/All, Animation, Comics (Trad.), Comics (Web), Teaching, Illustration (Kids), Illustration (Newspaper/Magazine/Freelance), Video/Entertainment.*

"Bee . . ." Julian said, staring at a chart comparing the benefits and drawbacks of various social media platforms as related to art. If Fabiana had handed him a folder like this—Well, she wouldn't have. Her version of helping him plan a career would probably look more like a single sheet of paper with *GET A FUCKING JOB, JACKASS* scrawled across it in red Sharpie. But looking at Beatrice's handwriting . . . the time this must have taken her . . . He was touched. And confused. No one but art teachers had ever told him it wasn't both stupid and financially irresponsible to pursue an art career.

"This is . . ." he began. "This . . . I . . . But . . ."

"I bet it's mostly stuff you already know," Beatrice said, ignoring his stammering. "And I sort of guessed at what you might want to head towards, career-wise. You seemed interested in the pictures-as-stories route, but I didn't want to assume you wanted to stick to comics just because that's what you wanted when you were younger. And you seemed really excited about teaching kids, so I thought that should get its own section. A lot of them would work well together, too, if you didn't want to box yourself in. I was going to do another section on different merchandising options, but a lot of it came down to how much you wanted to do yourself versus throwing a design up on a website, and I wasn't sure if you even wanted—" She seemed to get embarrassed again, and tried to tug the folder out of his fingers. "I'm sorry, this is really pushy, isn't it?"

"Hang on," Julian said, closing the folder and holding it out of her reach. "At least let me look at it before you start apologizing. When did you even have the time to do all this?"

"Hardly anyone came into the coffee shop this weekend, and I'd already done most of my homework," she said, adjusting her bag as the train clattered in. "It's not a big deal."

"Yeah, it is," Julian said. There had to be at least twenty pages, all packed with information. "Thank you, Bee."

She shrugged, tucking a strand of hair behind her ear. "No problem."

"You seriously did all this on top of your homework?" Julian asked, frowning. "Do you ever sleep?"

"Sleeping is for after graduation," she told him, lifting her chin sagely.

They pushed onto the train with everyone else and found their seats. Julian slid over to make room for Beatrice. She dropped into her seat with a poorly-stifled yawn.

"You do realize it's not healthy to run on nothing but caffeine, right?" Julian asked as they settled in.

She shot him one of those sly smiles that tended to knock the breath out of him if he wasn't prepared. "I was joking, loser," she said, kicking his shin lightly. "Stop worrying about me. I get at least four solid hours of sleep every night. *Also a joke,*" she added when he cut her a disapproving look.

"Sure, weirdo," Julian said.

She shook her head, still smiling, and shuffled through her textbook for the right page without removing her mittens.

Julian suspected there was more truth to the jokes than she let on. She had faint circles under her eyes, which didn't exactly indicate a weekend of rest and recuperation. And he wasn't sure why she was claiming she'd finished her weekend assignments before working on that folder if she still had statistics problems to do on the train.

"You know," he said thoughtfully, "I don't think I've ever seen you *not* working."

"What are you talking about? You saw me at the coffee shop that one time."

Julian snorted, mostly because of the exaggerated wink and finger guns that punctuated the joke. "That was weak."

"So's our coffee," she said, breaking out the finger guns again.

"Stop," Julian begged. "They're getting worse."

"You're laughing," she pointed out.

True. He tried to assume a straight face. "It's a pity laugh at best."

"You're going to have to wait for me to finish my coffee before I have the brainpower to break out the good stuff," Beatrice said, scribbling the date at the top of a fresh page in her notebook. "Actually," she said, turning to him and poking his arm with the end of her pencil. "I have a question for you."

He wished she'd stop doing that. The casual touching. It made him want to do stupid things. Like denude her hand of its glove and press his lips against the base of her thumb.

Julian cleared his throat and drew a random circle on an empty page of his sketchbook, trying to seem busy, and not like he was imagining any part of Beatrice nude. "What's that?"

"What are you doing for Thanksgiving next week?"

His pen slowed on the page. The art center was going to be closed over the holiday. He was pretty sure Fabiana was planning on going to their step-father's penthouse for dinner. She hadn't said as much, but that's what she did every year. Julian wouldn't be surprised if she was scheming to use the softness that came over Walter on the holidays to get back in his good graces.

Julian had cut off all contact with his step-father and his dick of a step-brother after Julian broke his hand and left that place for good. Even if he thought he would be welcome—which he didn't—the mere idea of talking to his step-brother after everything that happened made Julian's chest constrict. He didn't have any inclination to go back. Ever. Even for a holiday.

Which meant Julian would be spending Thanksgiving eating ramen and working on his portfolio in his shitty apartment, alone. And that scene was depressing enough without admitting it to Beatrice.

"I'm not really sure yet," he lied instead.

"You're not going to see your family?" Beatrice asked.

"There's . . . not really any family to see," Julian said, scrubbing the back of his neck. "It's just me and my sister. We lost both our parents, and the only other relatives we have are some second cousins in South Korea who we only met once, when we were three. And a step-dad and step-brother I don't talk to anymore."

"Oh, I'm sorry. About your parents. And the step-family situation, too."

"Thanks." Julian shrugged and tried to power through the awkward before he completely shattered his no-talking-about-the-past rule. "Why were you asking about Thanksgiving?"

"Well, *my* step-dad is going to be out of town working," Beatrice said, accepting the subject change without comment, "and my mom is going to visit her sister in Maine, and a couple of my friends are in similar boats—sans parentals—so Kinsey is going to host a dinner at her parent's house, and she and my other friend and my brother and I are going to try to pull together a kind of Friendsgiving thing *on* Thanksgiving, and if you don't have plans, you'd be more than welcome to come. You can bring your sister, too."

Sure. Perfect way to ensure disaster—bring the brash, confrontational twin sister. "I, uh . . . I think she's already got plans," Julian said.

"Then just bring you. You could come meet me and Nath at our place and we'll all pile into Sasha's car."

Julian fumbled around halfheartedly for a reason to say no. The rational part of his brain was running out of objections. "Are you sure your friends will be okay with me coming?"

"Sure, why not?" Beatrice said, beaming at him. "Nath will be happy there's another guy there, and the more people we cram in, the less chance we'll have to be cranky about missing relatives."

So no boyfriend in attendance? Interesting. "Um. Okay. Yeah."

"Really?"

"Sure." He wasn't technically breaking any of his rules, agreeing to come. Thursday was still a weekday, after all. And it sounded a damn sight better than moping alone in his dingy apartment. "Should I bring something?"

"That'd be awesome. Let me just check with Kinsey and see what we still need and I'll let you know this evening?"

"Okay."

"Awesome," Beatrice said, bouncing a little in her seat as she turned back to her homework.

"Don't kill me," Beatrice said, joining Kinsey and Sasha outside their statistics class. They were all a bit early today, and the TA hadn't shown up yet to unlock the door.

"No promises," Kinsey said, rubbing her eyes. Her checkered blouse looked a bit rumpled under her coat, and she was wearing jeans and sheepskin boots—a sure sign she hadn't gotten enough sleep. "I was fighting with Photoshop all night, and I've got a design hangover. You know how violent those make me."

"She's threatened to punch me at least three times in the last five minutes," Sasha said. "But she hasn't followed through yet, so I wouldn't worry."

"I'll punch you once I'm more awake," Kinsey said. She blinked and turned back to Beatrice. "Wait, why am I murdering you again?"

"I may have invited another misfit to Thanksgiving."

"I thought Greyson was spending Thanksgiving with his dad and his sister," Kinsey said.

"Not Greyson," Beatrice said, feeling her cheeks warm. "A friend of mine who takes the train with me."

"Have I met her?" Kinsey asked, frowning.

"No, but I think you'd like him."

"'*Him?*'"

Beatrice flushed deeper at the sudden curious expressions on both of her friends' faces. "Shut up. He's just a friend. Straight girls are allowed to have guy friends they're not trying to date."

"Is he gay?" Sasha asked, cocking her head to one side and hooking her thumbs in the pockets of her bomber jacket.

"No. I mean, I don't think so. I can usually tell."

"So you, a straight girl, have been secretly hanging out with a presumably straight guy, and neither of you have any interest in getting in each other's pants."

"You two hang out all the time and *you're* not going out," Beatrice said defensively.

"Not for lack of trying," Sasha said, tossing Kinsey an exaggerated eyebrow waggle.

Kinsey threw back a quelling look. "Don't make me punch you again."

Sasha laughed. "'Again?' You haven't even followed through with the first one."

"I just want to know," Beatrice said, trying to get the conversation back on track, "if it's okay if I bring my new friend to Thanksgiving. Because I kind of already asked him."

"Who even is this just-a-friend, and why haven't I heard of him before?" Kinsey demanded.

"His name is Julian, and I only met him a few weeks ago. He lives near me and works at an art studio thing in the Village. He doesn't have anywhere else to go. It sounded like even his sister was going somewhere without him. He's really nice, and he's funny, and he's really good at drawing, and I really think you'd both like him. He offered to bring food," she added, concerned she was still detecting some resistance. Kinsey was squinting at her suspiciously, though Beatrice couldn't tell how much of that was her Photoshop hangover. And Sasha's eyebrows had raised incrementally over the course of Beatrice's ramble until they were partially obscured by her hair.

They hadn't minded when Beatrice looped her brother into the Friendsgiving plans after he came home. They hadn't even minded when she'd felt obligated to invite Greyson last weekend. And Greyson didn't tend to fit in well with their group, any more than Beatrice fit in with his friends. She was pretty sure both

Kinsey and Sasha had been relieved when it turned out he already had plans. Quite frankly, so was Beatrice.

But she couldn't see Julian causing any problems. He was quicker to laugh than Greyson, and easy to connect with. And he didn't argue every little point. Beatrice was sure Kinsey and Sasha would like him if they just gave him a chance.

"I don't know, Bee," Kinsey said, scratching her nose.

Beatrice clasped her hands together and pressed them under her chin, adopting one of Nath's puppy dog looks. "Please? He doesn't have anywhere else to go."

Sasha and Kinsey exchanged a glance.

Sasha shrugged. "I don't mind. It's your house, though. Up to you."

"Fine," Kinsey groaned. "Just-a-friend can come to misfit Thanksgiving."

"Julian," Beatrice corrected, her shoulders relaxing. "And please be nice. He can act a little prickly at first, but he's really great. You'll like him. I promise."

ELEVEN

Julian decided he was going to wait outside Beatrice's building for her and her brother to come out. It was fucking freezing, but he couldn't get himself to climb the stairs and knock on the door.

He'd been in a knot of nervous anticipation over this stupid Thanksgiving dinner since he woke up this morning. There was no good reason for it. It wasn't like he hadn't seen Beatrice nearly every day for the past three weeks. But telling himself how irrational his nerves were didn't make them go away.

He'd gone from nervous anticipation to low-key anxiety somewhere around the time Fabiana had left for the train to Manhattan. And as he walked the half-mile trek between his apartment and Beatrice's, his feelings had warped again into a nagging dread.

It wasn't just about Thanksgiving, either. He was already aware that agreeing to come meant he was ignoring the point of all his made-up rules regarding Beatrice. Going to this dinner—seeing Beatrice in her element—could only make it harder to remember that he should keep his distance. Sure, he was being stupid, but he didn't really care. All it took was a little bit of rationalization and he could get his reason to shut up for hours at a time.

No, the dread he was feeling now didn't seem to have a cause. Things had been going too smoothly lately. That had to mean another disaster was imminent. The foreboding gnawed at his stomach and sent two words through his head on a loop: *Don't go.*

Julian pulled his coat closer around him, releasing a white puff of air. He tried to imagine all his dread had gone out of his lungs with it, dissipating until it didn't matter anymore. Nothing but superstitious bullshit.

But the dread wasn't in his lungs. It was in his gut, and in the bones of his hands, and in his blood. It couldn't be dismissed so easily.

He pressed his back against the wall, watching heavy clouds drift by overhead, willing his heart to slow its rapid pace.

He hated feeling this way. The sick, hovering foreboding. It was exactly how he felt when he was seven years old, clinging to his dad with all his strength. Begging him not to leave for his tour of duty in Iraq. He'd known, somehow, that it was the last time he'd ever see his dad. He'd been too afraid that saying the words would make them come true. Not that it had made any difference in the end.

It was exactly how he felt that day in the tenth grade when he was so anxious to go home, he made himself sick. Not for any clear reason, that time. Just this awful, tight feeling that something was wrong. He'd been sitting in the nurse's office when the principal came in and told him his mom had been in a car accident and she was in the hospital. She'd died a few hours later.

Julian yanked off his gloves, shoved them in his pocket, and took out his phone. The grocery bag on his arm slid to his elbow as he typed out a quick text to Fabiana, telling her to text him when she got to Walter's safely. She'd probably think he was crazy, but he was too wound up not to say *something.*

Why, she replied, seconds later.

He frowned at the screen. **Humor me.**

She sent him a rude emoji. Followed by several more emojis

that Julian guessed were meant to show Fabiana dying in a horrible train derailment. Complete with far more fire and skulls than necessary.

Not funny, he wrote.

omg chill

A few seconds later, a photo came through of Fabiana, looking pissed, standing on a street he recognized as being just a couple blocks from Walter's penthouse in Manhattan.

Proof of life, Fabiana wrote underneath the photo. **Happy?**

Not really. The dread in his gut didn't ease, but at least it didn't seem connected to his sister.

That just left him. He'd felt like this just a few days before he dropped out of high school, too. It had started in the morning, and by the end of the day, he was in the hospital with a broken hand, three broken ribs, and some serious internal bleeding. More than one stressed-looking doctor had informed him afterward that he was very *very* lucky to be alive.

Julian pushed off the rough stucco of Beatrice's building, rubbing the palm of his left hand with his right thumb to rid himself of the remembered pain. Maybe he should call this whole Thanksgiving thing off. It would give him a chance to work on an illustration he'd been struggling with. Get ahead of schedule on his portfolio. It wasn't like he hadn't spent the last three Thanksgivings on his own. It was depressing, but it wasn't the end of the world.

And it would shut up the words chasing themselves around his head.

Don't go.

Julian pulled up Beatrice's number on his phone. He'd just tell her he had the flu or something. She'd probably only asked him to come to dinner because she felt sorry for him. She wouldn't mind if he canceled.

"Julian!"

He looked up. Beatrice was coming down the sidewalk, her silly Java Mama hat clutched in one hand. Her hair was wilder than usual, and a big grin lit up her face. She waved her hat at him, and he found himself smiling back, some of the tension going out of his shoulders.

He didn't know what it was about her that made him believe everything could work out for the better. Nothing about his life so far had proved he wasn't destined to forever fall from one shitty disaster to the next.

But somehow, when Beatrice was around, it seemed like his shitty luck didn't have to define his life. When she looked at him, she didn't see some screwup with no chance of making something of himself. She saw someone who deserved to hope for something better. She'd told him once that all he needed was a plan and some hard work and he could do almost anything. And when she was around, Julian actually believed it.

"Hey," he called back, locking his phone and shoving it in his coat pocket. It was too late to cancel plans now, even if he had still wanted to. "I thought you said your shift was supposed to end twenty minutes ago."

"It was. We had this crazy rush and I got stuck."

"A rush?" Julian repeated. "At *Java Mama*?"

"I know. Something must've exploded at the Starbucks down the street, because why else would a whole flock of desperately under-caffeinated people descend on Java Mama screaming for coffee?" Beatrice stopped when she reached him and frowned, puffing out a cloud of air. "What are you doing down here? Didn't Nath let you in?"

"I thought I'd just wait out here," Julian said, trying to sound casual. The cold had flushed her cheeks an enticing shade of pink.

His chest ached suddenly, with something he couldn't name. He wanted to tuck her against his chest and hold on tight. To keep her safe. Or to absorb some of that comforting, stubborn optimism. He didn't know which.

Her eyes flicked over his face, a tentative smile pulling up one side of her mouth. "You okay?"

"Yeah," Julian said, pretending to check the contents of the grocery bag he was carrying. "I—Yeah. Fine."

"Okay." Beatrice sucked in a brisk breath and clapped her mittens together. "In that case, you better just come upstairs with me." She pulled at the collar of her polo shirt under her coat. "I have to change still, and Sasha won't be here for at least another ten minutes. If you stay down here, you'll freeze your butt off. Come on."

Don't, said the dread still lingering in his gut. But its voice wasn't so strong anymore, and Julian was able to squash it back down.

Beatrice led him upstairs, launching into a story about a particularly cheerful, chatty customer who'd attempted to steal the tip jar, not realizing it was nailed down. By the time they reached her front door, on the third floor, Julian was too busy laughing at her recounting of the incident to feel much dread at all.

Beatrice switched into checklist mode as soon as they were inside. She'd barely apologized for the 'mess' and introduced Julian to her younger brother before she disappeared into her room to change.

Nath, who'd muted the show he was watching when they came in, narrowed his eyes at Julian from the couch. "She didn't say you had ink."

Julian couldn't tell from his expression whether this was a good or a bad thing. "Uh . . . yeah."

"Huh," Nath said. Then his expression cleared and he shrugged.

"Well, if Bee likes you, you're probably cool. Put your stuff on the table there and sit down."

Julian left the grocery bag on an empty space on the kitchen table and sat down on one of the two sofas crammed into the living room. Nath had turned up the volume on the TV again, but Julian's attention wandered around the apartment. Despite Beatrice's apology, it wasn't all that messy. There was some clutter, and there was maybe more furniture in the front rooms than they'd been designed to hold, but it mostly made the space feel lived-in. Homey.

His heart ached. The last few years, he'd been in survival mode. Not trying to make a home, just trying to keep his head above water. He'd almost forgotten what homey felt like.

Beatrice whirled out of her room in a plumb-colored sweater and black skinny jeans, with neon pink socks bunched above her usual floral hiking boots. "Are you gonna get ready to go, Nath?" she asked, not glancing at either of them as she made her way to the kitchen.

"You're telling me sweatpants aren't acceptable Friendsgiving attire now?"

Beatrice swung around at the kitchen archway to shoot her brother a glare. "Seriously?"

"A joke, Bee. It was a joke." Nath dragged himself off the couch. "I'll get ready right now."

Beatrice muttered something to herself and disappeared into the kitchen.

Sensing that Beatrice might need another pair of hands—or at least a sounding board—Julian followed her to the kitchen, hesitating in the archway. "Can I help?"

"Um . . ." Beatrice paused her frenetic sweep around the small kitchen, her eyes darting every which way. Probably re-sorting her checklist to see which points she could delegate. "Can you grab me a couple of bags from that cabinet there?" she asked, pointing, while opening the fridge with the other hand. "Help me load up the food?"

Julian shook out two of the bags, stacking the casserole dishes inside as Beatrice passed them over. Four in total, including what Beatrice called the 'emergency backup lasagna.' Apparently, her friend, Kinsey, was afraid she was going to burn the turkey and ruin everything.

"When did you have time to make an emergency backup lasagna?" Julian asked once the casserole dishes were all neatly stacked in their bags. He crouched to scratch the ears of the vocal gray cat who had appeared to wind around his ankles. Probably in the hopes that Julian would drop the casserole dishes and create a feline buffet. Though from the loud, instant purring, it didn't mind the head-scratching alternative. "When did you have time to make *any* of this?"

"My mom helped," Beatrice said, frowning around the kitchen distractedly.

"Your friends are providing some of the food too, aren't they?"

"Kinsey's on turkey, gravy, and dessert. Sasha doesn't have a kitchen to speak of, so she went over early to help with the baking. I took most of the side dishes because I could do them ahead of time. Oh!" She pulled open a cabinet in the far corner of the kitchen and retrieved a bag of mini marshmallows. "Almost forgot."

Julian caught the bag out of the air when she tossed it to him. "You didn't have to do all of this. I could have taken care of the lasagna, at least. And the marshmallows," he added, reaching up to deposit the bag on top of the casserole dishes.

"Yeah, but I guess—I guess I wasn't sure you'd really want to come," she said, a blush creeping over her cheeks as she plucked at the cuff of her sweater. "You don't know anyone else, and . . . I don't know. I thought maybe you'd realize you'd rather spend the holiday with your sister after all."

Julian couldn't figure out how to react. He'd assumed she'd only asked him because she was collecting misfits. Not because it mattered if he actually showed up. His heart clenched in his chest again, heavy with something that felt a lot like homesickness. Only he wasn't longing for the past, he was longing for . . . for *this*. For a house that felt like home. For someone wanting him around. For caring about people and knowing they cared about him too. It took all his reason to stop him from crossing the small kitchen to where Beatrice stood and kissing her, boyfriend or no boyfriend.

The cat threw its whole body at Julian's knee, nearly knocking him on his ass. Julian, thankful for the excuse to break eye contact, scratched the cat's chin with one hand. "Trust me. Your friends could try to recruit me into their satanic cult and I'd still rather be there than at my step-dad's."

Beatrice wrinkled her nose at him, but she seemed to relax for the first time since she stepped into the apartment. She pointed at the cat. "I see you've made friends with Sunny."

"As in sunshine?" Julian guessed, laughing. The cat looked more like a gray, little raincloud than anything.

"Obviously," Beatrice said, grinning.

Her phone chimed as she spoke, and she took it from her pocket. "It's Sasha. She's downstairs. Gnat!" she shouted down the hall to her brother. "Ride's here! You have thirty seconds, and then we're leaving without you!"

"I'm *coming*," Nath shouted back, his voice muffled through the door.

"Lasagna, green beans, potatoes," Beatrice recited under her breath, ticking off her fingers as she listed them. "Where'd I put my bag? Oh, there." She shifted a mountain of hats and gloves to the edge of the kitchen table and retrieved her school bag.

"You're not planning on doing homework on Thanksgiving,"

Julian said, yielding to the cat's increasing demands for affection by scruffing his back with both hands. "Thanksgiving is all about going into a food coma. Not doing school work."

"I've got a paper due on Monday that I'm only half finished with, and two midterms on Tuesday I'm way underprepared for," Beatrice said, thumbing through the contents of her bag. "Proper lazy Thanksgivings are for after graduation. Crap. Where'd my laptop get off to?"

"Okay, I'm ready," Nath announced, coming back out into the living room, now wearing jeans in place of his sweatpants, and a cardigan over a teeshirt with a superhero on it. He held his arms up. "Good enough?"

Julian bit his tongue to keep from pointing out that, based on her own wardrobe, Beatrice was probably not most people's first choice to ask for advice on outfit acceptability.

Beatrice barely glanced at her brother, though. "It's fine," she said, brushing past him into her room again. "Have you seen my laptop?" she asked, her call accompanied by the sounds of rummaging.

"It's right here." Nath picked it up from the coffee table and waved it over his head. "Ten seconds, then we're leaving without you."

"Ha ha," Beatrice said humorlessly, returning from the bedroom. She plucked the laptop out of Nath's hand. "Good luck convincing Sasha to abandon me. Can you get the food, please? It's on the counter."

Julian gave Sunny one last pat, stood, and grabbed his meager bag of Thanksgiving offerings from the table. Nath got the casserole dishes while Beatrice threw her coat back on.

She checked her mittens were in the pockets and slung her heavy school bag over her shoulder. "I think that's everything . . ." she said, patting herself down. "Okay. Yeah. Let's go."

Beatrice herded them out of the apartment into the open air of the long balcony. The floor shook when she dropped her bag by the door so she could lock up. Julian felt like a jerk for only carrying the comparatively light grocery bag dangling from his own hand.

"Can you hold this a second?" he asked, holding the grocery bag out to her as she pulled her keys from the door.

She took it automatically, still preoccupied with whatever mental list she was double checking. "Sure, but why—"

Julian slung her bag over his shoulder and started for the stairs before she could finish.

"Hey," Beatrice protested, hurrying to catch up to him.

Nath laughed. "Oh, that was *smooth*. Did you see that, Bee?"

"You don't have to do that," Beatrice said, ignoring Nath as she chased Julian down the stairs.

Julian swung the bag out of her reach when she grabbed for it. "What do you have in here, anyway? Bricks?"

"It's not *that* bad."

"You should think about getting a backpack," Julian said. "They're easier on the shoulders."

"All the cute ones are ridiculously tiny," Beatrice complained.

"You only need it for school," Nath pointed out. "You could get a normal-sized, not-cute backpack."

"I happen to like that bag, thank you," Beatrice said. "I'm used to it. I don't want a stupid-looking backpack. I can carry it if you don't like it."

"And let you throw out your back on Thanksgiving?" Julian asked. "I don't think so."

"You both suck," Beatrice said.

"You're welcome," Julian replied cheerfully.

Beatrice rolled her eyes as they stepped off the stairs, a small smile escaping from one side of her mouth. She led the way to a dinged-up minivan parked in the loading zone. She tapped on the window and waved to the driver, who had been frowning at her phone.

The driver popped the locks, allowing Beatrice to swing the side door open.

"Hey, Bee!" She turned the '80s music she'd been blasting down to a reasonable volume. "Happy Thanksgiving!"

"Thanks for the ride, Sasha," Beatrice said. "You remember my brother, Nath, right?"

"The bum brother?" Sasha said, grinning. "Sure. How's things, Nath?"

"Hilarious," Nath said sarcastically, strapping himself into the back seat. "Happy Thanksgiving to you, too."

"Don't be such a grump," Beatrice said. "And this is Julian."

"Nice to meet you," Sasha said, twisting in her seat so she could shake Julian's hand as he climbed in after Nath. She was an athletic-looking girl with a kind of cheerful, wholesome Midwest look about her. "You're the artist, right?"

"Sort of," Julian said, shooting Beatrice a what-did-you-tell-these-people look.

"Yes, he is," Beatrice said firmly, catching the expression and lobbing back a don't-contradict-me look. "You're too modest."

Sasha pulled out of the loading zone and edged the van to the edge of the parking lot. Her phone chirped from the cupholder where she'd stashed it. Sasha groaned.

"Kinsey?" Beatrice guessed.

"She's freaking out about this turkey," Sasha said, passing the phone to Beatrice. "Would you please explain to her that I can't text her while I'm driving? You'd think she'd never seen one of those stupid PSAs in her life."

"'*Come on, Todd,*'" Beatrice said in a dramatic narrator voice, unlocking Sasha's phone. She didn't need to ask for the passcode,

Julian noted, with a weird pang of jealousy that didn't make much sense.

"Oh man, I would *really* not want my last recorded conversation to be about a turkey," Sasha said, turning onto the street. And then she winced and waved a hand at Beatrice. "Don't tell Kinsey I said that."

"Way to blow what I was going to open with," Beatrice replied, tapping out a text. "I'll see if I can get her to text me instead, hang on."

Beatrice ended up on the phone with Kinsey for most of the ride, while Julian and the others got into a debate over whether '80s music was better or worse than '60s music. Julian didn't participate much, not following the conversation very carefully. He couldn't seem to stop listening to Beatrice patiently trying to talk her friend down from the brink of panic.

It was . . . nice, watching her with these people she was so comfortable with. And it hurt, too, even though it shouldn't. He ached from not knowing her as well as these other people. From being so far outside her orbit that he couldn't reach all the light and warmth she radiated out to her friends.

Well, he was here, wasn't he? She had asked him to come. Maybe she wanted him in her orbit too. Not in quite the same way as he would like, but that was probably for the best. She deserved someone who could give her the world. Someone good, and kind, without the heavy drag of past mistakes threatening to pull him and everyone around him down to hell.

Someone better than Julian.

The dread in his gut flared, but Julian pushed it back down. It was just one dinner. Nothing bad was going to happen.

TWELVE

Kinsey answered the door of her parents' house in a miasma of soap-opera despair. "I hope you all like lasagna, because I've ruined the turkey."

Beatrice could tell Kinsey was playing her freak-out up for laughs, but her dark eyes were just a little too bright, and her eyelashes were damp. Beatrice would've given her a hug right then and there, but then Kinsey might end up crying for real. She knew Kinsey wouldn't want to do that in front of guests. Even if half of them were her best friends.

"I'm sure that's not true," Beatrice said, while everyone stashed their shoes against the wall in the entryway and hung up their coats.

"Oh yeah?" Kinsey challenged. She wore a flour-smeared, pink polka-dot apron over her white blouse and flared, fox-print skirt. Her usually immaculate black bob was disheveled, a few flyaways sticking to her forehead. "Come and see."

She led them through the dining room of the colonial-style house into the spacious kitchen—which did smell a little singed—and marched up to the stove, where sat a large roasting pan covered with aluminum foil. She whisked off the foil with a morbid flourish. "Behold the atrocity that ruined everyone's Thanksgiving."

Sasha made a horrified strangled sound before she managed to cut herself off.

It looked like Kinsey had tried to cook the turkey with a flame thrower. Beatrice wouldn't have believed it was possible to both overcook *and* undercook a turkey if she hadn't seen the evidence with her own eyes. Half of the skin was charcoal black, and it was somehow still raw in the middle where Kinsey had cut into it.

"Oh," Beatrice said, searching desperately for something diplomatic and supportive to say. No one else seemed to dare say anything at all. "My," she finally said.

"You can all skewer me with pitchforks now," Kinsey said, slumping into a chair at the small kitchen table and covering her face with her hands.

"Don't be silly," Sasha said. "Where would we even *find* pitchforks on Thanks—*ow*."

Sasha rubbed the place where Beatrice's elbow had just dug into her ribs while Beatrice pulled up a chair next to Kinsey's.

"You didn't ruin everything," Beatrice said. "We still have a load of side dishes. Nath and I brought potatoes and yams and green beans."

"And lasagna," Nath drawled unhelpfully.

Beatrice shot him a warning glare. She was trying to cheer Kinsey up, not imply that they had so little faith in her ability to cook a turkey that they'd brought an emergency backup lasagna. Even if the lasagna had been Kinsey's idea in the first place.

"And we've got corn pudding and bread," Sasha put in. "And pie. Everybody loves pie."

"And cranberry sauce and cupcakes," said Julian, his shoulder against the doorjamb. He seemed unsure where he was supposed to fit. He hadn't even removed his coat. As though he expected to be kicked out into the cold at any moment. He'd gotten along with Nath and Sasha in the car, but even then, he'd been quieter than usual. It made Beatrice nervous. She really, really wanted him to like her friends. And she really, really wanted them to like Julian.

"Cupcakes?" Kinsey echoed, peeking through a gap in her fingers to shoot Julian an incredulous look.

He shrugged. "I'm not a pie person."

"Heathen!" Sasha exclaimed with a melodramatic gasp.

Julian snorted, lifting an eyebrow at Sasha, who shrugged a cheerful apology.

Kinsey's head went down on the table, among the mess of dirty mixing bowls and utensils that she and Sasha must have used for the pies and bread before Sasha left to pick the rest of them up. "It doesn't matter," she wailed, her voice muffled. "You can't have Thanksgiving without turkey. Everyone knows that."

"Vegetarians don't eat turkey on Thanksgiving," Nath pointed out.

"I don't even *like* turkey that much," Sasha said.

"That's a lie, and you know it," Kinsey said. "Nothing matters if you don't have the turkey. And I ruined it."

"I don't know," Julian said. He wandered over to the hideous turkey and prodded at it with the carving fork Kinsey had left out. "I think this might be salvageable."

They all turned to stare at him as one, disbelief written over every face.

"I'm not saying it's going to be the quintessential, Norman Rockwell, entire Thanksgiving bird you were expecting," Julian said, rolling his eyes at them. "But I think it can be made to be edible."

"Setting our expectations high," said Sasha in grand tones. "But can he follow through?"

"I'm not promising good when I haven't done it before," Julian said, shedding his coat and throwing it over a kitchen chair. "But don't throw the lasagna in the oven until I've given this a shot, okay?"

He wasn't wearing his usual sweatshirt, Beatrice noted with some surprise. Instead, he wore a cream-colored sweater over a red-and-black checked flannel shirt. He pushed his sleeves up, revealing the start of that tattoo that always peeked out of his collar. A slim black point on the inside of his left wrist that twisted around his forearm. Beatrice's eyes followed the lines as it began to plume before it disappeared under his sleeve.

"Where do you keep your saucepans?" he asked.

Beatrice realized she was staring and turned back to Kinsey, hoping no one had noticed.

"Who cares," Kinsey said, setting her forehead down on the table again. "It's not like it'll make any difference."

"I'll show you," Beatrice said, patting Kinsey on the head as she got up to help.

Sasha took over the task of cheering Kinsey, scrubbing her back and claiming that no Thanksgiving was really Thanksgiving until some horrible fiasco happened. When Kinsey didn't believe her, Sasha launched into a long story about the year when one of her uncles tried to deep fry a turkey and ended up setting his wife's rhododendrons on fire.

Beatrice pressed Nath into service manning the oven and juggling kitchen timers, and set to work getting all the food in the oven and helping Julian save the turkey.

"Aren't guys supposed to watch football on Thanksgiving?" Nath complained as he set a timer on his phone for the potatoes.

"Not when they're busy saving the day," Beatrice said, taking a peek at Julian's progress with the turkey.

He had cut the entire thing up, putting the worst of the raw pieces back in the oven. The dry, overcooked parts—the ones that weren't blackened and useless—were simmering on the stove in a can of gravy.

"That certainly *smells* amazing," Beatrice said.

Julian shrugged. "It's a little leftover-y, but it's turkey and gravy. And it shouldn't give anyone fatal food poisoning."

"Again, with the grand promises," Sasha said dryly.

"Hey, I'm doing my best here," Julian said, laughing. "You think you can do better?"

"She can't," said Kinsey, wiping her nose with a napkin. She took a deep breath and squared her shoulders, grabbing a few dirty mixing bowls from the table. "She's a worse cook than I am."

"Uh, *rude*," Sasha said, though she was laughing herself.

"The leftovers are the best part, anyway," Beatrice said, relieved that her friends were all getting along.

Kinsey finished clearing the dishes and put on one of her famously eclectic playlists. This one seemed to lean heavily into classic Motown and selections from the '40s, peppered with songs from obscure musicals. And then, declaring she didn't trust herself in the kitchen, Kinsey volunteered herself and Sasha to set the table in the dining room. Nath floated off after a few minutes, playing some game on his phone, no doubt to disappear until the second food touched the table.

Only Julian and Beatrice remained in the kitchen, falling into an easy rhythm as they negotiated the counter space.

"Where'd you learn to cook?" Beatrice asked, during a lull. She stood near the oven, with her hip pressed against the counter.

"My mom," Julian said, hooking his thumbs in his pockets and leaning against the counter on the other side of the oven. He lifted his shoulders in a half shrug. "She thought cooking was an important skill. I've never been able to get her kimchi recipe right, but I can heat things up without burning down the house."

"Kimchi is some kind of Korean pickle thing, isn't it?"

"Sort of? It's fermented vegetables. It tastes better than it sounds."

"Fermented vegetables?"

"Yeah. It's like—You know sauerkraut?"

"Sure . . ."

"Fermented cabbage. It's basically the German version of kimchi. Not exactly—kimchi usually has radishes or other vegetables in addition to the cabbage, and I don't think you put fish paste in sauerkraut—but it's the same idea."

"I'm not actually German," Beatrice blurted.

He blinked. "What?"

"Everyone thinks I'm German because my last name is Bauer, but I'm not," she said in a rush. "Just my step-dad. My mom is Welsh and Irish and French, and my birth dad was English and . . . something. I forget."

"What happened to him? Your birth dad? Or should I not ask?"

Beatrice shrugged, taking a sudden interest in the narrow chalkboard by the kitchen door that Kinsey's mom used for meal planning. "Last I heard, he was living in some compound in Arizona."

"You don't talk to him much?"

"I used to get cards from him on my birthday," she said, trying to steer away from the obnoxious self-pity. Julian didn't have either of his parents, and his step-dad sounded like a grade-A jerk. She shouldn't have brought this up in the first place. Telling people about how much simmering anger she had towards her birth father didn't tend to go over too well. "I'm pretty sure it was just my mom buying cards and disguising her handwriting so I would stop crying, though. It's not a big deal," she added quickly, seeing a flash of sympathy in Julian's eyes she wasn't sure she wanted. "He was supposed to be a jerk, anyway."

"Still sucks," Julian said.

The way he was watching her was making her nervous. The whole point of this dinner was to *not* mope about absent relations. But if he kept looking at her like that, she was going to end up sobbing in the kitchen and ruining everyone's evening.

"I'm just a little stunned by how much you know about fermented vegetables," she said, in one of the most awkward conversational course-corrections she'd ever made. "It's not normal."

"Stunned?" Julian asked, one side of his mouth quirking up. "Or impressed?"

She smiled, thankful at how quickly he jumped back to their old conversation. "Try 'appalled.'"

Julian pressed a hand over his heart, failing to keep a straight face. "You wound me."

Beatrice snorted, wrinkling her nose. "You're ridiculous."

"One of my better qualities." He reached over and squeezed her shoulder as the timer on the oven went off. It was such a simple gesture, but Beatrice felt some of the threatening darkness lift. She felt like she could breathe again.

She rocked off the counter to pull out the sweet potatoes. No more pity parties, she decided. Her family might be a complicated mess, but she was surrounded by people she cared about, and she was determined that all of them would have a good time.

While she was spreading a nice thick layer of mini-marshmallows on the sweet potato casserole, Rosemary Clooney came on singing "Come On-A My House." Beatrice, unable to help herself, started dancing, bouncing from one foot to the other in a weak approximation of the Charlie Brown dance.

Julian glanced over and broke into another grin, shaking his head. "You look like a nerd."

"A nerd having fun," Beatrice retorted. Impulsively, she

dropped the bag of marshmallows and grabbed his hand, pulling him away from the stove. "Come on, you *have* to dance to this song."

"You're so weird," he said, not quite joining in, but not quite resisting her efforts, either.

"Ah, *yes*," said Sasha, appearing in the kitchen doorway. "Are we having a kitchen dance party?"

"*No*," Julian said, attempting a retreat.

"Heck yeah," Beatrice said, grabbing his other hand too and redoubling her efforts to make him do the Twist with her. "Dancing makes the gravy come out better."

"That doesn't make any sense," Julian said, laughing, as Sasha called Kinsey in to dance too. He was dragging on Beatrice's hands a little, but she wasn't about to let go. Not when he was so close to giving up and joining in. She could see it in his eyes.

"Uh, hello," Kinsey said. "You can't do the Twist on Thanksgiving. You have to do the Mashed Potato."

"That's not a real thing," Julian protested.

"Is so," Sasha said, joining Kinsey in demonstrating. "See?"

"We're not dancing for the potatoes, we're dancing for the gravy," Beatrice said, laughing so hard she could feel a stitch forming in her side.

"Which goes on the mashed potatoes," Sasha pointed out. "Doy."

"You're all crazy," Julian said, sliding one foot back toward the stove.

"Dance with us," Beatrice said, leaning in and waggling her eyebrows at him. "You know you want to."

"Good grief." For a second, he looked flustered, and she thought the dancing had upset him and he was going to flee the kitchen. But before she could pull away and apologize, the tense expression was gone, replaced by bright determination. He adjusted his grip on her hands, pulling her close. "Okay, if we're doing this, we're going to do it right. Keep your hands up like this, loose, and follow my lead. Ready?"

"Uh," said Beatrice, alarmed by the sudden mischief in his eyes, and the sudden shortness of her breath. They were close enough she had to tilt her head up to look at him. The kitchen seemed to grow five degrees warmer in the space of a second. "I don't—"

"Trust me," he said.

She did trust him. So she nodded.

And then they were *dancing*.

Beatrice squeaked as he pulled her into a complicated series of turns and twirls, twisting her out and back to his arms again. She didn't know how she kept up with it, or managed not to step on his toes, or lose her balance and fall like a top in a bad spin. She barely felt the floor under her feet. The only solid thing in the world was Julian's hands.

"Holy crap," Beatrice said, when he spun her to a stop, the last notes of the song jangling in the air. Her breath was coming in gasps. She turned her face up to him and clung to his hands while she tried to find the floor again.

"You okay?" Julian asked, grinning down at her while Kinsey and Sasha applauded.

"I . . ." Beatrice wasn't sure how to respond. Her face was flushed, and she felt like a swarm of birds was spiraling up from her abdomen to the top of her lungs.

She didn't know what was wrong with her. It wasn't like she'd never been this close to Julian before. They sat next to each other on the train, bumping arms and knocking knees, almost every day. She must be dizzy. From the unexpected twirling. That was all.

But God, if he didn't have the loveliest eyes she'd ever seen. They were a rich, warm brown, and when he looked at her, she felt . . . understood.

The grin on his face softened a fraction as she stared, tongue-tied. His gaze flicked down to her lips and back up again, his thumb skimming over her knuckles. Her stomach skipped as her entire body flushed in anticipation.

Slowly the world seemed to tilt—

"Where in the hell did you learn that?" Sasha asked, bringing reality crashing back down.

Julian cleared his throat and stepped back, breaking contact. "My high school gym teacher was really into swing dancing," he said with a shrug. Beatrice didn't know what to do with her hands, now that they were empty. What did she usually do with her hands? She couldn't remember. "I'll tell you, there's nothing like forty high schoolers trying to swing dance on a basketball court dressed in gym clothes."

"Okay, but you have to teach me how to do that," said Sasha. "That was epic."

Julian laughed as one of Beatrice's timers went off. "Remind me after dinner. I think this is almost ready."

Yes. Food. She was supposed to be making food.

Beatrice wiped her tingling palms on her jeans and went to throw another handful of marshmallows on the sweet potatoes.

Kinsey came to stand next to her, her eyes wide. "Whatcha doin', Bee?"

Beatrice sent her a censuring look. "What? Too many marshmallows?"

"No such thing," Sasha put in, gathering silverware from the drawer.

"I think there is, actually," Kinsey said, lifting her eyebrows in a way that made it clear to Beatrice she wasn't talking about the marshmallows. "But as long as you know what you're doing."

Beatrice's face warmed. She glanced at Julian, who was

searching the spice cabinet for something. If he'd picked up on Kinsey's veiled lecture, he didn't give any indication.

"The sweet potatoes just need a few more minutes," Beatrice said, turning away from Kinsey and sliding the casserole into the oven.

She wasn't doing anything wrong. She and Julian were just friends. If her heart beat a little too fast, it was from the dancing. If her face was flushed, it was from the oven. If she was scattered and lightheaded, well . . . maybe she was dehydrated.

She realized she had meant to check on the green beans when she put the sweet potatoes in, spun around—

—and slammed right into Julian's chest as he came the other way.

"Oh," she gasped, springing back like she'd been burned. Her elbow banged the counter. Pain exploded down through her fingers. "Ow. Crap—"

"Sorry," Julian said, touching her arm. A jolt of . . . *something* shot up to her shoulder and straight down, all the way to her toes. She tensed, hissing in a sharp breath, and Julian withdrew his fingers, leaving them hovering in the air between them. His eyebrows drew together like he couldn't quite read her. "Small kitchen."

"Right." Except Kinsey's kitchen wasn't that small. And they had been navigating it without any issues before Beatrice's insides decided to ping and light up like a pinball machine possessed by a hyperactive demon.

Good lord, what was *wrong* with her?

"I have to—I—Potatoes," she said. And with that elegant witticism, she darted out of the kitchen.

'Potatoes??' she wailed at herself, dashing into the living room and pressing her back against the door. *Your big excuse is 'POTATOES???'*

She let her head drop against the door and squeezed her eyes shut. This was ridiculous. There was no reason for her to be flipping out right now. So Julian had spun her around the kitchen a couple of times. So she felt jittery and light and awkward and conspicuous. So she had thought for a split second that he might want to kiss her.

So what?

They weren't *going* to kiss. She had probably imagined that look on his face. Some sort of nervous reaction from wanting Thanksgiving to go well. She'd never seen him look at her like that before, after all. Never for one second had she thought they were anything but friends. Buddies. Coincidental commute acquaintances.

Well . . . Maybe for *one* second. Maybe even two. Every so often, when they were waiting for the train together, or both supposed to be busy with studying, she would glance over at him, and their eyes would meet, and there would be this split second of . . . *what if.*

She'd always dismissed it. Brushed it away before it stuck. She'd been certain it was a weird, one-sided fluke. Another episode of *Beatrice Gets Way Ahead of Herself and Drives People Away.*

Not that it mattered. She had a boyfriend. She wasn't going to *cheat* on him. She wasn't that kind of girl.

Even if she *did* keep trying to figure out ways to slip out of the relationship without Greyson noticing.

She pressed both hands over her face and groaned into her palms.

"What's with you?"

Beatrice pulled her head from the door. Nath was tucked in one corner of the couch with his phone in his hands. He raised one eyebrow in typical brotherly you're-insane fashion. She hadn't noticed he was in here, somehow. Even though he was sitting on the couch right in front of her. And watching football. She hadn't noticed the TV was on, either.

She was all over the place.

Beatrice made a concentrated effort to pull herself together. "I—uh—I need to know how much longer on the potatoes."

Nath gave her a Look before pulling up the timer app on his phone. "Six minutes."

"Great. Thank you."

"Are you okay?" Nath asked. "You look weird."

"I'm fine," Beatrice said, in a voice that sounded strange even to her. "I'm *fine*," she tried again. "It's fine."

"Okay . . ." Nath said, clearly not buying it.

"Everything's fine." Every time she said it, she sounded less convincing. "Dinner soon. Okay? Okay."

"Bee," Nath said, calling her back as she turned to leave. "Breathe."

Beatrice closed her eyes and made herself take a slow breath. It helped, a little. She still felt like fireworks were going off inside her, but it felt less like they were also shooting out of her ears and fingertips.

"Did something happen?" Nath asked. "You want me to come out there?"

"No, it's fine," Beatrice said again. At least she sounded halfway credible that time. "I just had a moment. I'm better now. Thanks."

Nath gave her a thumbs up and turned back to his phone.

THIRTEEN

Things had—for the most part—gone back to normal by the time they all sat down at the dining room table. Kinsey's mood had lightened, and Nath had decided to make an effort to be social again. Beatrice had even managed to convince herself all her excess energy was due to nothing but nerves over wanting Thanksgiving to go well for everyone.

She thought she had, anyway. Sitting next to Julian when she was so agonizingly *aware* of him was making her feel like a neurotic squirrel. She had scooted to the far side of her chair, just so she wouldn't accidentally brush his arm, afraid of what embarrassing thing she'd end up doing next. It was so bad that when she tried to pass him the gravy boat, she almost knocked it over.

"Whoa, there," Julian said, his hand darting out to save their gravy once again. His fingers brushed hers and she jerked her hand back at the shock. He froze for a moment, turning his whole attention on her with that same strange look on his face he'd worn when she knocked into him.

This was ridiculous. She'd touched Julian dozens of times before. Maybe hundreds, by now. Kicking him to get his attention, or poking at his arm, or pressing against his shoulder to try to sneak a look at his sketchbook, or pushing his hand aside to make sure he was studying and not just doodling energetic chibi characters in the margins of the study book. None of that had ever set her heart racing. What was so special about a glancing touch over a gravy boat?

Slowly, he set the dish down, never once taking his eyes off hers. "Sorry," he said. "Did it burn you?"

She shook her head tightly. "I'm sorry. I didn't sleep that well last night." For some reason, her cheeks warmed at the excuse, and she turned away, stabbing a green bean with her fork and shoveling it into her mouth.

"So what's the verdict on the turkey?" Sasha asked Kinsey, pulling Julian's befuddled attention from Beatrice's burning face. "Is Thanksgiving ruined after all?"

"I appreciate the vote of confidence," Julian said.

Sasha bowed her head towards him with a little flourish of her fork. "No trouble."

"Well," Kinsey said, with the air of a queen about to make a pronouncement, "I think that this Thanksgiving, the thing I am most thankful for is this Julian guy that Bee found—probably in a gutter or something."

"Kins," Beatrice objected.

But Julian shrugged. "She's not far off."

"The point being," Kinsey said loudly, "that Sir Guttersnipe has indeed saved Thanksgiving." She raised her glass in Julian's direction. "The turkey is excellent, sir. You'd never even guess I ruined it."

"Huzzah!" Nath said as the rest of them raised their glasses at the toast.

"Good grief," Julian said, his shoulders going up in embarrassment. "You people are far too easy to please."

Beatrice kicked the leg of his chair to get his attention. He fixed his gaze on her at once, sending a strange little thrill through her. "You're too modest."

"You're right," he said with a growing smile. "I should start my own cooking show. Every episode, I'll take a seemingly ruined item of food and simmer it in gravy for half an hour."

Beatrice snorted.

"I think I'll start with the obvious—turkey, meatloaf, tofu—"

"Chicken fried steak," Nath suggested. "Mashed potatoes. Shrimp."

"Shrimp?" Sasha repeated, half disgusted.

"Why not?" Julian said. "And after that, I'll start including more unusual choices. Sandwiches, cabbage, scrambled eggs, pancakes. All simmered in a nice brown gravy."

"Ew," Kinsey said. She picked up a roll and shook it at Julian. "Some of us are trying to eat real food here."

"I haven't even gotten to the desserts yet," Julian said.

A collection of groans and laughs went up around the table. And just like that, like magic, everything clicked into place. Kinsey threatened to revoke her endorsement of Julian's turkey if he kept describing his imaginary cooking show. Sasha perked up and told a story about a cousin back in Wyoming who'd almost gotten on a Food Network competition. Nath ratted Beatrice out for bringing homework to Thanksgiving, and the whole table teamed up to stop her from actually doing any. Everyone was talking. Everyone was happy.

It was perfect.

When they were finished eating, everyone pushed their plates back and kept on talking and laughing. Someone floated the idea of Pictionary, which had Beatrice claiming it wouldn't be fair for whichever side had Julian because he was an artist. That turned from Julian trying to deny his art skills would give his team an advantage into the whole table trying to make him draw something for them.

"Okay, okay!" Julian relented, pushing back his chair. "My sketchbook is in my coat. Please calm yourselves while I get it. I don't draw for crazy people."

"When did you adopt that policy?" Beatrice asked, twisting in her seat to follow his progress into the kitchen. "I make you draw stuff all the time."

"You're not crazy," Julian said, his voice muffled by the swinging kitchen door. He emerged a moment later, coat in hand, and started digging in the pockets for his sketchbook. "You're just weird. I don't mind drawing for weirdos."

She wrinkled her nose to hide a giddy grin as he threw his coat over the back of his chair and dropped into his seat. He tucked a ballpoint pen—this week's favorite drawing implement—behind his ear and started to flip through the book for a blank page. Beatrice knew most of the sketches already, from sneaking peeks while he was drawing, and prodding him into showing her what he'd been working on between train rides. But then a little portrait whipped by that she hadn't seen before, but snagged her attention.

"Wait wait, go back," Beatrice said, swiping the sketchbook from him. She turned the pages until she found the loose drawing. It was of a girl in a fluffy sweater, enjoying a hot beverage while a flock of birds nested in her abundant hair.

A weird feeling seized her chest. It was that stupid joke she'd told him on their first train ride into the city. But he hadn't made the girl in the drawing look crazy, or frumpy, or riddled with pigeon mites. She looked sort of . . . cozy. It was like something out of a picture book.

Beatrice pointed at the page and looked up at Julian, her heart thumping against her ribcage. "Is that supposed to be me?"

"Of course not," Julian said, plucking the sketchbook out of her hand before anyone else had the chance to see it. He flicked to a new page. In one corner, he doodled a bee wearing a massive wig. He tapped it with the back of his pen. "*That's* you."

Beatrice made a face at him, relieved he was turning this into a joke. "Original."

"No good?" Julian asked, squinting at the sketch sideways. "No, you're right. I'll try again."

Beatrice rested her head on her hand and let her gaze follow the loping movements of his fingers. She liked watching him build up shapes from something completely random-looking to an actual drawing. It didn't usually make her feel so strange. But then, she'd never seen him draw *her*.

Not that he was drawing her actual likeness. The new sketch looked suspiciously like a bird.

"Don't forget the hair," Nath said, leaning in to point. He seemed to think it was hilarious his sister was being drawn as various implausible animals.

"Well, obviously," Julian said, sketching in another floof of hair on the bird's head.

"I feel personally attacked," Beatrice said, more to preserve her dignity than from any real offense.

"And her floral boots," Kinsey suggested as she and Sasha leaned over the table to watch.

"Good idea," Julian said, adding them to the masterpiece. He turned the sketchbook in Beatrice's direction. "Better?"

"One problem," Beatrice said, looking from the drawing to Julian's self-congratulatory face. "I'm not a pigeon."

"Ah, yes, I see where I went wrong." His pen flew across the paper, building up the shapes until it became a coherent image of a lion with a voluminous mane and an abundance of freckles, wearing what looked like Beatrice's favorite Fair Ilse sweater. "There. How's that?"

Her heart was thumping so hard she was surprised no one was looking around for the source of the noise. She'd thought, when he'd called her Simba, that it was some kind of dig at her appearance. But maybe she'd misunderstood. Maybe it was because, for some unknown reason, he thought she was brave.

"It's . . ." She struggled to find a joke that would put the world back on its axis. "But . . . I'm a girl."

"I noticed." Julian held her gaze for a long moment, something unreadable hiding behind his grin. "But lionesses don't have manes."

She couldn't have looked away if she wanted to. She bit her lip, wishing she knew what he was thinking. What he thought he saw in her face that had him watching her like he was waiting for an answer.

Then he coughed and turned away, running his thumb down the open spine of his sketchbook. Beatrice's hand twitched on the table with a sudden urge to catch his wrist and drag her teeth over the fleshy part of his thumb.

Whoa. What the heck?

She shoved her hands under her knees, shocked by the impulse. What in the world was *wrong* with her tonight?

"Do Sasha next," Nath said, oblivious to any prolonged staring that may or may not have just occurred.

"What, as an animal?" Julian asked.

Beatrice felt a twinge of annoyance that he could be so unaffected while she was freaking out. Although she wouldn't have felt any better if he was *also* freaking out.

She resisted the urge to face-plant on the table. The last thing she wanted was everyone demanding to know why she was acting so weird.

"Ooh, yeah," Kinsey said, her eyes lighting up. "What animal's good at soccer?"

"People," Sasha offered, bemused.

"Horses?" Nath suggested. "No, wait. Elephants."

Sasha snorted. "Now *I* feel personally attacked."

"What, because of your giant schnoz?" Kinsey teased.

"My schnoz is not giant!" Sasha protested, tenting her fingers over her nose and laughing.

"You're all wrong, anyway," Kinsey said. "Obviously, Sasha is a cheetah."

"Fast but lazy," Sasha said, squinting at a spot on the ceiling. "Yeah, sounds about right."

"Who said you were lazy?" Kinsey asked, scowling at her.

"*I* did," said Sasha. "Just now."

The doorbell rang before Kinsey could answer. Rolling her eyes, she excused herself and walked out to answer the door.

"So the consensus is cheetah in a soccer jersey?" Julian said, brushing imaginary eraser dust off a new page.

"Yes," Nath said, while Julian put a few light lines down.

"Hang on, I need a reference," he said, taking out his phone. "I'm going to get the face all wrong and I can't remember how the spots look."

"Just put Sasha's actual face on top of a vaguely cat-looking body," Beatrice suggested.

"That sounds terrifying," Sasha said as Julian laughed, eyes on his phone.

Kinsey's voice drifted from the foyer, indistinct.

"Aren't the spots sort of like crescent moons?" Nath asked.

"I thought that was leopards," said Sasha.

"No, leopard spots look like donuts," Nath said, grabbing his phone off the table and unlocking it.

"Ooh, can you give cheetah-me a donut?" Sasha said, distracted. "I love donuts."

"Sure, why not?" said Julian, glancing at Beatrice sideways as he picked up his pen. There was a spark of mischief there, like they were sharing a joke.

And . . . God. She wished she'd met him before she and Greyson got paired up on that stupid project. Or that she'd found the backbone to end that relationship a long time ago. Or that she would have looked up from all her lists and work schedules and class assignments long enough to realize exactly how hard she was falling for the kind, hardworking artist beside her.

"Look who I found," Kinsey said grandly, returning from the foyer.

Beatrice was still watching Julian's face when he glanced past her to see who had come in. So she saw the sudden change in his demeanor from cheerful mischief to utter dread. The color drained from his face, and his body went rigid as he pushed back from the table.

Beatrice's stomach knotted. She recognized that fear in his eyes. She'd seen it once before, back in the library when he'd first barreled into her life.

Beatrice flattened her hand on the table and spun in her seat, convinced the guy who'd been chasing Julian weeks ago had found him again. She was already rifling through her mental repertoire of referee tricks for something she could say to convince one person not to murder another in her friend's parents' dining room when she set eyes on the tall figure standing in the doorway behind Kinsey.

Dark, tousled hair, expensive jeans, and a fitted, dark blue dress shirt that leeched his pale eyes of color.

Beatrice's throat went dry in recognition. It wasn't a dangerous stranger with a knife. In fact, it was someone she knew quite well.

Her boyfriend had decided show up to Thanksgiving after all.

FOURTEEN

"Greyson." Beatrice sprang to her feet, her chair scraping the floor.

Greyson's expression was stony, and he was staring at Julian with a dark look in his eyes that Beatrice didn't like at all. It didn't make sense. If Greyson was going to be angry at anyone, it should have been her.

All the cozy warmth of a few seconds ago had fled the room. The tension coming off Julian was almost palpable, although he hadn't moved since he first pushed back from the table.

Confused and fighting a tight, guilty feeling in her chest, Beatrice switched into referee mode. Just keep everyone calm and reasonable, and the rest would be easier to sort out. She summoned a smile for Greyson, though it felt more like a grimace. "I thought you weren't going to be able to come."

"Clearly," Greyson said in clipped tones, never taking his eyes off Julian. "What's he doing here?"

"You guys know each other?" Sasha asked. She hadn't jumped out of her chair as Beatrice had, but she was poised to do so, both hands pressed against the table.

"Sure," said Greyson. "Julian and I go way back. Don't we, Jules?"

Beatrice had to bring all the stress in the room back down somehow. She took a step towards her boyfriend, reaching out a calming hand to lay on his arm. "Greyson—"

"Relax," Julian said, snapping his sketchbook closed and getting to his feet. "I was just leaving."

"Wait, really?" Nath asked. "What for?"

Beatrice tried to send Julian a silent apology, but he wouldn't look at her.

"I just realized what time it is." He jerked on his coat and thrust the sketchbook into a pocket. "Thanks for having me over, Kinsey."

"Yeah, of course," Kinsey said, eyes wide as they darted from Julian to Greyson and back. "But—Hang on, don't you want some leftovers to take home? Or some dessert?"

"No. Thanks." Julian headed for the foyer, his gaze on the ground, shoulders tight, like he wanted to avoid touching Greyson as he passed.

Greyson seized Julian's coat, dragging him around so they were almost nose to nose. "I asked you what the hell you're doing here," Greyson said, his voice pitched so low it felt like thunder.

Julian shoved Greyson back, nearly sending him sprawling. Beatrice jumped out of the way, clapping both hands over her mouth to catch a frightened squeak. A chair hit the floor. Sasha barked a warning, and someone let out a curse.

"*Don't touch me,*" Julian spat at Greyson, his hands fisted at his sides. Beatrice had never seen that look on his face before—the mingled hate and fear. Even in the library all those weeks ago, he hadn't looked so cornered and desperate and furious. "I said I'm fucking leaving."

Greyson's lip twisted as he shifted his stance, his eyes hard. Beatrice knew what was going to happen next. The shove would turn into a blow, and the blow would turn into a second—

"Stop," she begged, grabbing Greyson's wrist and tugging him toward the dining room. "Just stop. Tell me what's going on."

He didn't budge. He didn't even look at her.

Julian, though, caught the movement, and his gaze snapped to hers. Something flickered behind his eyes for a split second, too fast for her to understand if it was anger or pain, but it tore through her like a knife. She was just making him more upset. But she didn't know what else to do.

"Julian—" she began.

He turned on his heel. Kinsey dodged out of the way to let him by.

"You win, okay?" Julian shot over his shoulder at Greyson. "You win."

Beatrice had no idea what he meant. But she couldn't let him leave like this. She dropped Greyson's hand and started after Julian.

Greyson caught her arm and wrenched her back. "Let him go," he said, his eyes like ice.

"But—" Beatrice threw a *help-me* look in Sasha's direction as the front door slammed behind Julian.

Sasha was already on her feet. "On it," she said, slipping into the foyer.

"Let him go," Greyson said again.

"I'm his ride," Sasha called back impatiently.

"Okay, look," Kinsey said, holding up a hand as Sasha followed Julian out of the house. "Let's all just take a breath, here—"

"What was he doing here?" Greyson snapped, yanking Beatrice's arm again.

She stumbled half a step closer, a flare of pain shooting through her shoulder, her heart pulsing against her ribs. The way he was looking at her made her breath seize. There was a darkness behind all that ice that she'd never seen before.

"Greyson," she said, surprised at how calm she sounded. Her hands shook so badly that she was sure Greyson could feel it. His fingers dug into her skin like a tourniquet. She felt as small and breakable as a brittle twig. "Let go."

"Tell me what the fuck he was doing here, Beatrice," Greyson growled, his breath hot on her face.

She flinched. "Greyson—"

"*Answer me.*"

"She told you to let go," Nath said, appearing at Beatrice's shoulder and wedging himself between them. "Back off, man."

Greyson turned his threatening snarl on Nath. He was going to hurt her little brother. Beatrice grabbed Nath's sleeve with her free hand, so she could drag him out of danger—

Greyson dropped Beatrice's arm. His expression cleared as he stepped back. "Sorry," he said, rubbing his jaw with one hand. "I'm sorry. I didn't mean to hurt you."

Beatrice held onto Nath's sleeve, her instinctive move to protect him truncated. She didn't want to let go. Although whether that was because she was still worried about him or herself, she didn't know.

"You okay, hon?" Kinsey asked, not-so-subtly putting herself between Beatrice and Greyson.

Beatrice nodded. She wasn't okay. It hurt, where Greyson had grabbed her, and she was shaking all over. But it made her anxious to have Kinsey and Nath so close. Like if they took her side, it would make things worse for all of them. She wanted them to decide this wasn't their fight and let her handle it.

But she didn't feel equipped to handle Greyson on her own right now, either.

"I'm sorry," Greyson said again. He threw out a hand toward the front door. "I just don't understand what he was doing here. Last I heard, he was in Philadelphia. And suddenly he's chatting up my girlfriend at this sorry excuse for a Thanksgiving dinner?"

Kinsey's head snapped around to glare at Greyson, and defensive anger sparked in the back of Beatrice's mind. She had worked hard—all of them had—to salvage what could have been a really crappy Thanksgiving. And right up until Greyson walked in and started terrorizing everyone and throwing aspersions around, Beatrice would have said that the dinner was a resounding success.

Anger lent her false bravery. She let go of Nath's sleeve and stepped around Kinsey so she was facing Greyson head-on. "He was here," she said, her voice gaining strength, "because I asked him to come. He's my friend. And he didn't have anywhere else to go."

"Well, he lied to you about that one," Greyson said, his lip twisting in disgust. "If he wasn't so hellbent on playing the victim, he would've been having Thanksgiving dinner at my dad's place with the rest of us. Julian is my step-brother."

"Julian! Hold up!"

Julian didn't slow his stride. He had to keep moving. If he was forced to stop, he would have to start punching things to get rid of some of the excess *everything* that was making it so hard to breathe.

"*Julian!*" Sasha ran up to him, her boots unlaced, her coat open to the cold, and fell into step beside him. "My car's the other way."

He was *not* walking past that house again. "I'll get a cab."

"In this weather? On *Thanksgiving*? Yeah, good luck with that."

"Bus, then."

"Oh my God, at least let me drive you to the train station. I don't mind. Promise."

Julian came up short, balling his hands into fists. He made himself take a deep breath and think like a reasonable person.

Not an easy task, in the face of an unexpected Greyson Sayer-Crewe confrontation.

Old memories hurled themselves at him in vivid, incomplete flashes. An offhand comment twisted into cursing and shoving. The taste of blood in his mouth. Unyielding pavement scraping his back. Sunlight searing his skin as he fought to get out from under the hard blows raining down on him. Meeting his step-brother's eyes and knowing with black certainty that he would think nothing of taking Julian's life.

Julian felt sick. He hadn't laid eyes on Greyson since the day he decided he'd rather take his chances alone on the streets than risk another night sleeping under the same roof as his step-brother. He would have been thrilled if he'd never run into Greyson again. It was just Julian's shitty luck that Greyson would turn up right when Julian was starting to believe he was getting his feet under him.

"Both Kinsey and Bee will kill me if I go back in without taking you home first," Sasha said, bending to tuck her shoelaces into the tops of her boots. "If I have to chase after you in the ass-freezing cold to do that, I will. I could use the exercise after all that food."

"I don't need a babysitter," Julian said, not managing to sound as venomous as he'd intended. "I can get myself home. Go back inside."

"Eh," Sasha said with a shrug. "Greyson's a dick if you ask me. I'm happy for an excuse to avoid him."

Julian looked at her, surprised. Greyson was capable of turning on the charm when it suited him. But she seemed sincere.

Her pale eyebrows drew together when he hesitated. "I can get the car and meet you at the corner."

Part of him wanted to take her up on the offer. It was cold, and the clouds blocking out the stars above threatened snow. Not fun weather to try to hail a cab in. And that was before thinking about the amount of money he'd have to dish out to make it home. His eyes slid to the house.

He shouldn't have left Beatrice alone with Greyson while he was like that. If anyone knew what happened when Greyson decided you'd betrayed him, it was Julian. It had taken a broken hand and a near-fatal beating to teach him not to challenge his step-brother, but it was a lesson well learned.

Julian reached up to push his hair back and discovered he was shaking. Fat lot of good he'd do Beatrice now, even if confronting Greyson would smooth things over, instead of making them worse.

"No," Julian said, a grim clarity overtaking his panic. "I need you to go back inside. You have to make sure Greyson understands that Beatrice didn't have a clue he and I knew each other."

"I think Bee can cover that without my help," Sasha said.

"No, listen," Julian said, gripping her sleeve. "He has to understand this isn't her fault. Okay? Blame it all on me if you have to."

"What are you talking about?" Sasha asked, eyebrows shooting toward her hairline. "Blame you for *what*? How do you guys even know each other?"

"Please," Julian said, ignoring her questions. It would take too long to explain. And she had no reason to believe him. "You don't know what he's like."

"He wouldn't hurt her, though. Right? I mean, Nath and Kinsey are still right there, and neither one would let anything happen to—"

"Greyson is plenty patient," Julian insisted. "And he's slick. If he thinks he's been slighted, he'll keep that slight close until he sees a way to get even without getting his hands dirty. Please," he said again, when Sasha hesitated. "If I thought there was a chance I wouldn't make everything worse, I'd do it myself."

Sasha sighed, but Julian could see she was close to relenting. "Are you *sure* you'll be okay getting home?"

"I'm sure."

Sasha shook her head, then dug in her coat pockets and brought out a couple of hand-warmer packets and a Sharpie. She scrawled something on one of the packets and then pressed both warmers into Julian's hand. "If you can't get a cab or whatever, you text me and I'll make an excuse and come pick you up. And don't frigging die of hypothermia, or Bee's gonna kill me. For real."

"Understood," Julian said, knowing he wasn't going to text her, even if he found himself walking home.

He'd spent all evening letting himself believe maybe it wouldn't be so bad to let himself like Beatrice. He'd even started entertaining the idea she might like him, too. There had been a moment in the kitchen when she looked up at him, and he thought, if they'd been alone, she might have let him kiss her. He'd started to hope . . .

And then Greyson walked in. And Beatrice had reached for *his* hand.

Well, fine, Julian thought, watching Sasha jog back to the house. He could take a damn hint. If Beatrice wanted Greyson, Julian sure as hell wasn't going to stop her.

Even if that meant he'd probably never see her again.

He turned and started walking, head bent against the chilly wind, blind to the warm, homey light pouring out of the windows of the middle-class houses on either side. How many times had he told himself that hope only ever let him down? That his shitty luck was too fucking shitty to be overcome with plans and hard work? How many times had he told himself to stay the fuck away from Beatrice before he got attached? Before he got himself hurt?

He held the dark vindication against himself like a shield. But it did nothing to soothe the tearing pain in his chest.

He knew he shouldn't have come to this damn dinner.

FIFTEEN

Beatrice sank into the nearest chair. Her legs shook too much to support her any longer. This wasn't like the arguments she mediated at home, where she could function as a neutral third party. Where she could shut down her own feelings and steer the fight into some semblance of rationality.

She was smack in the middle of this one.

"I don't understand," she said, pressing cold fingers to her cheeks. She couldn't look at Greyson. A weird combination of guilt, nerves, and resentment made it impossible to look at anyone. Her eyes settled on the pepper mill near the end of the table. "You—You never told me you had a step-brother."

"It's a sore subject," Greyson replied, gripping the back of one of the other chairs. He tapped a hard staccato rhythm with one finger. "We . . . don't get along very well."

"Really," Kinsey said, crossing her arms beside Beatrice. "You seemed so happy to see each other."

"I don't understand," Beatrice said softly, trying to sort the chaos into some kind of pattern. How hadn't she known they were step-brothers? She'd mentioned Greyson to Julian before. She was sure of it.

Except, now that she thought about it . . . maybe she hadn't.

Whenever Greyson came up in conversation, she'd just referred to him as her boyfriend. And the one time Julian mentioned having a step-brother, he hadn't offered a name either.

Greyson released the chair and crouched at Beatrice's side. "I'm sure this wasn't your fault," he said in a low voice, freezing her in place with his gaze. "I know Julian. He has no trouble convincing people he's just a good guy who's down on his luck. But he's bad news. You shouldn't be hanging around with him."

Beatrice flushed. She wasn't stupid. She knew Julian had a rough past. He got quiet and tense as they neared the city every day—he'd stop drawing, his pencil tapping a rapid rhythm against the paper as he scanned the faces of the people around them, and it took him an extra beat to respond if she asked him a question. That tension tended to still be with him when they got on the train back home. For goodness' sake, they'd met because he was fleeing a guy he claimed was capable of killing both of them. That didn't exactly scream *wholesome lifestyle*.

"What do you mean, 'bad news?'" Beatrice asked, gripping the seat of her chair with both hands.

Greyson sat back on his heels, a warning flashing in his eyes. "I guess he didn't mention to any of you about how he got in trouble with the FBI for running drugs for a gang."

"Are you serious?" Nath asked.

"No," Beatrice said in flat denial. She didn't care if Greyson got angry. Julian may have had a tough life, but he wasn't a criminal. He just wasn't. "No way."

Greyson's expression softened into something close to pity. Beatrice turned her head sharply and blinked away an unexpected onslaught of tears.

"Okay." Greyson stood, rubbing his face. "Maybe I'd better explain. I was thirteen when my father married their mother— him and his sister. We got along at first. It was good having other kids around the house, after so many years of being an only child. I considered both of them real siblings. But . . . things started going wrong after their mother passed. The trauma—it was so sudden. She was driving home from work one day and got hit by a drunk driver."

Beatrice touched her fingers to her lips, fighting the well of sympathy pushing against her lungs. Greyson was so upset already, and she was afraid of what he would do if he thought she was taking Julian's side. But she couldn't imagine what it must have been like to have your mom snatched away from you so quickly. She swallowed, keeping her expression as still and neutral as she could.

"Julian, in particular, started acting out after that," Greyson went on. "It was like he became a completely different person. He got mixed up with these guys at school who were always getting in trouble. I tried to warn him about them, but he wouldn't listen. He didn't want anything to do with me. I think he resented me for still having my dad when both his parents were dead. And he was always so stubborn. There was nothing I could do." Greyson picked up a spoon from the table and turned it over in his fingers. "One day these guys he was hanging around turned on him and messed him up pretty bad. Broke his collarbone and a couple of ribs. Punctured a lung. Shattered a few bones in his hand by closing it in a car door."

"Oh God," Beatrice said before she could stop herself. Julian had told her he'd broken his hand in high school, but she had no idea it was that serious.

Greyson nodded, his frown somber. "It was awful, but . . ." He dropped the spoon and turned to Beatrice, a chilly sort of anguish twisting his expression. "It sounds terrible, but part of me was relieved when it happened. I thought he would see that messing with those guys was a bad idea, and he'd calm down, and come back, and everything would go back to how it was before. My dad was going to put him in physical therapy so that he could start drawing again. He could've gotten into an art school. He could've done something with his life.

"Instead, somehow he came to the conclusion that I was the one to blame for those guys attacking him. I think he resented the fact that I'd warned him about them. He refused the physical therapy. He stopped talking to me at all. And then he left. Packed up his things and left the day after he was released from the hospital. We kept tabs on him for a while, but he kept getting in trouble—drugs, gangs—and then the whole thing with the FBI . . .

"I'm—I'm sorry if I seemed not quite myself," he said, smoothing his shirt front. "I haven't spoken to him in years. It was a shock, seeing him after all this time."

Beatrice dropped her gaze. She didn't know what to say. She was having a hard time parsing how much of Greyson's story was fact and how much was . . . not *lies*, per se, but . . . embroidered. Skewed. She'd been the complaint receptacle for her own family long enough to know that when things got emotional, the story of what happened didn't always line up with the facts. Memories shifted. Some more than others. And this wasn't something that happened a couple weeks ago. This was years.

She kept seeing Julian's face in her mind's eye. That terrifying moment when she thought he was going to fight Greyson right there in Kinsey's dining room. How the color had drained from his face when he saw Greyson standing in the doorway. You didn't look at someone like that just because you had some misplaced anger at them from three years ago that you hadn't worked out yet.

Greyson took her hand. "Can you understand why I'd be worried to find out he's been trying to get close to you?" he asked, his voice oh-so-gentle.

No. I don't understand any of this. "I—I guess."

She looked up at him, but she couldn't read him. The tilt of his head, the furrow of his brow, should have signaled understanding. Sympathy. A hint of guilt for how he grabbed her, even. But there was something in his eyes—a sharpness that wouldn't blunt—that unsettled her.

He pressed his lips to her knuckles. "I just don't want you getting hurt."

"I appreciate that," Beatrice said, sliding her hand out of his grip and wrapping her arms around herself. "But I can take care of myself. I don't—"

The front door banged open. Beatrice pushed back from the table and darted to the foyer. Sasha blew in the front door with a gust of air that smelled of oncoming snow. She was flushed and breathless, and there was no way she'd had enough time to take Julian all the way back home.

"Sasha?" Beatrice said, meeting her at the coat rack by the door.

"He got a cab," Sasha said, without even waiting for Beatrice to ask. She kicked her shoes off but didn't remove her coat before touching Beatrice's shoulder and searching her eyes. "Everything okay here?" she asked in a whisper, as though making sure the others couldn't hear.

Beatrice nodded, surprised at the seriousness in Sasha's expression. But before Beatrice could ask her what Julian had said to make her look so worried, Sasha plastered on a smile and swept into the dining room.

Beatrice glanced at the front door before she followed, hesitant to go back in. Part of her wanted to slip out the door and catch up to Julian, even though it would just make Greyson angry. But what could she say that would make up for how much she'd hurt Julian by putting him in a situation where he felt so cornered?

Chest tight, Beatrice slid into the dining room behind Sasha.

"Sorry about all this, Greyson," Sasha was saying, her tone too bright, as though it was forced. "I don't think any of us realized you two knew each other. I mean, you don't seem like you would have run in the same circles."

"No, it's not anyone's fault," Greyson said, all his earlier agitation gone. He even offered up an apologetic smile.

"What do you say we all get some pie and think about something else?" Sasha suggested briskly, cutting Kinsey off when she opened her mouth—probably to say something sarcastic, from her expression.

A look passed between the two of them, and Kinsey narrowed her eyes. "Yeah, fine," she said, picking up the dish of stuffing and heading into the kitchen. "Pie it is."

Greyson volunteered to help clear the table, and that was it. They were all going to have dessert and act like nothing had happened.

But Beatrice didn't want any stupid pie. She shut her eyes and tried to breathe. For all her doubts about her relationship with Greyson, she never thought he'd try to hurt her. She wanted to go home so she could lock herself away and have a good cry. She felt agitated and confused and guilty and unaccountably sad.

"Bee?" Nath asked. He'd come to stand next to her, his arms crossed, his eyes big and worried.

"I'm fine." Beatrice forced a smile. "Let's get these dishes cleared, okay?"

Her gaze wandered to the window as she collected a butter dish and the gravy boat from the table. Outside, in the yellow light of the streetlamps, it had started to snow.

A few hours fighting public transit to get home hadn't improved Julian's mood. He didn't even feel human anymore. Just a sack of skin containing a dense vortex of angry, confused devastation.

He couldn't get his movements under control. They were too fast, too violent. He forced his way through the sticky door of his apartment, letting it bang against the wall.

"*Fuck!*" Fabiana was perched on one of the wobbly kitchen chairs with one leg drawn up, a bottle of nail polish in her hand. A hot pink streak slashed across her bare foot. She grabbed for a napkin as Julian slammed the door and wrestled his coat off. "Look what you—" She cut herself off when she looked up at him, her frown sharpening. "The fuck happened to you?"

"Thanksgiving fucking happened to me," Julian spat, shoving his coat in the closet. His sketchbook fell out of the pocket. Fucking useless piece of crap. He was fooling himself thinking he could get out from under a lifetime's worth of shitty luck with one sketchbook of shitty art. He snatched it off the floor and hurled it at the trash can. It hit a cabinet instead and landed pages-first on the linoleum.

"Hey, whoa," Fabiana said, eyes wide. "Chill."

Julian rounded on her before he could think better of it. "I thought I told you to text me when you left Walter's."

"I forgot," she said, wetting the napkin with nail polish remover and dabbing at her foot. By the looks of it, she'd been home for a while. She had changed into yoga pants and a sweatshirt, and her long hair was tied in a high knot. "So sue me."

"How hard is it to type two words on your way out?"

"Shit, Jules. Give me a break. You're not the only one who had a rotten night, you know. I was counting on Greyson bringing his new girlfriend to dinner so he couldn't be as much of a dick, but she was—"

"In White Plains?" Julian finished for her. "Having dinner with her friends? Yeah. I know."

"You—What?" Fabiana lifted her head, napkin suspended in midair. "How?"

Julian spread his arms. "Guess who else was there."

Fabiana's lip twisted in confusion. "In White Plains?"

"I take it Greyson left dinner early? Maybe said something about dropping in on his girlfriend?"

"Wait. You were there? With the girlfriend?"

"Yep."

He could see the moment the realization dawned, her expression going slack. "And then Greyson—"

"Yep."

Fabiana paled. "Fuck. *Fuck*. Are you serious? How do you even *know* his girlfriend?"

"She lives up here. We take the same fucking train. Every fucking day."

"Holy . . . Since when?"

"I don't know. Since I started at the art center. About three weeks."

"You've been screwing around with Greyson's girlfriend for the past *three weeks*?" Fabiana's bare foot hit the floor as she leaned toward him in her chair. "After all that shit he pulled with you in high school? Are you *stupid*?"

"I didn't—I wasn't screwing around with her. It wasn't like that. We're just—We were friends. That's it. Commute buddies." Julian tangled his fingers in his hair, his frenetic, directionless anger leeching out of him.

Were.

Beatrice was the first person he'd allowed himself to get close to—to trust—in years. And look where it landed him.

He sank to the floor and let his head fall against the wall behind him. "I didn't know she was dating him. I knew she was dating *someone*, but I never . . ." He let out a low growl, pressing his hands over his eyes. How hard was it to ask what her boyfriend's fucking name was? He could have put a stop to this ages ago if he'd asked one simple question. "I'm such an idiot."

Fabiana didn't say anything for a few long moments, just tapped her little bottle of nail polish on the table. Doubtless because he was so pathetic that even she could find no joy in arguing with him any longer.

Then, with a sigh, she pushed to her feet and padded to the fridge. After retrieving a couple of the Italian sodas she'd splurged on after her first paycheck—the ones she'd warned Julian not to touch, on pain of death—she shut the door with her heel and dropped down next to Julian on the floor, stretching her legs out in front of her. She cracked open one of the bottles and passed it to him.

A hard lump formed in Julian's throat. Fabiana could be difficult to deal with. She was blunt and demanding, and she was even worse at talking about feelings than Julian. She hid her kindness and affection under so many insults and judgmental comments that it was sometimes hard to see. But it was there. You just had to know how to spot it.

Sometimes it looked like sitting on the floor, sharing one of her jealously hoarded drinks, and not saying anything at all.

He hadn't expected her dinner with Walter to go well—when had their step-dad kept his promises to either of them?—but part of Julian had been hoping Fabiana could convince Walter to take her back. Not to get her out of the cramped apartment, but because she deserved better than sleeping on an old mattress in a shitty apartment. She deserved better than being let down by the Sayer-Crewes again and again.

At least one of them should be allowed to be happy.

"I'm sorry Thanksgiving didn't go the way you wanted," he told her, staring at the fizzy drink in his hands.

She shrugged, opening the second bottle for herself and taking a swig. "No big loss. Didn't care much for the new ultimatum."

Ah, yes. Walter's infamous schemes to 'better Fabiana's life' by threatening to disinherit her if she didn't get accepted into competitive colleges in fields she had no interest in pursuing. "What crazy program did Walter want you to get into this time?"

"No program. He wanted me to cut off contact with you. I guess they found out I've been crashing here. Greyson thinks you're a '*bad influence*.'" She cut air quotes around the last two words and scoffed. "Ridiculous."

Julian's heart sank. He didn't want to be the reason she was trapped here with him. They had a hard enough time dealing with each other without adding another layer of resentment. "Fab—"

"I said it was a shitty ultimatum," she said, in a false, light tone that meant she didn't want to talk about it. She threw him a half smile, one brow lifted. "They clearly don't know either of us very well if they think *you're* the evil twin."

Julian wasn't willing to blow past it so quickly. Not this time. "I'd understand," he said, even though it hurt like hell, "if you wanted to—"

"Too late. I already told Walter to shove it." She elbowed him, but not hard. "You're stuck with me, jackass."

Julian knew the routine. He was supposed to elbow her in turn and call her a brat. And it would mean he loved her, too.

Instead, he looped his arm around her shoulders and pulled her into a hug. Fabiana made a gagging noise, but leaned her head on his shoulder. He didn't know how to tell her how much it meant to him that she was still here, with him, when she could have been reveling in the reacquisition of her upscale Brooklyn apartment instead. He didn't know how to tell her how much he wished they could dispose of all the broken things between them and go back to when they didn't spend half their time bickering. He didn't know how to tell her how much he cared about her.

So all he said was "We sure know how to celebrate a holiday, don't we?"

"Fuck 'em," Fabiana said, slipping out of the embrace. "Fuck 'em all."

Julian let his head fall back against the wall. He still couldn't think about Beatrice without his chest aching. But it was nice to feel like he and Fabiana were in sync again, at least for tonight. It was nice to feel like he had someone in his corner.

He shook his head, eyes on the ceiling. "What a shitfest."

Fabiana huffed a laugh and held her bottle aloft. "To another Moon holiday clusterfuck."

Julian's lip curled in a rueful smile as he tapped his drink to hers. "Condolences."

SIXTEEN

That's your boyfriend?" Nath asked, the second he shut the apartment door.

Greyson had insisted on driving Beatrice and Nath home, despite Sasha's protestations that she was happy to do so. It had been a nightmare. Nath was frustrated at having to ride home in Greyson's cramped sports car, and only opened his mouth to make the occasional snide remark. Beatrice spent the whole ride trying to play down Nath's caustic attitude, worried that, given the chance, the ride home would turn into a nasty argument. She had a hard enough time keeping her impulse to cry under control without having to go full referee on the two of them.

Now she and Nath were home, her nerves were still on red alert, even though they'd left Greyson in his car downstairs. Nath's accusatory glare wasn't helping. She'd sensed him ramping up to some kind of rant as they climbed the stairs, but she didn't have an ounce of patience left in her. If he pushed her any more, she was going to snap.

She grabbed the bag of leftovers from Nath and swept into the kitchen, hoping if she didn't respond to the question, he'd let it go.

No such luck.

"Is he usually that much of a dick?"

"Drop it, Nath," Beatrice said, shoving the food Kinsey had sent home with them into the fridge.

"You realize you didn't make a single joke from the time he walked in the door," Nath said, shrugging off his coat. "Not one."

"So?"

"So it was weird." He hung up his coat and sat at the table to pull off his shoes. "You weren't acting like you."

Beatrice yanked a carton of orange juice out of the way so she could crowd the last of the casserole dishes inside. "I apologize if the lack of constant entertainment put a damper on your evening."

"Shit, Bee, no one would miss your jokes less than I would," Nath said, tossing one shoe at the pile near the wall. "They're all terrible. I'm just saying—"

"Well, don't," Beatrice snapped, slamming the fridge shut and rounding on him. "I'm sick and tired of arguing with everyone tonight. So *drop it.*"

"Fine! Jeez."

"*Fine,*" Beatrice shot back. She crossed the living room, ignoring a welcoming mew from Sunny, and slammed her bedroom door shut behind her.

She collapsed on her bed, still in her coat and shoes, and squeezed her eyes shut, waiting for the dam to burst.

She had been pushing so much of this mess to the side for so long. Pretending she and Greyson were fine. Keeping her friendship with Julian to herself. Feigning confidence in her ability to keep up with all her coursework. Like if she could just keep all the pieces in her life in separate corners—if she acted like everything was under control—they'd never have a chance to crush her.

She touched her arm where Greyson had grabbed her. It only

hurt when she put pressure on it, but she was sure she'd have purple marks tomorrow. And still she found herself trying to explain it away. Greyson hadn't meant it. She was overreacting.

But there was no getting around that hateful look on his face when he stopped her from following Julian. That moment, before he got control of himself, when he almost hurt Nath.

Beatrice pushed the images away and dug out her phone. Sasha and Kinsey both asked her to text them when she and Nath got home. Kinsey had asked her three different times, in fact, and had given her a tight hug as she left that hadn't eased Beatrice's nerves. If everyone else was scared for her, it meant she was right to be afraid herself.

She opened the group chat between her, Kinsey, and Sasha, and tapped out a short text saying she and Nath were home safe. Seconds later, Sasha texted back with about twenty purple heart emojis.

Everything okay? Kinsey texted under that. **Wanna talk?**

No and no.

Everything's fine, Beatrice wrote. **I'm going to bed. Early shift tomorrow.**

Okay. I'm here if you need me. ♥ ♥ ♥

Ditto, Sasha added.

Beatrice sent a heart emoji to indicate her appreciation, and then locked her phone and let it fall to the bed.

It worried her that Julian hadn't let Sasha take him home. It was so cold out, and she was afraid he hadn't been able to find a cab in the snow. Even if he made it to the White Plains train station okay, it was a long trip home. And with it being Thanksgiving, who knew how long he would have had to wait for a train.

She wanted to text him, too. Make sure he got home. Make sure he was okay.

Make sure he wasn't angry with her.

That look on his face before he left—the one that shot through her and made her want to cry—she couldn't get it out of her head. And every time she thought about it, she couldn't help but feel that it was too late. She'd broken whatever fragile thing they had into deadly shards. And if she reminded him of it now, she would either get her number blocked, or be on the receiving end of a nasty rant she wasn't emotionally capable of handling tonight.

But she wasn't going to see him in person again until Monday.

Beatrice wiped tears from her eyes with one hand. Whatever had been going on at dinner, she was supposed to be Julian's friend. If it was Sasha or Kinsey in the same situation, she'd check in on them.

And God, she didn't want Julian to walk out of her life. She didn't want to let him go without a fight.

She tapped to Julian's number on her phone.

I'm sorry about dinner, she said. **I hope you got home okay.**

She stared at her phone for a long time after she hit send, waiting for the screen to light up with a reply. She was still waiting when she dragged herself into the bathroom to get ready for bed. Still waiting as she lay curled up under the covers, staring at the wall in the dark, her mind and heart tangled in too many knots. Still waiting, hours later, when she drifted into uneasy sleep, eyes gritty with tears, phone cradled under her hand.

Beatrice spent her entire weekend trying not to drown. She worked full shifts at Java Mama every day, most of them on only four or five hours of sleep. When not at work, she spent most of her time trying to keep Greyson at arm's length without making him fly off the handle. He had started texting her more than ever, and he got weird when she didn't respond right away, or with the right level of enthusiasm. She wanted to scream at him to leave her alone, but whenever she thought about the fight that would trigger, her hands would shake, and tears would spring to her eyes, and she couldn't get enough air in her lungs.

So she put it off. She would have to break it off with him sometime. But not this weekend. Not when Thanksgiving was still so fresh in her mind.

She had barely had time to study. The paper she needed to write never got longer than five sentences—not counting a pretty spectacular keyboard-smash at the end when Greyson texted her at the wrong moment and destroyed a brief stroke of focus. No way she was turning that paper in on time. At some point, she'd had to make her peace with the fact that she was unlikely to do well on her last two midterms. She could only look over her study guides during lulls at work. Even then, she couldn't get the information to stick in her brain.

And in all that time Julian hadn't texted her once.

She'd almost marched over to his apartment building to make him talk to her. She didn't know his exact address, but she knew which building he lived in. If she could get inside, then she was sure she could find him.

But something always seemed to stop her. On Friday, it was Greyson showing up at her apartment building after her shift to take her to an 'apology lunch.' On Saturday, it was her mom coming home and getting in an argument with Nath about whether he had an acceptable plan for his future. On Sunday, it was simply that Beatrice was exhausted and overwhelmed and didn't want to show up at Julian's door and immediately burst into tears.

She figured he *had* to talk to her on Monday morning. It was hard to avoid anyone in the small local station, never mind on the long ride to Grand Central Terminal. She had a whole speech prepared in her head by the time she walked onto the platform.

But he wasn't there. Beatrice hung back as the other passengers filed onto the train, hoping he was just running late. That he'd burst onto the platform at the last second and she could catch him before he had a chance to ignore her again.

He never showed.

Beatrice sat by the window, a stranger in the seat beside her, a neglected study guide open on her lap. She could only stare at the passing foliage, fighting back tears, wondering what she could have done to keep everything from crashing down.

On her way to Statistics, she stopped at a small cafe and splurged on a white mocha, hoping the caffeine and sugar would be enough to get her to focus on school, and not just on her own miserable ruminations.

She slipped into her desk with two minutes to spare. Instantly, Sasha twisted around in her seat.

"Hey," she said with an uncharacteristic frown. "You okay?"

Beatrice nodded, turning her attention to her bag. She'd thought she had the impulse to cry under control, but she felt it threatening to break free again with the prospect of interacting with her friends. They both looked so worried. And she didn't want to burden them with her weird, self-inflicted problems.

"Are you sure?" Kinsey asked, leaning across the aisle. "I barely heard from you all weekend."

"Just busy," Beatrice said, trying not to let her stress come through in her voice. "I'm fine."

"So Greyson hasn't—"

"I don't want to talk about it," Beatrice snapped. "Not now. Okay? Please?"

"Okay," Kinsey said, sitting back in her seat and exchanging a worried glance with Sasha.

Beatrice dropped her bag at her feet, guilt tearing at her throat, but she didn't have the chance to apologize. The professor started calling roll, and Beatrice spent the rest of class just trying to copy down whatever he wrote on the board. She didn't understand a word he said. So much for the sugary latte plan.

Beatrice threw her stuff back in her bag after class and walked out before Sasha or Kinsey could corner her again. She was afraid, if she was forced to talk, she was going to take out all her pent-up frustration on them. The last thing she needed was to push any more of her friends away this week.

Kinsey caught her in the hallway before she could escape. "Come on," she said, grabbing Beatrice's hand and dragging her into the nearest bathroom. "We have to talk."

"I don't want to talk," Beatrice said, as Sasha followed them inside. "I don't have time to talk."

"Make time." Kinsey pulled her to the far end of the bathroom and turned to face her, dropping her hand. "What's going on with you?"

"Nothing," Beatrice lied, clutching the strap of her bag. "Just— It's nothing. I'm fine."

Sasha leaned against one of the sinks, thumbs in her pockets, that serious look on her face again. "You sure? 'Cause I'll kick some ass if you want me to."

Beatrice swallowed, her eyes sliding to a line of graffiti on the wall beside her. Someone had written *SMILE* in Sharpie. Someone else had scrawled it out with blue ink and wrote *fuck that* above it, digging the words into the paint. The letters swam in Beatrice's vision.

Whatever control she'd managed to hang onto since Thanksgiving snapped. She went from trying not to cry to great, heaving sobs in less than a second. And then she was spilling everything. The stress of coursework she couldn't keep up with, compounded by the tension at home, and a job she hated, and a *major* she hated; the persistent exhaustion; the feeling that she couldn't wrestle any part of her life under her control.

"And I think Julian's—mad at me," she hiccuped, pushing tears from her eyes with the wad of paper towels Kinsey had passed her. "He won't talk to me. He wasn't even—on the train this morning."

"Oh, honey," Kinsey said, squeezing her shoulder.

"I can't even blame him," Beatrice said, unable to look either of her friends in the eye. "It's my fault everything blew up."

"No, it's not," Kinsey said, with a sharp shake of her head. "Everything was going just fine until Greyson showed up."

"And who invited him?" Beatrice countered, pointing to herself.

"He told you he wasn't going to show," Kinsey said, bristling on Beatrice's behalf. "No one here holds you responsible for his behavior."

"I don't know if it makes a difference," Sasha put in, "but I didn't get the impression Julian blamed you, either. He seemed more worried about you than anything."

"Then why won't he talk to me?" Beatrice asked, unable to keep a lid on her self-pity.

"I don't know, Bee," Sasha said. "I'm sorry."

Beatrice wiped her nose. "It's not just that. I've made a huge mess out of everything. If I'd just . . . broken up with Greyson sooner. Instead of running around trying to keep anyone from getting angry. If I'd just had some backbone, this wouldn't have happened."

"Honey, if Greyson getting angry means he jerks you around like that, no one's going to blame you for wanting to avoid upsetting him," Kinsey said, planting her fists on her hips. "That was *not* okay."

Beatrice shook her head. "He doesn't—He's never like that. I've never seen him that angry." She usually just let him have his way before it got that far. Because she was a big fat chicken who couldn't handle conflict even on a small scale. She rubbed her forehead, a fresh wave of tears filling her eyes. "I don't know what to do."

"Well . . . what do you *want*?" Sasha asked, fetching a few more paper towels.

Beatrice accepted them and blew her nose. "What do you mean?"

Sasha shrugged. "What would make you happy? Never mind how anyone else might feel about it or what you'd have to do to get there. Just stop for a second and ask yourself what you, Beatrice Bauer, want."

"I . . ." Beatrice stared down at the paper towels in her hands. What she wanted—what she'd always wanted—was a place where she could breathe. She'd invented a little house in her mind. Where it would just be her, with Sunny to keep her company, her family far enough away that she wouldn't be constantly entangled in their arguing, Kinsey and Sasha close enough they could see each other often. It had always seemed enough. If she could get that little house to herself, she could breathe. She could be happy.

Except . . . she had found pockets of oxygen on the train every morning, and every night, for weeks. In silly jokes texted back and forth at random intervals throughout the day. In bursts of laughter and patient commiseration. In a comforting hand on her shoulder at just the right moment.

Her little imaginary house seemed lonely now, without Julian in it.

"I have to break up with Greyson," she said, gripping the paper towels. It still terrified her to think about, but it was something she could control. She couldn't force him to take it well, but he couldn't force her to stay in the relationship, either. Not unless she allowed it. And she was done with letting Greyson get everything he wanted.

"Do you want backup?" Kinsey asked, her arms falling to her sides. Her eyes were wide with worry.

"I don't—I don't know."

"It's not cowardly if you bring backup," Kinsey said. "Not under the circumstances. I thought I was going to have to call the police when he grabbed you."

"Dude's got issues," Sasha agreed. "At least make sure you break up with him when there are plenty of people around."

Beatrice nodded, but she didn't want to put either of them at risk. She had gotten herself into this mess by being too much of a pushover. She was going to have to get herself back out.

She just had to figure out the best way to approach the problem.

Maybe she could work up to it. If she was going to grow a backbone, it made sense to start on smaller conflicts and work her way up.

"I want to see an adviser," she said.

Kinsey exchanged another glance with Sasha, as though they thought Beatrice was losing it. "Wouldn't a counselor be more helpful?"

"No, I—I think I want to change majors," Beatrice explained. "I need to talk to someone about it so I know what I'm getting into before I drop the news on my parents." She might get yelled at for going into education when she could have had a nice job at her step-dad's friend's marketing agency, but it was likely to be less volatile than the blowout after Nath dropped out of his premed program with no alternate plans. And much as she hated the yelling, at least she was used to her family's fights. It would give her a chance to test her own resolve, and maybe make the idea of facing Greyson seem a little less scary.

And then there was Julian. She couldn't make him forgive her, but she could try to explain the situation. And if he refused to answer the phone, well . . . she was just going to have to track him down and make him talk to her face-to-face. Whether he liked it or not.

SEVENTEEN

Julian was well aware he was taking the coward's way out, riding a different train to work. But he couldn't face Beatrice again after Thanksgiving went to shit. He couldn't even send her a goddamn text. What was he supposed to say? There was no way she would believe his side of the story, even if he could somehow convince her to listen to him. No one ever believed his side. And why should Beatrice believe her ex-commute buddy over her fucking boyfriend?

Julian wasn't entirely sure he could face his job, either. He knew Mr. Fisk was likely to corner him and ask him about his progress on the damn portfolio. Julian wasn't up for explaining to his sort-of mentor that he'd lost the ability to draw *anything*. He hadn't even looked at his sketchbook all weekend. Fabiana had saved it from the garbage, but only by giving him a lecture about how it was rude to throw away gifts and stashing it under a stack of library books 'until he came to his senses.'

He'd thought about just quitting the art center more than once. But he couldn't stand the idea of disappointing his kids by not showing up one day with no explanation. They deserved better than that.

As long as Julian could avoid Beatrice, he figured the rest of it would be a lot easier. So he dragged himself out of bed at an ungodly hour on Monday morning to catch an early train.

It was a relief to get to work and discover several small emergencies waiting for him. The first floor bathroom was partially flooded. Someone had spilled an entire bottle of ink in one of the classrooms. A sparrow had gotten trapped in the staff break room. Problems he could solve. And he could solve them without talking to people. No one bothered him all morning, except when Kata, who ran the front desk, told him to go on his break already.

The physical work helped release some of his bad mood. The appearance of his first class helped, too. It was hard not to smile when he was greeted with delighted shrieks and fast-paced chattering about what everyone ate for Thanksgiving. His kids were rowdy and excitable after the long holiday weekend, and they kept him on his toes. He put a stop to several minor fights in the first class, and narrowly rescued one of the more sensitive kindergartners from having a full-on meltdown by persuading her to tell him all about her guinea pig, instead. His second class was less emotional, but they had a hard time sitting still, so he sorted them into teams and got them doing a monster-making game on some big pads of paper for the first half of the class.

He didn't think most of them even noticed that his smiles were less sunny, and his answers shorter than usual. Only one wide-eyed little girl seemed to realize he wasn't quite himself. She came up to him after class and stretched out a hand to offer up the drawing she'd been working on for the last ten minutes or so.

"What's this?" Julian asked, crouching down next to her so their eyes were about level. At the top of the page, in blue marker, she'd written *To: Mr. Moon* in her wobbly six-year-old handwriting. The rest of the page was crowded with crayon drawings of a pink-and-purple cat, a lopsided rainbow, Santa Claus, a cake, several fish, and a grinning yellow sun. Sprinkled in between were colorful little lines that could have easily been either gummy worms or confetti. "This is really good, Eva," he said, finding a small, genuine smile to give her. "Did you draw this for me?"

She nodded, the beads in her hair clicking together as they bounced. "I drew you happy things so you can stop thinking about sad things," she said, beaming. Then she scampered off to greet her dad before Julian could remember to thank her.

If only it were so easy, Julian thought as he filed onto the late train home a few hours later. If only his own list of happy things didn't begin and end with Beatrice Bauer.

He slumped into a seat, more exhausted than he had any right to be. He couldn't keep this up. If Fabiana didn't still need a place to crash, he might have just up and left over the weekend. There was nothing else keeping him here. Except a damn crush on the one girl in New York he should never have gone near.

Julian shut his eyes, thankful the smaller number of passengers on this train meant he had the whole row to himself. He needed the space. The pain he'd been avoiding all day had started to settle in his chest again, as raw and heart-twisting as it had been four days ago.

But, of course, his good luck didn't hold out for long. As the doors closed, another passenger slid into the aisle seat across from him.

Julian tensed and held his breath, his stomach knotting.

He knew it was her without opening his eyes. He knew the sound of her step. The way she settled into her seat. The drop of her heavy bag on the floor. The catch of her breath when she was right on the verge of speaking. The scent of coffee and floral soap.

He tried to brace himself to meet her gaze. But bracing himself didn't help.

He didn't know what it was he'd been expecting. Probably a big frown and a sound verbal beating. But the look she gave him now—sad and hurt—tore him apart.

"Hey," Beatrice said, tangling her fingers in her lap.

"What are you doing here?" he asked, his voice strangely flat.

One corner of her mouth pulled up in a tiny smile that didn't reach her eyes. "I had a hunch you were avoiding me."

He tore his gaze away, letting it fall on the threadbare upholstery of the seat in front of him. "Why would I go and do that?"

She was quiet for a moment. "I know it probably doesn't make any difference," she said, scooting forward to perch on the edge of the chair, "but I didn't know that you knew each other, or that you'd had a falling out."

He shook his head, pressing his lips together, unable to look at her. "Is that what your boyfriend called it? A falling out?"

"Not in so many words," she said.

"I suppose he told you I broke my own hand?" Julian asked, with the vicious bite that tended to creep into his voice when he talked about Greyson. He didn't care how sharp his words were. Directing some of his bitterness in her direction couldn't make things any worse than they already were. "That I'm some kind of self-destructive criminal who cast his poor, lonely step-brother aside in a fit of cruelty?"

"He did it, didn't he?" Beatrice asked, her voice so soft he wasn't sure he heard her right. "He broke your hand."

He looked at her, feeling his guard slip. "Why would you say that?"

"I—" She dropped her gaze and bit down on her lower lip. "Just—Am I right?"

"Not . . . not exactly."

The train lurched into motion, slowly picking up speed. The lights of the station outside the windows made way for blackness as they rolled into the tunnel that made up the first stage of the journey, the bright interior of the car reflecting a hazy overlay against the dark.

Beatrice didn't say anything. Just watched him with those compassionate gray eyes, waiting for him to continue.

"It's . . ." Julian let out a breath, crossing his arms. He stared at the seat in front of him. "I used to be able to handle him. He and Fabiana would butt heads all the time, but I could smooth things over. Fab butts heads with a lot of people, so I was used to it. It was just my job, keeping things balanced. I didn't even mind, most of the time. You crack a joke, or reroute the conversation, and it's no big deal, right? Who cares?

"And then my mom died. And I . . . I couldn't do it. I couldn't handle him anymore."

"You shouldn't have had to," Beatrice said. "You'd just lost your mom."

"Tell that to Greyson," Julian muttered. "I don't think I realized how bad it was until then. I thought all the fighting was just . . . growing pains. All of us trying to adjust to a newly blended family. But after my . . . When I stopped smoothing everything over, I found out that wasn't really what I'd been doing. I wasn't keeping the balance. I was just trying to stop Greyson from exploding. I was placating him. Letting him push me and my sister around. Just to keep the yelling to a minimum. It pissed me off.

"And—I don't know. Maybe it was a stupid move. Maybe I should have tried to stay out of his way until I could move out. But I was so sick of letting him push me around. So I started pushing back.

"Big mistake. He and I started fighting more. Over some of the stupidest things. It was just a lot of shouting and cursing at first. And then we were shoving each other . . ."

Julian rubbed his eyes, trying to scrub away the memories

playing through his head. "We got into it really bad one day. I don't even remember what I said to set him off. But next thing I knew, we were actually, physically fighting. Right by the pool of Walter's goddamn vacation house in Laguna Beach."

Beatrice lifted her hand, then pulled it back, like she wanted to reach across and touch him, but thought better of it. "Is that when it happened?"

"No." He slumped further down in his seat. "I think it's what pushed him over the edge, though. Walter had to come out and pull us apart."

He didn't tell her about the hard look in Greyson's eyes as they fought, or the sick feeling in Julian's gut when he realized Greyson wasn't going to stop trying to hurt him. He didn't tell her about how he had paced his room for hours that night, door locked, with a chair stuck under the handle, debating whether to pack up his things and climb out the window. How the only thing that stopped him was a fear that Fabiana would end up on the receiving end of Greyson's anger instead of him. He didn't know of a way to tell someone that he'd been convinced Greyson was going to kill him without sounding like a complete lunatic. Even his twin sister had thought he was blowing everything out of proportion.

"What did he do?" Beatrice asked.

"Nothing. Not at first. He kind of . . . switched off after that. He acted like I didn't exist, and I tried to stay out of his way. I was almost done with high school, and I was determined to go out-of-state for college. I just kept telling myself *it's only a few more months. A few more months and then you'll be out of here.*

"And then one day, I was on my way home after school, and these guys grabbed me and just . . ." He shut his eyes, curling his fingers into fists. He didn't want to tell her about that part. It was bad enough thinking about all the rest of it without reliving two of the worst minutes of his life.

"They broke your hand?" Beatrice asked, her voice soft.

Julian nodded, grateful for the means of blowing past the details. "I knew some of them from my art classes. Rich kid stoners, most of them. Not really my crowd, but I didn't think they had anything against me. How could they, when they barely talked to me? I still don't know why they jumped me."

"But you think Greyson got them to do it."

Julian turned his head to meet her eyes. There was nothing about her expression that indicated she didn't believe him. Didn't sympathize with him.

He felt sick. He didn't know what he was thinking, telling her all that. It was *better* if she thought he was at fault for that whole thing. It meant Greyson wouldn't have any reason to hurt her.

Julian didn't want what happened to him to happen to Beatrice. He wanted to protect her from that. And there was only one way that he could see to keep her safe.

Steeling himself, he sat up, twisting in his seat until they were face to face, with just the narrow aisle between them. He gripped his hands together between his knees, willing his voice steady. "I can't do this anymore, Bee."

She drew back, a line of tension stiffening her spine. "Do what?"

"This whole . . . thing. The . . . the trains and the talking and the . . . everything."

She shook her head, her eyes searching his face. She reached for his hand. "Julian—"

He jerked out of her grip, the soft brush of her skin scalding him. There were so few people in the world who cared if he lived or died. He wanted to be in her life. He wanted dancing in the kitchen, and trying to save disastrous cooking flubs, and watching her with her friends, and laughing at her jokes until his belly ached.

He wanted her. And he couldn't have her without getting her hurt.

Beatrice wrapped her arms around herself. "But—Why? Because of Greyson?"

"No," Julian said vehemently, making himself meet her gaze. But it was too much, the hurt in her eyes, and his gaze fell to his hands. "Yes. I don't know. A lot of reasons. I want to stop. I just want it to stop. I can't do it anymore."

For the space of a few agonizing breaths, she didn't reply.

He couldn't look at her. He couldn't, or he'd lose his nerve and take it all back. And this needed to end. Now. He'd already let it carry on too long. He thought he could handle it. Keep enough space between them so he'd never get a chance to let her down. Enough distance that the deafening chaos of his life would never rip her away from him.

What a fucking idiot.

"So . . . that's it?" Beatrice asked. "You just want to—to stop?"

"I think it would be the best thing for everyone if we just pretended we never met," Julian said.

"You don't really mean that," she said, her voice cracking. "Julian—"

"I really mean it," he said. His voice was gruff, but at least it didn't waver. "I think we have to cut ties. I'm sorry. I just—" He swallowed and found her eyes. "I can't risk it."

She blinked a few times, her eyes bright with unshed tears. Then she caught up the strap of her bag. "Okay," she whispered, sliding out of the seat and stepping away from him. "I get it. I do. I'm . . . I'm sorry."

It took all of Julian's remaining strength to stop himself from calling after her as she strode to the other end of the car to find a different seat. Someone should throw him under the train for making her cry. He scrunched himself into his seat, hood pulled over his face.

She'd be better off without him. People usually were. She'd be safe now. And that was more important than whether or not Julian's heart was breaking.

EIGHTEEN

Greyson decided he was going to drive Beatrice home the following Thursday night. Beatrice, apparently, didn't get a say. Not that she tried very hard to argue with him about it. She couldn't get herself to care enough to speak up.

She'd felt numb since Julian told her he wanted to cut things off a few days ago. Like that one last thing had overloaded her system and shut her down.

She tried not to poke the apathy too much. She could sometimes feel the edges of an overwhelming panic that threatened to reach out and drag her down. There were too many things in her life she couldn't control. Couldn't keep up with. And if she thought about them—and if she thought about losing Julian just when she'd started to realize how much he meant to her . . .

But giving in to the panic—and the gaping pain of losing him— wasn't an option. She couldn't let her life stop moving forward.

At least if she was numb, she could function. Sure, she functioned at the bumbling, unintelligent level of a zombie. With about the same emotional range and social grace, too. But at least she wasn't curled in a ball under her covers, nursing a hurt she didn't ask for and didn't know how to deal with.

She spent most of the drive staring at the same two pages of the play she was supposed to be reading for English Lit, not taking in a word. She just wanted to crawl into bed and go to sleep.

She came out of her trance when Greyson put the car in park. She looked up to find he'd pulled into her apartment's parking lot. She must have been nodding in all the right places during the drive, because Greyson didn't seem upset with her, but she couldn't remember most of the trip home. She couldn't remember if he'd spoken to her at all.

Mumbling a thanks for the ride, she shoved the play into her bag.

"Wait a second," Greyson said before she could climb out of the car and escape. He reached into the back seat and shifted something aside. "Here. Merry Christmas."

Beatrice stared at the garishly wrapped box Greyson slid in her lap. It was about the size of a board game, but lighter. The gift wrap was an elegant white and gold pattern—poinsettias or something—on paper so glossy it reflected the streetlights right into Beatrice's eyes. It looked like something you'd see in a department store window; pretty on the outside and filled with nothing but air and paper.

She angled the metallic glare away from her and looked up at Greyson. It took her a second to drag herself out of her apathetic fog long enough to find a reaction.

"You bought me a Christmas present." It was supposed to be a question, but she couldn't quite make her inflection go up at the end.

Greyson deigned to give her a winning smile. "Yes, I did."

A second reaction occurred to Beatrice. But opening the window and chucking the gift into the nearby shrubbery probably wasn't her smartest move.

"I thought we weren't going to do Christmas presents. We've only been dating for . . . for six weeks."

"Seven. But I thought you could use it next weekend." He nudged the gift. "Open it."

Beatrice bristled, fighting the impulse to shove the box in Greyson's face.

God. She had to get out of this car before she gave in to one of those angry impulses. And opening the stupid box seemed like the quickest way to do that. So she tore off the lid.

Inside the box, folded neatly, and surrounded by a cloud of tissue paper, was a dress.

Beatrice lifted it out and stared. She didn't know a whole lot about the prices of sleek, black cocktail dresses. She'd never had occasion to wear a cocktail dress in her life. But one touch of the material told her that it had probably cost more than she'd made in her last three paychecks combined.

She dropped it back into the box like it was a snake. "I can't take this."

Greyson frowned. Not much, but enough to put Beatrice on edge. "Why not?"

"It's too much," Beatrice said, replacing the lid and trying to pass the whole thing back to him. "We said we weren't going to do the presents thing."

Greyson huffed, his lip twitching. "Is it so wrong to want to shower my girlfriend with gifts?"

That word—*girlfriend*—coming from his mouth felt like steel bands pinning her arms to her sides. "I can't take this, Greyson," she said, struggling to keep her voice level.

"Besides," he said, ignoring her, "you need something to wear to the Christmas party."

Oh God. The stupid Sayer-Crewe Christmas party. He'd told her about it two or three weeks ago. Insisted she come so he could introduce her to his dad. She'd forgotten she'd let him bully her into accepting the invitation.

The bands around her tightened, threatening to crack her open.

"No," she said, in barely more than a whisper.

Greyson looked at her like he'd never heard the word before. "If you don't like that one, I can buy you another."

"No," she insisted, wedging the box between the dashboard and the windshield—anywhere she didn't have to touch it anymore. "I don't want another dress. And I'm not taking that one."

Greyson gripped the steering wheel. "I don't think you understand what this party is like. It's vital you show up looking the right way. And while *I* appreciate your . . . eclectic fashion choices, there's a time and a place. And my father's Christmas party is not the place, nor the time, to show up looking like you're an extra in a shitty, moth-bitten '70s movie."

Beatrice flushed, stung. She had suspected Greyson didn't love her thrift-store chic style, of course, but he usually left it alone.

"Wow," she said, angry at herself for feeling hurt. Angry at him for making her feel that way. She *liked* how she dressed. She knew it was a little eccentric, and it wasn't to everyone's taste, but she thought it suited her. "Okay. How about this: You don't have to worry about me embarrassing you at your dad's party anymore. I'm not going."

"Of course you're going," Greyson said. "You already said you'd come."

"I changed my mind." She made herself look him in the eye. One advantage of only being able to access anger was that she didn't feel the fear she probably should be. She was experiencing her usual physical reaction to conflict—rapid heartbeat, shaking hands—but it seemed disconnected from her feelings. She couldn't call a lack of fear real courage, but it was as close as she was ever likely to get. "I'm not going. I'm done."

"Oh, come on," he said, resting his hand on the back of her seat. "I didn't mean—"

"*No.*" She straightened her spine, gripping the door handle to assure herself that she had a quick escape if she needed it. She was supposed to do this with Sasha being intimidating on one side and Kinsey ready to call 911 on the other. She was supposed to have done this earlier today when they were all at lunch in the crowded food court. Or in the hallway after marketing class. Not while she was alone with Greyson in his car, with Nath and her mom three floors up, and Mike somewhere in Ohio, and no witnesses nearby. But she didn't care. If she didn't end this now, she was going to crawl out of her own skin. "I don't want to see you anymore. Not at your dad's party. Not dropping by whenever you feel like it. Not cornering me between classes. Not ever. I'm done. Okay? I'm done."

Greyson blinked. And then he smiled. Like it was a joke he didn't quite get. "Okay, you win. I'll take the dress back. You can wear whatever you want."

"It's not the dress," Beatrice said. He wasn't listening. He never listened. "It's . . . everything. You want me to be some . . . some . . . some docile, smiling girlfriend who will do whatever you say. And I'm sick of being that person. I'm sick of fighting with you all the time."

"Where is this coming from?" He was still smiling, like someone trying to humor a child they thought was particularly stupid. "When do we ever fight?"

That, for some reason, was the last straw. The idea that her attempts at arguing with him—about food, or rides, or whether she wanted to go out with him in the first place—were so pathetic he hadn't even registered them as fights was too much to deal with.

"You know what?" she burst out. "You don't get to do that anymore. You don't get to talk me in circles until I get tired of trying to explain myself and give in to whatever you want. This isn't a negotiation. I don't need to make an ironclad case for why we should break up so you can try to pick it apart."

"But—"

"No. I don't want to do this anymore. I'm through. Don't call me again."

She shoved her door open. Cold air spilled into the car, slicing through her jeans. But before she could climb out, Greyson seized her arm—exactly where he'd left a ring of bruises on Thanksgiving—and yanked her close.

Her heart jumped into her throat when she met his eyes. He wasn't laughing at her anymore. He wore an expression of tightly controlled fury.

Turned out she *was* capable of fear. Whatever spark of bravery Beatrice had found for that little speech was snuffed out in an instant.

"What did he say to you?" Greyson snarled.

"What?"

He jerked hard on her arm, and she let out a frightened little yelp before she could stop herself. Greyson didn't seem to care. "What did my little shit of a step-brother tell you? You know you can't believe a word he says."

"Greyson, stop." She tried to wrench her arm out of Greyson's grip, but he held her fast.

"He wants to turn you against me," Greyson growled. "He's a liar. He's always been a liar."

"Julian didn't tell me anything," Beatrice said, meeting his gaze, trying not to let him see the fear twisting her stomach. "This isn't about Julian."

"You probably think you're in love with him, don't you? Because he's so dangerous and brooding, and you think it's more exciting to fuck the bad boy than be with a man who's actually doing something with his life."

Beatrice was sure she had turned bright red, her face was so hot. But she wasn't going to let him drag her into an argument about whether or not she'd cheated on him. Or over whether Julian—who had danced with her because she'd asked him to, and who cracked up when she told terrible jokes—was 'dangerous and brooding.'

"Greyson," she said, in a voice that sounded like it belonged to someone else. "Let go. Right now, or I'll scream."

Greyson looked down at his hand as though he hadn't realized he was holding her. He let go. "I—"

Beatrice seized her bag and jumped out of the car before he could grab her again.

"Beatrice," Greyson said, getting out and following her toward the stairs. "Wait. Can't we talk about this?"

"Just leave it," she begged, wishing she didn't live on the third floor of the building. Wishing Mike would get home early, or Nath or her mom would come down to take out the trash and intercede. Why hadn't she listened to her friends' warnings about doing this alone?

Greyson caught her wrist and spun her around to face him. "Beatrice. Come on. You're overreacting. It's just a dress."

She jerked her hand back before he could feel how much she was shaking. "It's not about the dress."

"Then what's the problem?"

"It's—I don't—" She pressed her hands to her cheeks, trying to find the words that would make him understand. Make him stop arguing. Make him give up and let her leave. But all she could come up with was: "I don't trust you."

"You don't *trust* me?" Greyson said, his voice dripping with condescension. "I don't care if you fucking trust me."

"Well, I do," she said, ignoring the burn in her throat. "And I care that I act like someone I don't like when I'm with you. And

I care that I'm not happy. And that you make me feel like I'm not good enough for you. I'm sick of letting you walk all over me. I don't want to do this anymore."

Greyson's lip twisted into a snarl. Her throat closed as he stalked toward her.

"Greyson," she rasped, hoping if she said his name, he'd snap out of it.

"Don't lie to me." He didn't touch her, but he was crowding her, forcing her back. "Don't fucking lie to me, Beatrice."

Her shoulders hit the stair railing. She should scream, but she wasn't sure she'd be able to force one out. And she wasn't sure that it wouldn't make things worse.

He gripped the rail on either side of her head, boxing her in. The flat look in his pale eyes made her want to cower on the ground with her arms over her head. "He put you up to this. He's manipulating you."

"That's not—"

He slammed his palm against the bar beside Beatrice's head. She flinched, a breathy sob escaping her throat.

"Can't you see what he's doing?" Greyson demanded, his fingers digging into her coat collar, too close to her throat. His breath was hot on the side of her face, and she couldn't move. She couldn't see a way out. "Can't you see that—"

A neighbor's door burst open, letting out an older woman and two rambunctious dogs from two doors down. Greyson's attention was momentarily diverted, and Beatrice seized her chance. She ducked under Greyson's arm and fled up the stairs, ignoring his shout for her to come back.

Her heart pounded in her ears as she ran. She barely felt the concrete under her boots or her bag slamming into her leg. She kept expecting Greyson to catch up to her and grab her by the ankle and drag her down.

But when she finally checked over her shoulder, once she was at her door and fumbling her keys out of her bag, he wasn't there. It was quiet except for the echoing barks of her neighbor's dogs, and the muffled sound of a television inside her apartment. And the roar of Greyson's engine down below. Gasping for breath, Beatrice staggered to the railing to watch his car tear off into the night.

Another strange sob tore Beatrice's throat.

She held onto the banister with one hand, sinking to a crouch as she willed herself to calm down. Stop crying. Stop shaking.

She shouldn't be this scared. It could have been a lot worse. He hadn't followed her upstairs. He hadn't hit her. She was fine. She was safe.

She should feel safe.

She curled into herself, her hand pressed over her mouth to muffle the uncontrollable sobs shaking her body. She wanted to go inside and lock herself in her room, but she couldn't face her mom and Nath while she was having some kind of breakdown. She was supposed to be the rational Bauer. The one who never had any problems that she couldn't handle herself.

And now she was buried so deep that she couldn't even imagine reaching out for help. She didn't understand how she had let things get so bad. She'd been wary of Greyson from the start. She should have seen this coming. She should have shut it down right away, instead of waiting so long.

Somehow, she got her breathing under control, and the worst of the sobbing passed. She kept shivering, but it was as much from cold as fear, now. She thought she could make it to her room without an interrogation about why she was in hysterics.

It took her a couple tries to get the key in the lock, but finally she fumbled her way into the apartment. Sunny sauntered up to her at the door.

Beatrice scooped him up in her arms, burying her face in his fur. "Hi, friend," she breathed.

Her mom was at the kitchen table, arguing with Nath, who was standing by the kitchen sink with a soapy dish in one hand. Neither of them even seemed to notice Beatrice come in at first, but Joyce stopped mid-scold when Beatrice passed the table on the way to her room.

"Are you all right?" Joyce asked.

Beatrice nodded tightly, still walking, unable to answer. Sunny purred and rubbed his head on her shoulder.

"Bee?" Joyce called after her. "What's wrong?"

"Nothing," Beatrice said, wrenching her bedroom door open. But something made her pause and turn back, her fingers still on the doorknob. "I broke up with Greyson."

"Bravo!" Nath called, his head appearing around the kitchen archway.

"That nice rich boy?" Joyce asked, frowning. Piles of bills were spread out on the table in front of her. There were dark circles under her eyes, and her hair was coming loose from where she'd clipped it back. "Why?"

Beatrice instantly regretted the confession. Her mom had enough things to deal with without Beatrice dumping another burden on her shoulders.

"He wasn't nice, Mom," Nath said before Beatrice could start backtracking. "He was a dick."

"Language," Joyce said, waving a hand at him without taking her eyes off Beatrice. "What happened, Bee?"

"Nothing," Beatrice said, blinking back a fresh wave of tears. "It's fine. I can handle it."

She shut herself in her room before either of them could say anything else, and sank onto the bed, trying to take comfort from Sunny's persistent affection.

NINETEEN

Julian got all the way home before he remembered he didn't have any food in the apartment. He'd been meaning to get groceries all week, but it never happened. He'd been too tired, or too tense, or too apathetic. All that was left in the fridge after dinner yesterday was about half a glass worth of orange juice and a stick of butter. The pantry was even worse. There was nothing inside but an empty box of noodles, half a sleeve of stale crackers, and a cereal box containing a handful of sugary crumbs. He didn't even have any goddamn peanut butter.

Cursing under his breath, he wrestled the pantry door shut. He didn't want to have to go back out again and deal with more people. Fabiana was closing at work and wouldn't be home for a few hours yet. She would have figured out her own dinner, which meant he was only responsible for feeding himself. Technically, Julian could get away with not eating at all.

But he'd forgotten to eat breakfast. And all he'd had for lunch was a cold Pop-Tart.

Julian pulled his coat back on and headed out. He wasn't up for a whole grocery excursion today. Especially if he was going to have to cook once he got back. But there was a cheap Chinese place a couple blocks away, and the leftovers should hold him until tomorrow.

He might not be up for getting groceries tomorrow, either, but that was future-Julian's problem.

He'd been a cranky, miserable mess ever since that last god-awful conversation with Beatrice a few days ago. He was trying Fabiana's limited patience with him at home—he couldn't stop snipping at her and picking fights. Fabiana was doing a weirdly good job of not rising to the bait, but she was going to pull a muscle if she rolled her eyes at him any harder. And he suspected she'd only picked up the closing shift today so she wouldn't have to deal with him when he got home.

Thankfully, a lot of his duties at work didn't require him to interact much with other people. He'd gotten a few funny looks from some of the other staff, and a companionably sarcastic *don't look so excited* when he was caught glowering at his half-eaten lunch in the break room yesterday, but at least he wasn't driving all his co-workers up the walls. He could usually fake some good humor for his kids, but the effort drained him, and he was pretty sure the kids were starting to pick up on his mood. They kept squabbling over crayons, and three different kids in the past two days had burst into tears at the smallest provocations.

Julian didn't know why he hadn't cut Beatrice off when she was still just some random girl he kept running into. He'd known from the start their friendship wouldn't last. He'd known he was going to get hurt. He'd known he was going to disappoint her eventually. And it was so much worse now than it would have been if he'd just told her he didn't want to ride the goddamn train with her that first time.

Christ, but he missed her. Even more so, now that he couldn't pretend she'd taken Greyson's side. He'd left work right after his shift today, telling himself it was because he wanted to avoid an inevitable conversation with Mr. Fisk about his stalled-out portfolio. But in reality, it was because of a masochistic need to see her again.

Not to take back anything he'd told her. He still believed staying away was the right thing to do. He just wanted to be near her for a few minutes. He wouldn't have even cared if she'd told him to fuck off.

But she hadn't been there at all.

Which made sense. It was Thursday. Before the Thanksgiving fiasco last week, she used to sometimes text Julian on a Tuesday or Thursday to let him know her boyfriend was driving her home. So if she wasn't on the train, it meant Greyson must have taken her home.

The realization hadn't helped Julian's already stormy mood.

He tried to think about something else while he waited for his food at the restaurant. Like how the hell he was going to finish his portfolio before the deadline in two weeks. He'd been on track up until last week, but he was falling further and further behind. It was hard enough keeping himself from throwing out the pile of shit he already had. He'd started half a dozen new illustrations in the past week only to toss them the second he hit a complication.

On some level, he knew he was being too hard on himself. But he couldn't find a way to push through the self-hatred that stuffed up his mind like a bad cold.

Sometimes he just wanted to give up. He'd make himself finish out the rest of the semester for the sake of his kids, but he didn't see how he could go back next year. He didn't think he could handle the pain of avoiding Beatrice every day.

But God, he was so sick of running. It wasn't like he had a back-up plan. *Hop on a bus and go until you run out of money* didn't work so well when it wasn't only himself he had to worry about.

At least finishing his portfolio was something to focus on that wasn't Beatrice. He was probably going to end up losing the teaching gig, but if he was going to fail, he could at least make sure it wasn't for lack of effort.

Julian collected his food and pushed out the restaurant door into the bitter cold.

Beatrice would have told him—

No. He wasn't going to think about her anymore.

But that didn't mean he couldn't channel her weird obsession with study schedules. The same principles should work for completing portfolios. It was just a matter of breaking everything down into manageable steps.

He'd have to do the math on how much studio time he had left to finish the last few illustrations. *Not enough*, probably. But if he could just stop giving a shit whether they were any good, he could probably knock out a sketch or two tonight. He'd bought some Bristol board with his last paycheck so he could start illustrations at home. And he could beg Mr. Fisk for a few hours of studio space on Saturday, which would help make up for some of his wasted time this week—

The sound of a car engine tearing up the road from behind distracted him. This was a quiet street, in a quiet town, and it wasn't late enough for the speed demons. Julian had just enough time to register it was a shiny, dark sports car before it careened over the curb, brakes squealing, right up on the sidewalk.

Julian swore and jumped back, avoiding the fender by mere inches. "Watch it, asshole," he shouted as the driver's door swung open. "You could have—"

The rest of the reprimand flew out of his head as Greyson climbed out of the car. His lip was twisted in disgust, his eyes sharp with rage. Julian hadn't seen that look since the fight in Laguna Beach, shortly before his life went to shit the first time.

Greyson grabbed him by the front of his coat. Julian's shoulders and head hit the brick wall, sending a spike of pain through his skull. His dinner fell from his hand and burst open on the sidewalk.

"What the hell did you say to her?" Greyson snarled, his nose mere inches from Julian's. His knuckles dug into Julian's collarbone as though Greyson meant to crush him into the bricks.

Julian shrugged off the blind panic that had his heart in his throat and snapped into fight mode. He found his feet and threw Greyson off him, putting a few yards between them as Greyson struggled to regain his footing.

Julian could outrun Greyson, but he didn't see the point in trying. He'd be surprised if Greyson didn't know where he lived. If he was going to have it out with Greyson, he'd rather do it on the street, in front of businesses, where someone might think to call the police if things escalated.

And then, belatedly, Julian registered what Greyson had just spat in his face. "Say to who?" he asked, even though he had a pretty good idea.

Greyson came at Julian with a wild swing. Three years ago, it might have landed. But Julian had been in more than his share of fights since then. He threw an arm up and blocked it, adrenaline spiking, then jabbed Greyson hard in the jaw before falling back. He didn't want to turn this into a real fight, but he wasn't going to let Greyson pummel him, either.

"Son of a bitch," Greyson swore, staggering away and clutching his jaw. He wouldn't make that kind of mistake again. As shitty a human being as Greyson might be, he wasn't stupid. "You're more pigheaded than you used to be," he said, circling Julian in a slow prowl.

"Are you going to tell me what your problem is, or do I have to guess?" Julian asked, careful to keep Greyson squarely in his sights. He wasn't going to get backed into a corner.

Greyson growled and came at Julian, fast and controlled. Julian pivoted, slapping Greyson's fist out of the way at the last second. But it put him off balance. Greyson grabbed the hood of Julian's sweatshirt and rammed a fist into his stomach.

Julian doubled over, coughing. Greyson pressed his advantage, seizing Julian by the sweatshirt again and shoving him onto the hood of his car.

"What did you tell her?" he demanded, flecks of spittle hitting Julian's face in his rage. "What did you tell her, you little shit?"

"Nothing," Julian said through gritted teeth, struggling to get enough purchase against the car to leverage Greyson off him. "The fuck are you talking about?"

"I know you said something to turn her against me," Greyson said, redoubling his grip and pulling Julian close. "What was it? Did you feed her that bullshit about how it's my fault you got your hand broken? Paint yourself as the tragic hero?"

"That's more your move, isn't it?" Not his most elegant deflection—or his smartest—but it seemed better than grasping for a lie. "Or are you just so full of shit you've started believing your own lies now?"

Greyson made a primal sound between his teeth and seized Julian's throat, cutting off his air.

Shit—

Julian grabbed Greyson's wrist with both hands, but he couldn't pry free. Panic buzzed in his ears as his lungs worked fruitlessly to pull more air through his closed throat.

"You always wanted my things," Greyson said. "Even when you were a kid. You wanted my house, my dad, my money. You didn't get any of that, and you're not getting her, either."

Julian couldn't speak. The edges of his vision were doing dim. He threw a wild punch at Greyson's face—

Greyson swore and lurched back, dropping Julian in favor of nursing his eye.

Julian rolled off the hood, gasping for air and stumbling a safe distance away. "Fuck you," he rasped. "She isn't one of your *things*. You don't own her."

"Fuck you," Greyson shot back, wrenching his car door open. "You might have her fooled now, but you've never been anything but a worthless piece of shit. You're not going to win, so just stay the fuck away before I have to make you."

Julian flipped Greyson off as he slammed into his car.

Bracing one hand on the wall, Julian tried to catch his breath as Greyson revved his engine and swerved into traffic and took a sharp right turn toward the highway. It had all happened so fast Julian couldn't quite believe it had happened at all. The one thing he did understand was that Greyson was livid over something that had evidently happened between him and Beatrice.

If Greyson had hurt her—

Julian forgot all about his dinner, and his plans to finish his portfolio, and Greyson's threats. He took off running.

TWENTY

When Beatrice ventured out of her room again, her eyes puffy and tender, she found only Nath in the living room. Apparently her mom had already gone to bed. Nath, finished with the dishes, was playing a video game on the TV.

"You okay?" Nath asked, pausing the game as Beatrice padded around the coffee table, Sunny in her wake.

"Could be worse." Her voice was rough from crying. She fell into the couch cushions, pulling her fuzzy sock-encased feet up under her. She'd changed into her favorite bright pink pajama pants and an old firetruck-red sweatshirt with sleeves that went past her fingers. The visual dissonance felt like wrapping a soft, comforting blanket around her shoulders.

Sunny jumped up next to her the moment she was settled, and curled in a warm, fluffy ball at her hip, purring lazily. Beatrice wiped a lingering tear from her cheek and scratched Sunny's ears, pretending not to notice another anxious sideways glance from Nath.

"I'm sick of losing this level," Nath said, cutting back to the console's home screen. "Wanna play something with me? Your pick."

It was more or less exactly what Beatrice needed. The two of them smashing digital furniture and solving low-key puzzles while alternately goading and encouraging each other. Nath singing his weird video game songs to make her laugh. Sunny stayed nearby, where Beatrice could easily reach down and pet him during cut scenes. The last of the tension in her shoulders started to ease, and the knot in her stomach loosened . . .

A sharp rap on the door made her fumble the controller as every muscle in her body seized. Sunny's head whipped up. Nath paused the game, his expression clouding.

"Think he came back?" Nath asked softly.

Beatrice shook her head, the blood draining from her face. She felt like an idiot, believing she would be safe from Greyson's anger, at least for the rest of the night. "I don't know."

"I'll check." Nath threw his controller on the table and went to look through the peephole, grabbing the baseball bat they kept by the door as he went. He stashed it again after a second of frowning out the peephole and unlatched the chain on the door. "The hell?"

Beatrice sat up straight, reaching for her phone. "Don't open it."

Nath ignored her and threw the door open. "Julian?"

Beatrice's heart stopped. *Julian?* Why would Julian be at her house this late? He was supposed to be angry at her. He'd told her he didn't want to see her anymore.

"Is Beatrice here?" Julian asked. She could just see Julian's shoulder from her perch on the couch, and the flash of his hand as he braced it against the doorjamb. "Is she okay?"

"She's fine," Nath said, looking confused. "What the hell happened to *you*?"

Beatrice vaulted off the couch and shouldered Nath out of the way. Julian winced and looked away when he saw her, passing a hand over his mouth, but not before Beatrice had noticed that his lip was split, and his knuckles all scraped up.

"Oh my God," she said. "What happened?"

"Are you okay?" he asked, his voice rough. He met her eyes briefly, with an aching, desperate concern that squeezed her heart.

"Me?" He was disheveled and out of breath and *bleeding*. The only injury she had was a week-old bruise on her arm, which he couldn't know about since it was well hidden under her sleeve. "I'm fine. But what—"

"Greyson didn't hurt you?"

"No," she said automatically, her heart sinking as the truth of what must have happened washed over her. "What did he do to *you*?"

"Nothing," he muttered, backing away. "I'm sorry. I don't know what I was—Sorry."

"Julian," Beatrice called after him, but he was already walking toward the staircase, shoulders hunched against the gusty wind. She hung out the doorway. "*Julian!* Good grief . . ."

"What's going on?" Nath asked Beatrice.

Beatrice ignored him. She grabbed the nearest pair of shoes—her polka-dot rain boots—and yanked them on, nearly losing her balance in her haste.

"Bee, what's going on?"

"Stay here," she ordered Nath, and ran out the door after Julian.

She caught up with him halfway down to the next landing and touched his sleeve. "Julian, wait."

He spun around so suddenly that Beatrice nearly collided with him and sent them both tumbling down the stairs. His hand circled her elbow to steady her, his eyes searching hers with a desperation she hadn't seen before.

Her fingers brushed the zipper of his open coat. She just wanted his arms around her, assuring her everything was okay, even if it wasn't. That they were okay. That she could still fix this.

"You're really not hurt?" he breathed.

"I'm not the one with a split lip and a busted hand," Beatrice said, her hand drifting towards his face to better inspect the damage.

He flinched back, dropping her elbow and retreating down a step before she could make contact. "It's nothing," he snapped, glaring at the parking lot below. "Don't worry about it."

Beatrice rubbed her forehead with her rejected fingers, trying to smooth out the headache settling there from all the worrying she'd already done. She didn't know what to say to keep him from leaving. Her heart ached with how much she'd missed him and how much she hoped that—maybe if he was here, he hadn't really meant everything he'd said before. Maybe she hadn't ruined everything as much as she'd feared.

But she couldn't read him at all. He looked like he wanted to run, but he'd planted himself three steps below her, his hands clenching and unclenching sporadically. She didn't know what any of it meant, and he seemed determined not to explain himself.

"Can you—can you just talk to me?" Beatrice pleaded. "Was it Greyson? Did he go after you?"

Julian opened his mouth and got half a syllable out before he cut himself off and started down the stairs again.

"I'm sorry," Beatrice said, hurrying after him. Her throat contracted, but she told herself sternly that she wasn't allowed to cry. She had done quite enough of that today. "I didn't realize he'd go after you. I thought—"

"I don't care about that," Julian said, stopping at the landing and turning toward her. Though he wouldn't look at her. His gaze traveled over the railing. "I can handle him. I just—You need to be more careful with him. One of these days, he'll stop blaming me for this whole . . . mess, and he'll try to hurt you, instead. And if he—If something happened to . . . I . . . Shit." He pushed his hair back, pacing to the far end of the landing.

Beatrice stared, afraid to move. Those weren't sentence fragments people threw at you if they hated your guts. It sounded almost like—

She cut that idea short, before hope could set her up for disappointment. Her heart was already pounding, a weird, heady warmth making her feel light and not entirely real.

"But—" she stammered, struggling to stay rational. "But I just—"

"No, I mean it," he insisted, pivoting toward her. He still wouldn't look her in the eye. His gaze lighted on her shoulder before it landed on her stupid polka dot rain boots. "You don't want to get on his bad side. Trust me. I know that you . . . I know . . ." He growled wordlessly, fisting his hands at his sides. "I know you . . . care about him, but if he—"

"The hell I do."

Julian started to say something, then his eyes snapped up to meet hers. "What?"

"I don't care about him," Beatrice said, shaking her head. She clutched the banister, feeling like she might float right up into the sky if she didn't keep herself grounded. "I broke up with him."

Julian let out a puff of air. An expression Beatrice couldn't read flickered over his face before being replaced with an angry scowl. He climbed up a step, presumably so he could glare at her more effectively. "Are you insane?" he demanded. "What would you go and do that for?"

Beatrice bristled, scowling right back at him. She didn't expect him to jump for joy, but she would have at least hoped the news wouldn't make him yell at her. "Look, I'm sorry he went after you—"

"Better me than you," Julian snapped. "He's dangerous, Bee."

"I know." She pressed a fist to her chest. "I *know*. But what do you want me to do? I'm not going to apologize for breaking up with a guy who scares me, and walks all over me, and hurts people I—I care about."

Julian drew back, passing a hand over his mouth again. "He scares you?"

"Only sometimes." She pulled at the collar of her sweatshirt, wishing she hadn't let that slip. "It's fine."

A muscle jumped in his jaw as he clenched his teeth, but his expression softened. He climbed up another step, his fingers resting on the banister just centimeters from her own, his eyes pinning her in place. "Bee," he said, in a rough whisper, "what did he do?"

"Nothing," she said, echoing his own words back at him. His eyes were almost black in the weak yellow light of the sconce overhead. "Don't worry about it."

"Bee." His fingers touched hers on the banister. It might have been an accident, but he didn't pull them away.

"He just . . ." She slid her gaze away from his, searching for something to look at that wasn't Julian. "He just got a little loud. I don't handle conflict that well and I just . . . I overreacted. He barely even touched me."

Julian shut his eyes with a soft curse, pinching the bridge of his nose, the picture of exasperation.

"It really wasn't that bad," Beatrice said quickly. "He didn't hit me or anything."

"'Not that bad?'" he repeated. "The best thing you can say is that he didn't actually hit you and that's supposed to be '*not that bad?*'"

"I'm sorry," she said automatically.

It only seemed to make him more frustrated. "For *what?*"

"I don't know," she said, blinking back a fresh wave of tears. "Whatever it is you're angry at me about. Whatever made you want to cut me off. I don't understand what I did wrong. I thought—I thought we were—"

"I'm not—Christ, Bee, I'm not angry at *you*," Julian said, his frown sharpening. "I was never angry at you. I sure as hell don't want to cut you off. I hate taking the damn train without you. I hate that I can't tell you about weird shit that happens at work. I hate not seeing you every day. Not talking to you is killing me. It's like—like trying to function with this gaping hole in my chest. I just—" He dragged a hand through his hair, the frustration going out of him in a puff of air. "I thought I was protecting you."

"Protecting me?" Beatrice repeated, her voice cracking.

"I thought if he was only pissed at me, and I took myself out of the picture, he wouldn't . . ." He tore his eyes from hers, turning instead to their hands on the banister. "I thought you'd be safe." His thumb brushed the edge of her hand in a long, feather-light stroke.

Her breath hitched as warmth washed over her. She released the rail from her death grip and slid her fingers in his without thinking. "Julian—"

"I didn't want you getting hurt because I was too selfish to let you go," he said, tucking her hand against his chest and covering it with both of his.

His coat was cool and rough under her fingers. His eyes were dark and so sad. So lonely. Beatrice reached up and touched his face with her free hand. "But I don't want you to let me go."

"Beatrice . . ." Her name was barely more than a whisper on his tongue. He pressed his forehead to hers. "God help me."

She shut her eyes, breathing him in. That scent of crayons and citrus he carried with him after work had faded to almost nothing, but he still smelled like him. Soap, and something peppery, and Julian. Her chest ached. She hadn't realized you could miss the smell of someone before.

"Don't go." She pushed her fingers up through the short hairs on the back of his head. He was too important to lose again. His kindness, his laughter, his understanding . . . She loved him. She didn't know when it started, or why she hadn't noticed. But now that she realized, she wasn't going to let him slip away. Not again. "Stay here," she whispered. Pleaded. "Stay with me."

Julian groaned, his hands going to her waist, a gentle, hesitant pressure. "This is a really bad idea," he breathed against her mouth.

"I don't care," she said, tipping her face up.

His mouth slanted over hers, drawing kisses from her slowly, carefully, with an edge of desperation underneath. Like he was afraid he was going too fast, or that she didn't want this as much as he did.

She dug her fingers in his coat, catching his upper lip in her mouth. He made a noise in the back of his throat, and she remembered his lip was split and thought maybe she'd hurt him. But before she could even start to draw back, his restraint fell away. His hands slid up her back, warm and solid, as he pressed her mouth open.

Beatrice felt something loosen in her chest as their tongues met. Like she'd been struggling to breathe despite a heavy weight crushing her lungs, and finally the weight had lifted.

She made a sound somewhere between a moan and a sigh and wrapped her arms around his neck, arching up into him. She was desperate to hold onto him. Keep him near her. Keep him safe.

She didn't know how long they kissed before they came up for air again. She could have kept on kissing him for a long time yet. Julian's lips brushed hers once more before he pulled back to look at her, his mouth lifting in a half-smile. "Hi."

"Hey." Beatrice felt herself smile too as she gazed at him. God, she'd missed his smile. She wrapped her arms around him and pulled him close, burying her face in his shoulder. "I'm so sorry. I should have just broken up with Greyson sooner—"

"Shh, shh," Julian said, kissing her temple as he held her. "It's okay."

"It's not," Beatrice said, squeezing her eyes shut. "This is all my fault. You never would have run into him at all if I'd just broken it off with him last month."

Julian let out a heavy breath, one careful hand stroking her hair. "It's not your fault, Bee. I'd much rather he made me his scapegoat than you. I've dealt with him before."

"Yeah, and he nearly got you killed," Beatrice said, taking his face in both her hands and meeting his eyes. "That's not happening again. Okay? Not if there's one single thing I can do to stop it."

Julian's mouth quirked up in the smallest hint of a smile as he bent to kiss her again. He kissed her until she almost forgot the flicker of pain behind his eyes with that smile.

TWENTY-ONE

Julian sat in the back of an empty classroom in the art center the next morning. He'd wanted to get in a couple hours' work on his portfolio before his shift started. His sketchbook and several half-finished pieces were spread out on the table in front of him, but he'd barely touched them since he got in. He had his face planted on the desk with his arms over his head.

He felt like a complete ass. He didn't know what the hell was wrong with him. It was like his brain had switched off when he laid eyes on Beatrice last night. He'd been operating on instinct and wishful thinking alone.

Sometimes he was amazed by how stupid he could be. Just because a girl you were hopelessly in love with said she didn't want you to let her go didn't mean it was a good time to jam your tongue down her throat. *Stay with me* wasn't code for *I love you, too*.

She was obviously shaken from a breakup which happened less than an hour before their kiss. She seemed emotionally distraught, probably vulnerable. What she needed was the support of people who would help her get through the crap with Greyson. Not Julian dropping in, yelling at her, and then pulling that knight-in-shining-armor bullshit.

If anything, it just proved what a worthless excuse for a human being Julian was. Beatrice was this . . . beautiful, joyful ray of light. She didn't even swear, for God's sake. Julian was a black hole of bad choices and disappointment. No amount of pretending was going to change that.

The last thing he wanted was to snuff out all her joy and light. Though he was afraid he'd already started. She'd been a lifeline for him, with her plans and her dogged optimism. She'd made his life better, but he could only make hers worse.

He should have at least told Beatrice about how Greyson had threatened him last night. But he just . . . couldn't. He hadn't wanted to freak her out when she was already so upset and guilt-ridden. He didn't want Beatrice thinking he blamed her for Greyson being Greyson. And then—God help him—he just hadn't wanted to stop kissing her.

He wanted to pretend everything was fine, dammit. That Greyson was full of shit, and neither Julian nor Beatrice would have to deal with him again. That Beatrice's plans to keep them both surrounded by people until Greyson cooled off would work. That Julian and Beatrice could be together without everything falling apart. That he could hold onto her light without tainting it with his own clinging darkness. He wanted to pretend there was no reason to worry, no reason to listen to the loop in the back of his head telling him *this is exactly how it started last time.*

"Julian?"

He lifted his head, not bothering to make himself look busy.

Mr. Fisk stood in the doorway, a steaming mug of coffee in one hand. Smiling, he pushed his glasses up the bridge of his nose. "How's it coming?" The smile faltered. "Are you doing okay?"

"Fine," Julian lied. "Why?"

Mr. Fisk pointed vaguely towards his own face. "You look a little dinged up."

"Stupid accident." Julian stood and gathered up the papers in front of him.

"Are you sure?" Mr. Fisk said, his focus shifting to the scrapes on Julian's knuckles.

No. I got in a fight with my psychotic former step-brother because he thought I was trying to steal his girlfriend. And then I went and kissed her. Because I'm a selfish idiot.

He shut his sketchbook with a snap. "I'm sure."

The wind whipped at Beatrice's coat and hair as she walked up the quiet side-street where Greenwich Village Center for the Arts was located. Dark clouds had been building all afternoon, smothering the last few hours of daylight. Now, as twilight faded, the light of the city reflected off their low, rolling forms. Beatrice couldn't even make out the hazy indication of the moon beyond their bulk.

Meeting Julian after work hadn't been part of the plan. But Beatrice didn't really care. She hadn't spoken to Julian since last night, and it was stressing her out. If she could just talk to him in person, she would feel better.

She'd been wound too tight all day. She kept dropping things, and forgetting what she was supposed to be doing, and jumping out of her skin at every little noise. She'd been such a wreck at lunch that Sasha insisted they spend the break in her dorm with takeout instead of doing their usual cram-in-the-food-court thing.

It was amazing Kinsey and Sasha weren't fed up with Beatrice's frazzled nerves by the end of the day. It was almost worse that she hadn't heard anything from Greyson. No texts, no calls, no showing up unannounced. She felt like she was bracing for an inevitable battle. The longer she waited, the more she worked herself into knots.

Maybe if Beatrice had slept better, she would've been able to at least *pretend* to act normal. She couldn't close her eyes last night without reliving the scariest parts of her argument with Greyson. She kept having to remind herself she was safe in her room by sitting up and turning on the light.

When she'd tried to think about something else, she just ended up fretting over whether she'd somehow pushed Julian into kissing her. Nothing he'd said had explicitly expressed any romantic interest in her. She'd been wearing a sweatshirt and pajama bottoms, for crying out loud. And stupid rain boots. Who'd want to kiss that? He was probably being nice because she was a mess and practically begging him to kiss her. He was just too kind to rebuff her when she looked so pathetic.

She'd drifted off only a few hours before her alarm went off, curled up under a crocheted afghan and a fleece blanket at the foot of her bed with her light on, like she used to do when she was little and had nightmares.

She woke up shivering, exhausted, and disoriented. And with no chance to talk to Julian again. They'd agreed, before he left, that it probably wasn't a good idea to take the same train to the city. What if Greyson tried to meet Beatrice when they got into Grand Central? Greyson already thought something was going on between her and Julian. If he found out there really was, it would make everything that much worse.

So Julian had taken his early train again. Without her. And Beatrice asked Sasha to pick her up from Grand Central Terminal. Just in case.

She hadn't told Sasha or Kinsey about Julian appearing on her doorstep last night. At first, because it seemed easier to explain in person than over text. But Beatrice found it was hard to talk about in person, too. Her friends were supportive of her breakup with Greyson, but that didn't mean they'd be on board with her getting together with Julian the same night.

Beatrice herself was fed up with her frazzled nerves by the time her last class let out, fifteen minutes early. She couldn't wait around for Kinsey to be free, panicking about what she was going to do if Greyson cornered her again during the single fifteen minutes she didn't have either of her friends nearby. And she couldn't stand not being able to talk to Julian anymore.

The art center was only a few blocks away, she reasoned. Even if Greyson had meant to corner her after English Lit, she'd be more likely to avoid him successfully by getting off campus than waiting around for Kinsey to meet her.

Not that she thought any of that through before she was leaving Washington Square Park behind. It didn't even occur to her to text anyone about the change of plans until she was waiting for the Sixth Avenue crosswalk. Sasha and Kinsey got a lie about wanting to head straight home. Julian got a short text informing him she was coming to meet him—mostly to make sure he didn't take off for Grand Central before she got there. She wanted to see him, and she didn't want anyone to talk her out of it.

A cold raindrop landed on her cheek when she spotted the art center—a stout brick building halfway down the block, welcoming light shining out of the windows, with a colorful hanging sign above the door. Cars were parked all along one side of the street, but there wasn't much traffic going through. A woman with a small dog was letting herself into an apartment building across the street. The only other pedestrians were those scurrying past on the busier thoroughfares on either end of the block.

Turning up her collar against the weather, Beatrice quickened her pace. She could wait in the lobby for Julian, where there would be no rain or icy wind cutting through the thin wool of her coat.

She was maybe a couple dozen yards away when Julian came out of the art center, looking over his shoulder as he said something to someone still inside.

She let out a breath that she felt like she'd been holding since she left him at her front door last night. All that fretting from being insecure about a kiss flew off her shoulders with a gust of wind. He didn't look like someone who thought she was being too needy, or who wanted to push her away at the next opportunity. He just looked like Julian.

"Hey!" she called, waving to get his attention.

A worried frown drew his eyebrows together as he jogged down the front steps onto the sidewalk. He opened his mouth like he was going to call back to her—probably to lecture her for sneaking off by herself—but as he neared the corner of the building, his attention snapped to the narrow alley next to the art center.

It all happened in the space of a few seconds. Julian backed up, toward the street, one hand going up in a gesture that was somewhere between placation and defense, his mouth forming words Beatrice couldn't hear from this distance. Figures in dark clothing darted out from the alley. Julian turned on his heel to run, but they grabbed him. There was a shout, and a struggle, and they disappeared into the alley, leaving the street in silence.

It didn't seem real. One second Julian was standing there, and the next he was . . . gone. That kind of thing didn't happen. Not here. Not to Julian.

Not again.

Her feet started moving before her brain fully processed what people were supposed to do when this impossible thing did happen. All she knew, deep in her gut, was that she needed to get to Julian. Now. She dropped her bag and broke into a sprint as rain came sheeting down with an all-encompassing hiss.

"Julian!" she cried, skidding into the alley too fast. Her shoulder slammed against the art center's wall.

The alley was dark and hazy with rain. A streetlight behind Beatrice reflected off the raindrops and slick alley floor, giving just enough light to see. Three men in dark coats and hoods had Julian backed up against a wall behind a dumpster. He was fighting all three at once, but didn't have enough room to move. Two vicious blows to his stomach and he was on the ground, trying to protect himself from the onslaught of kicks and stomps.

Fury shot through her, pushing out the shock and fear. "*Hey!*"

She darted forward, seized the scruff of the nearest man with both hands, and yanked him back as hard as she could. "Get *off* him!"

The guy swung around and grabbed her arm, jerking her close. "Stay out of this, bitch," he spat in her face.

Beatrice flinched. She knew him. She'd only seen him once, but having an argument with a rough-looking stranger in a library study room wasn't an experience she was going to forget anytime soon.

It didn't seem to be something Vito did often, either. He did a double-take, his eyes darkening. "I know you," he snarled.

Crap. Beatrice didn't stop to make proper introductions. Planting her feet, she slammed the heel of her free hand into his nose. The crunch of bone made her stomach turn, but she ignored it. She could freak out later. Right now, she just wanted to get Julian and run.

Cursing, Vito released her, clutching his nose. "*Bitch.*"

Beatrice shoved the smaller, scrappier of the last two men off Julian, into his friend, and grabbed Julian's sleeve, hauling him to his feet. He was bleeding from a gash near his eye, and one of his arms circled around his ribs.

"Bee," Julian began, gripping her arm. "Get out of here."

The look in his eyes frightened her. She would've understood if he was scared, or angry, or in shock. She could've handled that. But he looked like a man who'd accepted he'd lost. He looked like he'd already given up.

She redoubled her grip on him. "Not without you."

"Wrong answer." Arms seized her waist and hauled her up and back, tearing her away from Julian.

No, no, no, no—

Beatrice dragged in a lungful of air and shrieked, the sound ripping at her throat as she kicked out. The heel of her boot connected with something hard. The guy grunted and threw her to the ground.

Jolts of pain screamed up her elbow and knee where they struck the pavement. She scrambled to her feet—better to be upright and limping than cowering on the ground.

"You chose the wrong fight to get involved with, princess," Muscles said, making a fist with one hand.

Beatrice's throat went dry. The stupidity of what she'd just done hit her, far too late. Her phone was still in her bag where she'd dropped it on the sidewalk. She was unarmed and outnumbered, she didn't have a plan, or anything she could swing at the attackers that would cause them any harm. The litter in the alley was useless—strips of cardboard, an empty beer can—or too far away to grab. She pressed her back against the wall, racking her brain for some kind of solution that would get both herself and Julian out of this alley alive. "Please—"

"Stop!" Julian shouted, throwing himself between Muscles and Beatrice. "Just *stop*. She doesn't have anything to do with—"

Muscles threw a punch at Julian's face. Julian blocked it and jabbed him lightning-fast in the stomach, then knocked his legs out from under him. Beatrice clapped her hands over her mouth.

"Leave her alone!" Julian rounded on Vito as Muscles, groaning, rolled to his feet. "*I'm* the one you have beef with. Don't drag her into this."

"Julian," Beatrice breathed, shutting her eyes and gripping the back of his coat. Puddle water was seeping into her sleeve and the knees of her jeans. Her hair was plastered to her face. She didn't know how to get them both out of this. She wasn't big, or strong. She wasn't even brave. All she had going for her was her stubborn, stupid resolve that she *wasn't going to let them die here.*

"You were plenty willing to drag her into this back in that library," Vito said, swiping his sleeve across his bloody face. It didn't so much wipe the blood away as smear it around.

"You leave her the fuck alone," Julian growled, taking a step toward Vito with his hands curled into fists at his sides.

"What's the matter?" Vito asked, cocking his head and smirking. He flicked his wrist, and a knife appeared in his hand like a deadly magic trick. "Suddenly too noble to let the little cunt fight your battles for you?"

Julian started toward Vito. "You fucking—"

"No," Beatrice begged, dragging him back. She was sure Vito wouldn't hesitate to use that knife, and all Julian had were his fists. "Julian—"

Vito made a motion to the other two. "Hold them."

"No," Beatrice said, as Muscles and Scrappy bore down on them. Her fingers ached from gripping Julian's coat, but she held on still tighter. "No."

"Fuck," Julian swore under his breath, dropping into a fighting stance. But both men came at them fast. Beatrice couldn't hang onto Julian and drag herself out of Scrappy's grip at the same time. Julian was torn away from her in a matter of seconds. Muscles pushed him face-first against the wall, twisting his arm behind his back.

"No!" Beatrice cried, lunging for him.

Scrappy caught her from behind and dragged her deeper into the alley. His hands gripped her wrists, pinning them under her chin.

"STOP IT!" she screamed, fighting to get free. Scrappy was

using his height to force her to hunch over, and he wouldn't put his stupid face close enough for her to throw her head back into his nose. She let out a wordless shriek, half panic, half frustration.

"Shut her up," Vito snapped, striding towards Julian. "I'll deal with her next."

Scrappy adjusted his grip on Beatrice, covering her mouth and nose with his forearm. She could barely breathe, and the air that filtered through his damp sleeve was sharp and acrid. She tried to wriggle free, but it only made him tighten his grip.

"Let her go, you son of a bitch!" Julian shouted, struggling to throw Muscles off him. "She never did anything to you!"

"Too late for that now." Vito pointed the blade at Julian's face. "You should never have tried to screw me, my friend."

No. She was not going to stand here and watch Julian get murdered. In sheer desperation, she bit down on Scrappy's arm as hard as she could.

Scrappy swore and released her. Beatrice stumbled, one palm smacking the ground before she recovered, and slammed into Vito. They tumbled into the grimy water draining down the center of the pavement in a heap. People were shouting, but she couldn't parse what they were saying.

She grabbed for the knife, but Vito was faster. He caught her wrist with one hand and slammed the other into her side, once, and then again.

She couldn't pull free. She made a fist and went for his bloody nose instead.

Vito swore, cupping both hands around his face. The knife skittered across the pavement.

Beatrice dove for it and snatched it up. She scrambled to her feet as Julian threw Muscles off him. The bigger man stumbled, smacking his head on a wall and going down hard. Julian leaped on Vito before he could get up, hitting him over and over.

"Julian," Beatrice said, her voice much, much softer than she anticipated. They should leave. This was their chance to run. Before Scrappy dragged Muscles to his feet and the fighting started all over again. She drew in a breath to shout for Julian to stop so they could get away.

But she felt strange and off-balance. Time seemed to slow to a crawl.

Maybe it was the shock setting in. Maybe that's why she felt like everything around her was unraveling.

She wasn't in pain. Not really.

The knife must have missed her, somehow.

If she'd been stabbed, she should be able to feel it.

She just couldn't explain why the blade in her hand was slick with blood now, when it hadn't been before.

Rain pounded against her head and shoulders. Icy rivulets ran down her face and the tips of her fingers and fell to the ground, where they joined thicker, red drops that bloomed like ink in the puddle at her feet.

The knife fell from her hand. But the blood continued its lazy spread across the pavement. It seemed to be dripping from the edge of her coat.

With abstract curiosity, she touched her side. It was warm and wet, but not with rain. Her fingertips came away stained crimson.

Oh, God.

Pain tore into her side, knocking her back into the alley wall. She needed to focus. She needed to get Julian and get out of there. But her legs wouldn't listen to her. She was transfixed by the blood on her fingers.

Her knees gave out, and she sank to the ground.

She was dimly aware of things happening around her. Shoes slapping wet pavement. A shout.

She should pay attention. She had to help Julian.

But the pain made it hard even to breathe. It took all her concentration just to stay conscious.

"Bee?" Julian's voice broke through the wash of meaningless sound. He dropped to his knees in front of her and gripped her shoulders, panic in his eyes.

The people behind him were wrong. Muscles and Scrappy had been swapped out for a middle-aged man with glasses and a young woman with pink hair.

"Talk to me, Bee," Julian said, his voice cracking. Blood cut a line down his face from the nasty gash under his eye. "What happened?"

Disoriented, she reached out to touch his cheek. "You're hurt."

Suddenly angry, he pushed her hand away. Something about her coat, near her waist, drew his attention. His frown deepened. With a rough movement, he jerked her coat open.

The color drained from his face. He touched her side, below the point where the pain was concentrated. "*Shit.*"

Beatrice followed his gaze, feeling even more disoriented and disconnected from reality. It was like something out of a bad slasher flick. Her sweater and the inside of her coat were soaked red around two small tears in the fabric.

It was absurd. They were just tiny little holes. They shouldn't hurt this much.

"What the hell were you thinking?" Julian growled, pressing his palm over the wounds.

She bit back a sob as the pain exploded at the pressure. The fraying threads still tying her to reality snapped. She grabbed a fistful of Julian's sleeve to stop the world from spinning, and darkness swallowed her whole.

TWENTY-TWO

A phone was ringing, far, far off. **Beyond the heavy silence. Beyond the thick, black fog holding her still.**

It felt like she'd been kicked in the ribs by a vindictive horse. Who had then pulled out half her internal organs, twirled them around like spaghetti, and put them back in upside down.

She had the sense of being tucked into bed—blankets weighing her legs down, a pillow under her head. Which was odd, because she didn't remember going home. She remembered being at school, and leaving her last class . . .

Except she'd gotten out of class early, and she was worried about Julian, so she—

A flood of disjointed images crashed over her. Julian pushed up against the wall. Her hand slamming into Vito's face. Blood at her feet. Julian's eyes when he pushed her coat aside.

What the hell were you thinking?

Something shifted on the bed beside her. A warm hand covered her own. When she flexed her fingers, they closed around a thumb.

Another susurrus against the bedclothes. A second hand joined the first, clasping her hand. "Bee?"

She knew that voice, even rough and cracked as it was now. She liked that voice.

Beatrice fought her way through the sluggish haze and forced her eyes open.

Beside her, Julian exhaled, as though he'd been holding his breath. "Thank God," he muttered, bending over her hand like a man seeking benediction. He looked disheveled—exhausted—but he was here. He was whole. That was good.

She became aware of a pressure on her other finger—a monitor of some kind. She was in a hospital room, divided in two by a curtain. A narrow tube disappeared into her arm under a piece of medical tape. The clothes she'd been wearing had been replaced by a thin hospital gown. Gauze scratched her skin where it wrapped around her middle.

It took her a moment to work out what happened. She sort of remembered being in an ambulance. The motion of the vehicle. The sound of a siren. A sharp prick on the inside of her elbow. Hands curled tightly around one of her own.

She remembered people talking in clipped, professional tones. Fluorescent lights streaking past. Being told she was going to be put under for surgery.

She remembered someone telling her they'd had to remove one of her kidneys. Asking her if it was all right if people came in to see her.

But they were like the memories of a dream. The details slid away before she could examine them. Faces were blurred. Conversations indistinct. Pain or medication had kept her mostly out of it for . . . she didn't know how long. The light coming through the thin curtains was yellowish—artificial—but she had no clue how late it was. Or even what day it was.

She tried to speak, but her mouth was made of cotton balls. All that came out was a soft croak. She swallowed with some difficulty and tried again. "It's okay," she rasped, squeezing Julian's thumb. "I never liked that kidney anyway."

Julian rocked back in his chair, one hand pushing his hair back, the other still holding hers. He looked like she'd accused him of stabbing her himself.

Now didn't appear to be a great time for gallows humor.

"Hey," she said, pulling gently on his hand. The lingering effects of whatever she was on was making it hard to do anything with much gusto. "It's not your fault."

Julian shook his head. Still gripping her hand, he produced a cup of water from the bedside table and helped her take a few sips. "Your—Your family is on their way. They should be here any minute."

Oh, God. Her family. If they thought things were bad enough to come all the way down here, they were bound to be operating at Bauer Panic Level 11. No way was she going to be able to calm them down in her current state. "Well . . . shit."

Julian lifted an eyebrow. "Beatrice Bauer, did you just swear?"

"The drugs made me do it," she said, her voice still hoarse. She closed her eyes again. It was tiring to keep them open all the time. "Very bad, drugs are. First they make you swear. Then you're cooking meth and dismembering hapless construction workers behind the local diner."

"That's . . . quite an escalation," Julian said, his tone flat.

Something was wrong. Usually that would have startled a laugh out of him.

She turned her head, and the room seemed to flip briefly before it settled and she could get a better look at Julian.

There were stitches over the gash on his cheek. It looked like one part of his jaw had been attacked by a cheese grater, though the cuts seemed to be scabbing over. Dark splotches stained his coat. Blood. Some of it hers, probably. Her heart dropped when she noticed the wrap around his left hand.

"What—"

Julian drew back sharply, shoving both fists in his hoodie pockets. "Just a sprain."

Her stomach lurched, aggravating the distant pain in her side. He was shutting her out again, and she couldn't think clearly enough to figure out why.

"Julian?" she asked, her empty fingers curling around the bedclothes.

He swallowed, eyes fixed on a point on the floor. "That hard work theory . . . It doesn't work."

Beatrice blinked. Her grip on the real world was so questionable, she thought she'd grayed out for a few seconds and missed a topic shift. "What are you—"

"You're always talking about how if you just work hard enough, and you have a good enough plan, everything will turn out okay. But it doesn't work like that. Not when you're waiting for all your shitty mistakes to catch you up and screw everything over again."

Maybe she was dreaming. That might explain why this conversation made no sense. She reached for him, pushing past the heaviness in her limbs. "Julian . . ."

He scraped his chair back, his mouth twisting. "Don't—Just—" He let out a sharp breath. "I don't get it."

Beatrice withdrew her hand, curling it protectively around her ribs. "Get what?"

"What do I have to do to get you to wise up?" Julian demanded, meeting her gaze with eyes as hard as flint. "Actually murder someone in front of you? Would that do it? Or would you just find another excuse to explain it away?"

She couldn't get enough air in her lungs. "I don't—I don't understand."

"You could've died. You had no business jumping in the middle like that."

A little spark of defensive anger caught in her chest. "What was I supposed to do? Stand by and watch you get murdered?"

"It was *my fight*," Julian snapped, his voice too loud in the small room.

"He had a *knife*, Julian."

"No shit, Beatrice! Why do you think I told you he could've killed you back in the library?"

Beatrice's face warmed. She was willing to admit that throwing herself into the fray wasn't her smartest-ever move, but she didn't think she deserved getting yelled at like an idiotic child. "Stop it," she whispered.

"Did it ever even occur to you why a guy like Vito would want to kill me?"

"*Stop.*"

He leaned forward in his chair, elbows on his knees, so their eyes were level. "I got involved with his gang after I dropped out of high school. I ran drugs for him. For about nine months. And then I flipped on him to the FBI so they wouldn't prosecute me."

Beatrice shook her head. "No," she said, trying to sound firm. But her voice was torn at the edges, fraying and unraveling with every word. "*No.* You're not a criminal."

"Unbelievable," Julian said, throwing his hands up. "No matter what I say, you just go on thinking I fit somewhere inside your wholesome little organized life. Well, newsflash, sweetheart: Some of us have lives that are so chaotic and riddled with stupid mistakes that no amount of bullshit planning could pull us out of it. Stop being so goddamn naïve, Beatrice."

"I was only trying to help," she said in a small voice.

"Who asked you?" Julian shot back.

She bit her lip, fixing her eyes on the ceiling so she wouldn't cry. All she could think was *it's not fair*. She thought Julian was different. He didn't seem to mind that she was a little strange. He laughed at her jokes. He listened to her like everything she said was important. He understood her, in a way most people didn't.

At least, that's what she thought.

She had never asked for an explanation for that day in the library. She'd never pressed him for details about what he'd done with himself after he broke his hand. She hadn't even bothered to validate Greyson's accusation that he got in trouble with the FBI. There was a part of her that knew Julian couldn't have had an easy life, but she had rejected any explanation that didn't fit her image of him.

And why? Because he was cute and she liked the way he laughed? Because being in love with someone meant they couldn't make any mistakes?

She felt tiny and stupid and lost. Whenever she reached out for him, he pushed her away. And it hurt worse every time. She couldn't do it anymore. She couldn't keep throwing herself at his walls until she was a broken, bloody mess.

He was right. She was naïve. Any sensible person would have stopped chasing after him a long time ago, instead of deluding themselves into thinking . . .

She huffed out a breath. She couldn't make Julian love her. And it was long past time to give up trying.

She dug her fingernails into her palms. When she spoke, it was a thread of a whisper. "I think you should leave."

A muscle jumped in his jaw. He blinked, the flint in his eyes seeming to crack.

Then, without a word, he stood, swiping his backpack off the floor as he went by.

He hesitated at the door, and for one moment, Beatrice thought—she *hoped*—he would turn and say something else. Something that would explain everything and give her an excuse to forget the whole argument. Anything at all. *I didn't really mean it. I was lying.*

I don't want to go.

But the moment slipped by in silence. Julian jerked the door open and left, leaving it to close behind him with a dull, terminal thud.

TWENTY-THREE

There was a lot more *stuff* in the apartment than Julian had realized. All his things used to fit into two storage bins, his backpack, and his dad's old army bag. Now he was looking at having to throw a bunch of it away.

Some of it was easy. The furniture would stay. Most of it should have gone to a landfill long ago anyway. There wasn't much point in packing the food, either. Half of it was leftovers, and it'd be easier to replace the rest of it than figure out how to take it with him.

It was all the other stuff that was presenting the problem. At some point in the last few weeks, he'd started settling in. Buying impractical extra crap that was too heavy or bulky or useless to haul around.

Hefting one of the loaded bins onto the table, he started rummaging through it for anything he could toss. It had still been dark this morning when he gave up trying to sleep. He hadn't wanted to turn on a light, in case it woke Fabiana up, so he'd been clearing things off shelves without sorting through them.

A gray wash of early-morning sun filtered through the windows now, giving him enough light to figure out what could go. Old clothes. Assorted half-used office supplies. The last of his Bristol board. His sketchbook.

A slim stack of kids' drawings made him pause, a soul-wrenching sense of guilt battering at the cold practicality he was trying to maintain. Most of his kids wanted to take their art home with them, but there were a few who loved giving them away. Julian looked through the pages slowly. The subject matter ranged from dragons and unicorns and monsters to pets and self-portraits and illustrated snippets from their lives. He shouldn't keep them. He couldn't go back there again. He'd put those kids in danger, taking the job when he knew Vito was still after him. If one of them had been around when he got jumped . . .

He shoved the guilt away as best he could, setting the drawings aside to deal with later, and thrust his hand back into the bin.

His fingers closed around canvas and he pulled out a heavy tote bag. Inside was a cracked pan of watercolors, a tin of colored pencils, a handful of markers, an assortment of paper, and a folder full of plans and notes in Beatrice's clear, cheerful handwriting.

Julian's heart clenched in his chest.

I was just trying to help.

He could still see her back in that alley—freckles stark against paper white skin, eyes fixated on her shaking, blood-smeared hand like it belonged to somebody else. The tremor in her voice when she said *You're hurt.* Like some stupid scratch was more important than the fact she'd been fucking stabbed.

She should have been furious at him. She should have kicked him out of her hospital room the second she saw him. It was Julian's fault she got hurt. Beatrice wouldn't have come to meet him at the art center if he hadn't gone to her apartment the night before. If he'd made her understand how Greyson worked when he got angry. If he'd told her how easy it would be for Greyson to find out where Julian worked, track Vito down and pass on the information. If he'd told her how she was in danger of getting caught in the crossfire.

If he'd been honest with her from the beginning.

Somehow, she didn't seem upset at all. She just lay there, looking small and helpless, mumbling absurd jokes and insisting Julian wasn't to blame.

It was infuriating. He hadn't meant to start yelling at her, but he couldn't take that goddamn *sympathy* anymore. All he wanted was for her to give him some of the blame he deserved.

But she didn't. She didn't even get angry. She shut down. Pulled away. Julian hadn't been prepared for how much it hurt to know he'd finally found a way to let her down.

It shouldn't bother him this much. Beatrice should have realized a long time ago that Julian was nothing but a hopeless screwup. Now he wouldn't have to feel guilty for constantly fucking up her life. He wouldn't have to wonder how the hell he was ever going to give her that little house—that stability she wanted—when life was always knocking him down. He wouldn't have to worry about when he was going to lose her, like he'd already lost so many people.

But I don't want you to let me go. He remembered the warmth of her fingers against his cheek. The heartbreaking way she looked at him that night on the stairs. Part guarded hurt, part careful hope. *Stay here. Stay with me.*

"Shit," Julian swore, the word catching on the hard lump in his throat. This was all his fault. He seized the bag and threw it as hard as he could at the garbage, taking little pleasure in the loud crash when it knocked the entire thing over.

Behind him, Fabiana made a half-asleep sound of protest and mumbled something that sounded vaguely like a question.

"Go back to sleep," Julian said, striding to the trash can and yanking it upright. He started gathering the scattered scraps of paper and eggshells.

Fabiana groaned and pushed herself to her elbows. She

squinted one eye at Julian through a curtain of black hair. "The hell are you doing?" she croaked. "What's with the bin?"

"Don't worry about it." He threw the last of the scraps away and went back to rummaging for crap he didn't need.

Fabiana pushed her hair out of her face and scowled at her phone. "Jesus. It's the ass crack of dawn. Did you sleep at all?"

He ignored her. He'd slept. Not well, but he'd gotten a couple of hours in. And more sleep sure as hell wasn't going to change his mind about what he had to do.

Fabiana had met him at the hospital last night. Julian found her arguing with a nurse after Beatrice asked him to leave. Someone at the art center must have called her to say Julian was in the hospital, but since he'd been discharged after getting a few stitches, hospital staff figured he'd left. Fabiana had been in prime fighting form and was making it abundantly clear to the poor nurse that she thought the hospital losing track of one of its patients was beyond irresponsible when she spotted Julian.

She abandoned her tirade mid-word in favor of attacking him with a rare hug.

Followed almost immediately by a punch in the arm and a lecture about making her worry. She'd called out of her closing shift at work as soon as she heard and came straight down, apparently on the verge of a heart attack the entire time. Once she had satisfied herself that Julian wasn't at death's door—and trying at least half a dozen times to make him check back into the hospital for another round of x-rays—she'd asked him rapid-fire questions about what happened, barely waiting for answers. Julian lost what little patience he had and shouted at her to leave him alone.

Miraculously, it didn't trigger a new fight. The interrogation stopped. Fabiana didn't even bitch at him for snapping at her. She just stared at him for a moment, then said *okay* and focused on getting them both home. Her angry energy never dissipated, but it was all directed outward, like a hostile, confrontational force-field, keeping everyone else a good ten feet away.

Apparently, the peace had been only a temporary ceasefire.

"Hey," Fabiana said, throwing a pillow in his direction. It crashed into the kitchen chair to Julian's right and flopped to the floor. "Are you *packing*?"

Julian considered the paperback in his hand, not really seeing it. He couldn't look at Fabiana. They'd already done this. Him leaving. Her staying. He didn't know how to make her understand why he had to go, and he couldn't stomach a repeat of the blowout they'd had when he left the Sayer-Crewe's penthouse. Not after the shaky truce they'd developed lately.

"Jules," Fabiana said.

He tossed the book in the garbage. "The rent is paid up through next month. You can stay here until you find someplace else. Or we can go down and get you on the papers so you can keep it a while longer. Though if you tell Walter I'm gone, he'll probably reinstate your apartment for you."

Fabiana groaned again, and there was a soft thump, like she'd dropped back onto her mattress. "I'm going to kill Greyson."

A handful of old pencils joined the rest of the junk. "That wouldn't accomplish anything."

"Might stop you packing the apartment at stupid thirty in the morning." Cursing, she got out of bed and prowled past him into the kitchen. "Can you at least put the meltdown on hold until I've made some coffee? Your shit isn't going anywhere."

"I'm not having a meltdown," Julian snipped, snatching the plastic lid from the floor and snapping it in place. "This is the first rational thing I've done in weeks."

"Sure it is." She turned on the faucet and filled the coffee pot. "I always box up all my shit when I'm at my most rational."

"What do you want me to do, Fab?" Julian demanded. "Stick

around so Greyson can tell Vito's thugs where I live and get us *both* killed?"

"Have you considered *talking to the police?*" Fabiana shot back, shaking the coffee pot in his direction. Some of the water splashed onto the floor, but she didn't seem to care. "I'm pretty sure there's a case for conspiracy to commit murder, here. Or grievous bodily harm, at least. If Greyson told those guys where you worked—"

"They won't be able to pin it on him," Julian said, sliding the first bin off the table. "They couldn't last time."

Fabiana reached for the coffee tin. "Greyson's not God, Jules. He can't get away with everything. Don't you want to fight back?"

"Against what? It's my fault Vito was after me. If I hadn't gotten involved with him in the first place—"

"Yeah, Greyson couldn't have *possibly* convinced someone else to go after you instead," Fabiana said, slapping the filter shut and switching the coffee maker on. "He's never done *that* before."

Julian shook his head. "That's not—"

"I thought the reason you ran away last time was to get away from Greyson's manipulative bullshit." She crossed her arms and leaned against the counter. "What was the point of all that if you're just going to let Greyson walk all over you again?"

"Look, I'm sorry I let you down. Okay? I'm sorry. But I'm—I mean, look at me. I literally can't make a good decision to save my life, and I've just—I've been in this nosedive for years that I can't pull up from, no matter what I try. I didn't want you to crash and burn with me. I didn't want . . ." He paced away, pushing his hair back. "I just—I fuck things up. That's all I ever do. I fuck things up."

"Jules—"

"I can't stay here, Fab," he said, pleading with her to understand. "I can't. Beatrice is in the hospital because of me. What if she'd—"

He cut himself off with a curse, his stomach cramping with all the toxic fear he'd been trying to ignore all night. This was why he kept everyone at arm's length. This was why he'd sabotaged the few romantic relationships he had in high school, and why he had avoided dating since. This was why he picked fights with Fabiana instead of communicating like a reasonable human being. When he cared about people too much, bad things happened.

He couldn't take it anymore. Every time he lost someone, he felt like a part of his soul went with them. He was in tatters already. He didn't know if he could survive another loss.

"Hey," Fabiana said, pushing off the counter. "It wasn't your fault."

Julian shook his head to clear his mind of Beatrice saying the exact same words to him just hours ago. The same words of the police officer who took his fractured statement at the hospital while he was waiting to hear if she was going to be okay. Of course it was his fault. He'd set all the dominoes up himself. All Greyson had to do was flick his wrist and it all came crashing down exactly how Julian had known it would.

"I kissed her," he said in a hoarse voice. "Couple days ago. Greyson came after me, and it sounded like he'd had a fight with her, and I sort of . . . I guess I lost my mind, because as soon as he left, I went over to her place and I just . . ." He sank into a chair, pressing the heels of his hands against his stinging eyelids. "She said she broke up with him. And I—I missed her like crazy . . ."

Fabiana sighed and came to sit down at the table with him. "You really like her, huh?"

He had her imprinted on his brain. The way she wrinkled her nose when he said something she didn't want to admit was funny. The smug, crooked little smile she adopted when she startled him into laughing. The warmth of her hands. The way her mouth moved against his when they kissed. Her infectious joy. Her unflinching bravery. Her stubborn conviction that anything could be accomplished with the right plan of attack.

Like didn't begin to cover how he felt about Beatrice. He let himself hope, when he was around her. He let himself believe he could stitch the shreds of his life back together, somehow. She made him want to be a better version of himself. He felt like he *was* a better version of himself, with her.

"I love her," he admitted, his voice rough.

Fabiana lifted an eyebrow at him. "So why are you trying to bail, jackass?"

He blinked. "What?"

"You're bailing." Fabiana flicked her hand at the bins on the floor. "It's your move. Things get tight, you freak out, you internalize whatever bullshit Greyson's trying to pull on you, and you *bail*."

Julian opened his mouth to argue, but he had nothing to argue with. He couldn't claim he *wasn't* bailing. He didn't even know where he was moving to. He just felt like he needed to get out.

"I'm just—I've been waiting for her to realize what a useless piece of shit I am since I met her. Every day she didn't, I dreaded it more. And now—between me landing her in the hospital and—and everything I said to her . . . I fucked up. She got hurt trying to help me, and I threw it in her face. I know she hates me. And I can't . . ." He rubbed his eyes, suddenly feeling all the hours he hadn't slept. "I've let so many people down already. I can't stand the idea that I disappointed her, too."

"What do you mean, 'too?'" Fabiana demanded, leveling a scowl at him. "*I'm* not disappointed in you."

He let his hands fall on the table. "Don't try to tell me you're not still pissed that I left you with them."

"I'm not!"

He just looked at her. "Fab."

She rolled her eyes. "Okay, yeah, maybe I was pissed at first. I used to think if you'd just stuck around another few weeks I could have gotten Walter to . . . I don't know. Get you an apartment or something. Looking back, it probably wouldn't have worked even if you'd let me try. And it *clearly* wasn't good for your health to stick around anymore. I get why you had to leave.

"Besides, even if I *was* still pissed at you, how many times have you gotten me out of crisis since then? I know I can be a bitch, but I'm not completely unreasonable. You never, ever let me down. Okay?"

Julian swallowed, his gaze landing on a chip in the table, throat too tight to answer.

"Hey. Look at me," Fabiana said, slapping her hand on the table. "You are *not* a piece of shit, and you are *not* a screwup. The only people who think that are you and Greyson. And you know what? *That* pisses me off. You shouldn't listen to your psycho stepbrother over your own twin."

"But—"

"I haven't met Beatrice," Fabiana went on, speaking over him, "and I don't know what you said to her. But I'd bet cold, hard cash she doesn't think you're as much of a screwup as *you* think you are."

"You don't get it." If she'd seen the hurt in Beatrice's eyes, she wouldn't sound so confident. "I fucked up, Fab."

"So that's it? You're not even going to *try* to make it right?"

"How can I?" Julian turned his hands palm-up on the table. "Even if she could forgive me . . . She wants stability. I can't give her that. I've never even lived in the same house for more than five years running. I can't give her what she needs. I can't—I can't make her happy. If she hates me, she can move on. Find someone else who's . . . who's actually good for her."

Cursing under her breath, Fabiana ran both hands over her face. "Okay. Listen. I love you, but you're an idiot."

"Excuse me?"

"It's like you're *trying* to make yourself miserable. You risk provoking Greyson just to kiss this girl, and then the second shit hits the fan, you want to bolt. You know how controlling Greyson can be. Do you want to leave Beatrice to deal with him by herself?"

"Me getting involved isn't going to defuse the situation," Julian said, crossing his arms. "He's tried to get me killed twice now."

"I'm not telling you to get in a turf war with him. We're talking about a person, not a city block. But I gotta say, as someone who's dated some real class acts, it's always a hell of a lot easier getting out of shitty relationships if you've got a support system to fall back on."

"I'm not anybody's support system, Fab. She's already got her family. Her friends. She doesn't need me."

"You're *my* support system," Fabiana said, crossing her arms too and leaning back in her chair. One side of her mouth quirked up in a smile. "You're not even that bad at it, when you aren't having meltdowns before I've had my coffee."

Julian let out a half-laugh, pushing his hair back with both hands.

Fabiana was right. He was bailing. Trying to protect himself by ending things with Beatrice before the rug could get ripped out from under him. Because he'd rather she was alive and hating him than the alternative.

But maybe that wasn't the choice. Pushing Beatrice away didn't keep her safe. It was just another way of losing her. Made all the worse because skipping town meant leaving Beatrice to deal with Greyson—and the aftermath of last night—by herself.

He didn't know if there *was* a way to make things right with Beatrice. But that didn't mean he couldn't try. This thing with

Greyson was something he should have dealt with a long time ago. He was sick of running. Sick of letting Greyson win. He had to at least try to take the burden of how to handle Greyson off Beatrice's shoulders.

He hadn't bothered to bring Greyson up when he gave his statement to the police last night. No one had believed him last time he tried to accuse his step-brother of arranging to kill him. There hadn't seemed to be a point in bringing it up again.

Except that if Greyson was arrested, it'd be a lot harder for him to bother Beatrice.

Julian blew out a long breath. "What do you think the chances are I'll get laughed out of the police station if I go down there and tell them Greyson tried to set me up again?"

"I'll come with you," Fabiana said, brightening. "Just let me shower and caffeinate first."

"What about your job?" Julian asked. He was pretty sure he'd have to quit at the art center, even if he'd decided not to move for now. He couldn't justify staying when he'd put so many people in danger. Fabiana's part-time retail gig might be their only income for the next few weeks.

Fabiana waved this way. "You need the backup today. I'll get someone to cover."

"Really?"

"Yeah, really. You don't have to do everything yourself. And it's about damn time someone took that psycho to court."

"I don't know about court," Julian said. "I have to get someone to believe me first."

"They'll believe you," Fabiana said, in a tone that implied there was an *or else* hidden in her meaning. The coffee maker spat out the last of the water. She got up and poured herself a cup, then settled against the counter. "There should be a few domestic disturbance reports from high school that'll work in your favor.

Walter smoothed things over, but I'll bet there's still a police record from when the neighbors called about the noise. Plus, I'd be surprised if there isn't some kind of phone trail this time. People who get away with a lot of shit tend to start forgetting to cover their asses."

Julian stared at her. "Christ, Fab. How long have you been plotting this?"

She smiled, a glint in her eye. "Useful, having an evil twin, isn't it?"

TWENTY-FOUR

Greyson's father had set him up in a small, one-bedroom apartment in Greenwich Village when he started at NYU. Mostly as a PR move, according to Fabiana, to make Greyson seem more down-to-earth, or some bullshit. With no personal assistants or housekeepers to keep everything working like clockwork, the trust fund kid was practically working his way up from nothing.

Greyson's building was still a hell of a lot nicer than Julian's. There was an elevator, for one thing. The buzzer seemed to work, for another—though Julian had bypassed this in favor of slipping inside as someone else came out. According to a sign by the elevator, there was even a gym by the laundry machines in the basement.

Roughing it, by Sayer-Crewe standards.

Julian's heart pounded as he got in the elevator and hit the button for Greyson's floor. There was only enough room in the elevator for maybe five people, if they crammed in shoulder-to-shoulder. Though fortunately for Julian's nerves, there was no one else going up with him.

He massaged the palm of his left hand through the ACE bandage wrapped around it, trying to keep his breathing slow and even. His hand didn't hurt too much anymore—he was trying to do all the care procedures a nurse had walked him through at the hospital, and it was helping. It certainly wasn't as bad as when he actually broke his hand three years ago. He was probably imagining the ache getting worse as the elevator shuddered upward.

Julian had spent most of the weekend at a police station, trying to get someone to believe Greyson had been responsible for Julian getting jumped. No one had wanted to listen. But between Fabiana's tenacious lectures and Julian stubbornly sticking to his story, the two of them eventually annoyed one detective into checking a few facts. Detective Flores had found the case files from when Julian broke his hand, and even tracked down the domestic disturbance reports that Fabiana was convinced were going to help.

Unfortunately, none of it proved anything except Julian didn't get along with his step-brother. Compare Greyson's squeaky clean record to Julian's past involvement in running drugs—regardless of never being charged with anything—and Julian looked like a screwup with a jealous vendetta.

He wasn't surprised he got nowhere with the police. It was the same runaround he got the last time he accused his step-brother of trying to kill him. No one wanted to mess with an influential family like the Sayer-Crewes without some hard evidence.

And there wasn't any hard evidence to be had. Vito had confessed that someone had tipped him off about Julian's location, but Greyson hadn't been stupid enough to use his own cell to call him, much less give out his name. Without more to go on, the police weren't willing to drag Greyson in for a voice lineup.

Detective Flores hadn't been unsympathetic to Julian's frustration, but her attitude seemed to be that he should be happy the DA believed he was acting in self-defense when he attacked Vito, and should let the rest drop. And maybe stay away from Greyson from now on.

The elevator pinged and Julian strode down the fifth-floor corridor, glancing at the numbers on the doors as he passed. He found the one he wanted and stopped, rubbing a hand through his hair as he made a fruitless attempt to slow his racing heart.

Coming here went against every instinct. All his running, the past three years, had been a flailing attempt to never get caught in Greyson's net again. He couldn't rid himself of the feeling that he should accept the advice he'd been given and get out of the way before he got himself killed.

But there wasn't any other way around it, as far as he could tell. Running from Greyson hadn't stopped him screwing with Julian's life, or anyone else's. It was about damn time Julian dug his heels in and said *enough*.

Julian blew out a breath and checked his phone. Plenty of battery left. He hit record on the memo app he'd downloaded yesterday and watched it for a few moments as it counted out the time in milliseconds. He'd done a few test runs on the way down. There was no reason it shouldn't work now.

He swallowed down the dread building in his chest. He wasn't ready. He probably would never be completely ready. But he was here. He had to do this.

Stashing his phone in his pocket, he raised his right fist and pounded on the pristine black paint.

There was some shuffling inside, and the clatter of dishes. The lock turned and the door glided open.

"Julian." Greyson's eyes widened incrementally as he regarded Julian from the gleaming light of his foyer. "What are you doing here?"

Julian's hands curled into fists as dread turned to anger. "Surprised to see me?"

Greyson's mouth quirked up in a cruel smile as his gaze traveled over the healing injuries on Julian's face, and the wrap around his left hand. "I wouldn't say I'm surprised," he said, crossing his arms and leaning one shoulder against the doorjamb. "You never did have much of a survival instinct."

"And you never knew when to back the fuck off," Julian snapped.

The whole way down, Julian had told himself, again and again, that dealing with Greyson wasn't like dealing with other people. If you wanted him to listen to you, if you wanted to control the conversation, you had to be cold and cutthroat. Just like him.

But he couldn't match Greyson's cool indifference. All Julian's guilt and fear and pain and frustration—everything he'd been trying to ignore or control for the past week—smoldered in his chest, evaporating whatever thin layer of frost he may have succeeded in building up on the way over.

He dug his nails into his palms, trying to let the flare of pain in his left hand remind him to keep it together. "The fuck is wrong with you? Don't you even care that trying to get back at me almost got Beatrice killed?"

The only thing that changed in Greyson's expression were his eyes, which turned to ice. Probably thought it was bad form to accuse people of attempted murder where other people might hear. He pushed off the doorjamb and motioned Julian inside.

Julian strode past him into the living room, where he had some room to maneuver if this all went to shit.

A picture window on the far side of the room showed off a view of the city that matched the decor—all of it in grays, browns, and white, with the odd splash of red. Even the pristine fake Christmas tree in front of the window was a creamy white, draped with earthy red and bronze ribbons and glass ornaments. The furniture and wall hangings inside were placed so carefully, were so deliberately coordinated, it looked like Greyson was anticipating a fucking interior design magazine to photograph the place any moment. A single bowl by the sink in the marble-surfaced kitchen was the only thing suggesting anyone lived here at all.

Greyson shut the door and took a couple steps toward Julian, his hands in his pockets. "This victim complex thing of yours is getting old, Jules. You're always trying to blame me for your problems."

"Kinda hard not to, *Grey*," Julian shot back. His heartbeat thundered in his ears. This had to work. He had to make this work. "You do keep trying to have me killed."

Greyson scoffed. "Give me a break."

"First you get those boys at school to go after me—"

"I still don't know where you got that idea," Greyson said, brushing an imaginary speck of dust off his sweater. "This is what I'm talking about. You get yourself in these bad situations, and then you can't face the consequences and try to pass the blame off on someone else."

"So, what, I'm supposed to believe it was a coincidence that less than twenty-four hours after you threatened me, Vito and a couple of his friends just-so-happened to be waiting outside my work to jump me?"

"Maybe it was cosmic intervention," Greyson said, a smirk twitching the corner of his mouth.

Julian's stomach twisted as heat rose in his ears. "Really?" He was shouting by now, incapable of keeping his volume in check. "You want to fucking stand there and tell me *cosmic intervention* was responsible for putting an innocent person in the hospital?"

Greyson's eyes narrowed. "You're the one who thought screwing around with a gang would be a good idea," he said, a subtle edge creeping into his tone. "They wouldn't have given a shit where you were if you hadn't messed with them in the first place."

"That's your justification?" Julian demanded. "I screwed up three years ago and that makes it okay that you almost got Beatrice *killed*?"

"Look, I don't know what you're trying to accomplish, here," Greyson said, dropping his voice to a low growl as he strode the last few feet separating them. The look on his face was one Julian knew too well. It meant *push me any further and I'll push back. Hard.* "I tried to tell her to stay away from you if she didn't want trouble. It's not my fault she didn't listen. And it sure as hell isn't my fault you couldn't protect her."

Fuck the plan. Hot rage burned up the last of Julian's self-control. He seized Greyson's collar with both hands, ignoring the sharp flare of pain in his left fist. "She wouldn't need protection if it wasn't for you, you son of a bitch. You want to talk about responsibility? Own up to your own fucking choices."

"Get your hands off me," Greyson rumbled.

"Why didn't you kill me yourself, instead of hiding behind people you couldn't control? Didn't want to get your hands dirty? Or are you just that much of a coward?"

Greyson shoved Julian off him, lip twisting in disgust. "Let me spell this out for you, nice and clear," he said, prodding Julian's chest with one finger. "Because apparently you're too fucking stupid to understand how this is going to go if I don't: I want you gone. I don't care how you get gone, but you're going to get the fuck out of my way. And in case that's still too difficult for your tiny brain to understand, that means you either get your ass on the next flight out of here, or I make another call to your old friends and tell them about your little shithole upstate." He dropped his voice to a low rumble, getting in Julian's face. "And trust me when I say that the next time they find you, they'll do the job right. I'll make sure of it. Dumb luck won't save you a third time."

Julian knew he should be filled with dread that he'd gone too far. Instead, it was relief that made him stumble back a step. If he couldn't convince anyone Greyson wanted him dead with a recording of *that* speech, they'd never believe it. "Fuck you, Greyson," he rasped.

"Get out," Greyson said, jerking his head toward the door.

Julian didn't wait to be told twice.

TWENTY-FIVE

Beatrice sat in the back seat of her mom's car, watching the cold, steel architecture of the city give way to the dead, brown trees and lonely, weathered buildings of the highway. It had been five days since she was admitted to the hospital, and the ride home with her family was tense and too quiet. Even the classic rock blaring from the radio couldn't drown out the fraught silence inside the car.

Her family had been fretting over her nonstop since they arrived after her surgery. Beatrice couldn't remember if she'd ever had the full force of her family's attention before. She didn't like it. It was like being hunted down by three buzzing, panicked helicopters. She couldn't escape the searchlights.

Mike and Joyce squabbled over stupid non-problems whenever they were on hover duty at the same time. Nath seemed to sense this stressed Beatrice out, so he'd been trying to run interference on her behalf. But his prickly version of running interference just added fuel to the fire.

It wasn't his fault. He was as anxious as their parents, and had more practice picking fights than settling them. Beatrice just wanted to burrow under the blankets and cover her ears to block it all out.

True to form, getting out of the hospital this morning had been more of an ordeal than it should've been. If her parents weren't arguing amongst themselves, they were asking Beatrice a million questions she didn't have the energy to answer. Beatrice couldn't handle it. By the time they'd packed into her mom's '09 Honda Accord, she'd gone from monosyllabic to nonverbal to completely unresponsive.

Which was apparently more worrisome than anything that had happened so far, because the other three Bauers went uncharacteristically quiet in response. Beatrice could feel their searchlights gliding over her periodically, though she refused to meet anyone's gaze. Every ten minutes or so, her mom would remind Beatrice that if she needed anything, all she had to do was ask. Once or twice, Nath reached over and gave her arm an awkward pat that Beatrice thought was meant to be a reassuring gesture.

Beatrice couldn't take the attention anymore. She wanted to strangle the next person who asked her if she was *doing all right*. All anyone wanted to hear—her parents, her friends, even her nurses—was some brave, meaningless quip, tailored to put them at ease.

Oh, I'm hanging in there.

It doesn't hurt that much.

You haven't lived in New York until you've gotten stabbed a couple of times, right?

She was sick of coming up with new lies to tell. She was sick of taking care of everyone else when she was broken and angry and sad and just . . . *not all right*.

No one wanted to hear that the only time she wasn't in pain was when she was asleep. They didn't want to hear that sleep only made her feel worse, smeared as it was with heavy, claustrophobic dreams that she woke from with her heart pounding, tears staining her pillow. They didn't want to hear that she couldn't stop reliving those few minutes in the alley, convinced if she'd just done something differently—gotten there sooner, or kept some kind of weapon on her, or knew kickboxing, or if she'd run for help—then maybe she could've stopped anything bad from happening.

They didn't want to hear how she was only in the hospital because she'd been trying to protect someone she loved, who she'd discovered too late didn't care about her at all. Even thinking about that one made her face burn with shame. She had been so, so stupid.

She knew she was weird. She knew she put people off with her strange clothes and dorky sense of humor. She knew she had too many freckles and too much untamable hair to ever be called a beauty. Yet she'd still somehow convinced herself that Julian might actually come to love her.

Of course he didn't love her. How could she have even thought he would? Beatrice had always had a habit of throwing her heart at people who didn't give a crap about her. She'd been doing it since she was little, when she'd sit on the floor, crying, because she couldn't understand what she'd done to make her biological father walk out of her life.

She'd thought she learned her lesson after she turned nine. A birthday card had come in the mail—late, as usual—claiming to be from her biological father, who was supposed to be in Alaska at the time. Beatrice had found it on the table when she came home from school, and for a moment, looking at the return address, she felt relieved. Frank hadn't forgotten her after all. It had just taken a few days for the card to come.

Then she made the mistake of checking the postmark on the envelope.

It wasn't from Alaska. The card had been sent out from the post office down the street from her house.

In a haze of denial, she'd gone to her closet in search of an explanation. She took out all the other cards she'd tucked away in the folds of an old blanket, where her mom couldn't find them and toss them out. Six more birthday cards, plus a few odd Christmas cards she'd received since Frank left when she was just a few months old.

Every last one was postmarked from right around the corner.

It felt like the ground crumbled out from underneath her. All those years hanging onto this tentative promise that, despite all evidence to the contrary, she hadn't been completely forgotten. Maybe Frank never visited, or called, but he cared enough to remember she existed once or twice a year, and say *love you, kid* at the bottom of a brightly colored card.

But all the cards did was prove to what lengths her mom would go to stop Beatrice crying. *Here, stupid. Take this card and shut up.*

Beatrice had never confronted her mom about it. She didn't want to hear the lies. There was a small, anxious part of her heart that was terrified to hear the truth, too. She didn't want her parents to admit they'd never wanted her around. That she reminded them of a bad time in Joyce's life that everyone would have much rather forgotten. That it would have been easier on everyone if Beatrice had never been born. She wasn't strong enough to face that reality if it was said out loud. At least if it was only a thought in her head, there was a possibility she was wrong.

So she'd stopped asking for help. Stopped asking for attention. Stopped asking for love.

If she never needed anything, no one would ever stop to wonder how such a weird little duck as Beatrice had slipped into the nest unnoticed. And if no one realized she didn't belong, no one would push her out.

Beatrice's phone buzzed in her pocket as Mike exited the highway, but she couldn't bring herself to check it. She'd been getting notifications almost nonstop since her admittance into the hospital. Anxious get well messages from out-of-state relatives and random acquaintances. Texts from Kinsey and Sasha asking if she wanted them to bring anything the next time they came to visit, or valiantly trying to distract her with silly videos and memes. Emails from her professors with information about making up the finals she was going to miss during the month or so her doctors had told her it would take to recover. A flurry of texts from Greyson she'd never answered.

I heard what happened.

Are you okay?

I want to come see you.

Please don't stay mad at me. I love you.

Lies.

He didn't love her. He just wanted what everyone else wanted—a conflict-adverse, people-pleasing invertebrate who never objected to being pushed around. She'd blocked his number after that. And then went through her social media accounts to make sure he was blocked on all of those, too.

The really pathetic thing was that she couldn't stop looking for messages from Julian. She kept refreshing her texting app whenever she checked her phone. Thinking maybe she'd missed something. Maybe he'd tried to contact her and it had gotten lost in all the other notifications. Maybe . . .

Maybe she was a complete idiot, still wishing he would talk to her.

The moment Mike parked in front of the apartment, Beatrice got out, not giving anyone time to fuss over her. She could walk just fine, even if the fading bruise on her knee gave her a little trouble with stairs. Most of her other injuries didn't hurt so much anymore. Her bruises were greenish and dull. A few bumps and scrapes were nearly gone. Her side still ached, but it wasn't as bad as it had been the first few days. She'd been prescribed more pain meds if she needed them, but she planned on not needing them. The meds made her feel fuzzy and nonlinear, and she wanted to be able to think clearly again. Maybe then she'd have a chance to snap out of this horrible funk.

Nath caught up to her on the stairs, and climbed with her in a kind of silent solidarity, carrying her overnight bag on his shoulder. Their parents hung back near the car, talking in low voices. Probably fretting over what to do about Beatrice.

At least dealing with Nath by himself wasn't so bad. He'd gone very scowly and grumbly the past five days, but he never seemed upset with her for not being able to fake a good mood. That was more than could be said for most of her other visitors.

"Fair warning," he said when they reached their landing. He narrowed his eyes. "There's . . . *flowers*, inside. They came this morning before we left."

Beatrice gave him a blank look. The arrival of flowers didn't seem that odd, under the circumstances. She'd received a few bouquets at the hospital, including a few from relatives, one from her coworkers at Java Mama, and one from her statistics class that she suspected Kinsey had organized. It seemed plausible an aunt or someone would send flowers to the apartment on the day Beatrice was discharged, to welcome her home. There didn't seem to be any need for a cryptic warning if that was the case.

But Nath maintained his grim expression and unlocked the door, leading the way inside.

Beatrice froze on the threshold. The apartment was overrun with greenery. For a moment, she wasn't sure if it was possible to fight through the dense foliage to her room without a machete. Carnations, roses, gardenias, orchids, poinsettias—and a dozen other flower varieties that Beatrice couldn't name—spilled out of the vases that crowded the free space on the kitchen table and overflowed onto the floor in the foyer and kitchen. They had even infested part of the living room, blocking the lower half of the TV and sitting on top of old bills and dirty dishes on the coffee table. Her home didn't smell like home anymore, so thick was the scent of flowers in the air.

"We didn't know what to do with them," Nath said, shifting one of the vases in the foyer aside with his shoe so he could set Beatrice's overnight bag on the floor. "I thought we should chuck 'em, but Dad said you should get the final say." Frowning, he poked around in the blooms until he found a small white envelope. "Here. Three guesses who they're from."

Beatrice let out a shallow breath and took the card from him. She didn't need three guesses. There weren't too many people in her life who would try to suffocate her with over-the-top, expensive gestures like this.

She tore open the envelope with shaking fingers.

Please give me another chance, Beatrice. This wasn't how anything was supposed to go. I know you don't believe me, but I love you. I want to make this work. Let me see you. Please.
- G

A strange sound escaped Beatrice's throat. Somewhere between a high, humorless laugh and a yelp.

He'd terrorized her in front of her own home, spat curses in her face, and might have struck her if a neighbor hadn't interrupted . . . and she was supposed to get over it. Let it go like it had been some minor disagreement. Like she was still overreacting about some stupid dress.

"Oh . . . go to hell!" she snapped, tearing the note in half.

"Beatrice?"

She looked up. Joyce and Mike stood frozen inside the doorway, gaping at her. Like neither of them had ever heard the word 'hell' before.

Heat flooded Beatrice's cheeks. Everyone kept treating her like a delicate piece of china, perched on the edge of a high shelf. Like if they so much as breathed in the wrong direction, she would fall and break.

But they were too late. She'd already shattered. And the shards she was left with scraped the inside of her skin. Trying to keep it all in was tearing her apart.

"I can't—" She slapped the pieces of Greyson's note on the table, trying to find something to look at that didn't make her want to scream. The furniture and clutter and all the idiotic flowers were closing in on her. Even the walls seemed too close. "I can't—"

"Are you all right, sweetheart?" Mike asked, in the nervous tone they'd all adopted whenever they spoke to her.

It was too much. That last, well-meaning question pushed pressure levels to critical. She let out a frustrated, strangled scream and burst into tears.

Beatrice's personal fleet of helicopters sprang into action, trapping her in a whirlwind of comforting hands and soothing voices that only made it harder to breathe.

"Would you all just *stop*?" Beatrice cried, tearing herself away from them. "Just let me—" Half-blind with tears, she stumbled over one of the garish flower arrangements on the floor, knocking it over. Water soaked into the living room rug, leaves and petals scattering across the floor. "*Dammit!*"

Sunny zipped out from under the coffee table to the back of the couch and stared at the scene with wide, scandalized eyes. Even her *cat* was appalled with her.

"Honeybee—" Joyce began, catching Beatrice's sleeve before she could start cleaning up.

"And stop calling me that!" Beatrice sobbed, spinning around to face her mom. "You only call me that when you're pretending you give a crap about me, and I'm sick and tired of everyone pretending they give a crap about me!"

Joyce rocked back, as though Beatrice had physically pushed her. "Hon—Beatrice, you *know* we care about you. We all do."

Beatrice let out a strangled sob, curling her arms around her middle like the lie had cut her open again. "No," she said, shaking her head. "No, you don't. You put up with me because I never cause any trouble, and I never have any feelings, and the rest of you need a referee for your ridiculous sparring matches!"

"Bee—"

"When have you ever cared what I'm doing when I'm not in mortal peril?" she went on, refusing to acknowledge the hurt expressions on her family's faces. She couldn't hold all her broken pieces inside any longer. They tore through her skin like shrapnel, and she didn't care who else got cut. "You never ask me about school, or work, or if I'm handling things okay on my own. And I'm *not*. I can't handle everything by myself. I'm drowning. I'm *drowning*, Mom. And no one even notices. No one cares."

"But we do care, baby," Joyce said, her eyes bright with unshed tears. "How can you say that? We love you."

Beatrice choked on another scream. The words—*we love you*—tore at her heart. The only time she ever heard them was when someone wanted her to shut up, or stop fighting, or swallow everyone else's guilt in the interest of peace. No one actually meant it. No one ever meant it. And Beatrice could prove it.

She marched into her room and threw open the closet door.

"Beatrice?" Joyce ventured, following her into the room. "What are you doing?"

Beatrice didn't answer. She shifted a box out of the way—ignoring her mom's anxious reminder that she wasn't supposed to do any heavy lifting—and dropped to her knees to dig into the box underneath.

"Beatrice, honey . . ." Joyce tried again, hovering in the doorway.

The cards were shoved down at the very bottom of the box. Thirteen in total, all in their original envelopes, addressed to Beatrice in block letters.

She stood and shoved the multicolored envelopes at Joyce.

Her mother stared at her for a moment before she took the cards. Mike had come to stand at her shoulder. Nath poked his head through the door, watching the scene with wide puppy-dog eyes that Beatrice couldn't meet, afraid guilt would overwhelm her.

Joyce turned the envelopes over in her hands, a sharp line between her eyebrows. "What are these?"

"Birthday cards. Christmas cards." Beatrice dashed a rogue tear off her cheek. "You said they were from my birth dad, but I know it was you. I know you wrote them. You didn't even bother to send them out of a different postal code."

Joyce covered her mouth with her hand, eyes still on the envelopes. "Bee . . ."

"I'm not a kid," Beatrice said. "You can quit lying. I know you only sent me those so I'd stop bringing everyone down with my stupid feelings. I know you hate it that I remind you of when you were with Frank. I know—" She choked on the words, but forced them out anyway. "I know you would have rather I was never born."

"Oh—God, honey, no," Joyce said, sliding the cards on Beatrice's desk and gingerly touching her shoulders. "That isn't true at all."

Beatrice pulled out of her reach, shaking her head. "Then why did you send them, if you didn't just want to shut me up?"

Mike cursed under his breath, rubbing his jaw. "It wasn't your mom's idea, sweetheart. It was mine."

Beatrice felt dizzy. All her life, she'd known that her step-dad had serious issues with the way Frank treated Joyce when they were married. But there must have been a tiny piece of Beatrice that still hoped Mike didn't hold it against her, because the admission hurt. She gasped in some air and sat down hard at the foot of her bed. "God. Did you hate me that much?"

"What? No!" Mike said, pulling out her desk chair and sitting across from her. "Are you kidding? You're my little girl. I love you just as much as if we shared the same blood. I'd do anything for you. Those cards weren't supposed to shut you up, they were . . ." Mike scrubbed his hand over his jaw again. "You don't know what it was like, watching you hurting. You were a sweet little kid. You should've been happy about presents and cake and all that, and instead you'd cry and cry. It didn't matter what we said, you were convinced that lowlife didn't love you because you'd done something wrong."

Beatrice pulled her knees up to her chest, hiding her face in her arms and trying not to sob. She couldn't deal with this. She couldn't tell whether Mike was lying. Part of her *wanted* him to be lying. She couldn't take any more heartbreak.

"It killed me, seeing you like that," Mike said, gripping her wrist. "If I could've knocked some sense into him, I would have, but we didn't even know where he was half the time. There was nothing I could do to make Frank a better father to you, and you needed proof that it wasn't your fault. I didn't know how else to give it to you." He moved his hand to Beatrice's shoulder, squeezing lightly. "Maybe it was a mistake. I didn't know you kept them. I didn't know you thought . . ." His voice wavered, and he stopped to clear his throat. "I'm sorry," he said gruffly. "I never wanted to hurt you, sweetheart. Never."

Beatrice couldn't answer. There was no reason to doubt anything Mike said, but . . . Believing her parents secretly wished she didn't exist had turned into armor. It kept her safe from being hurt by the truth.

But if she was wrong about the truth, that belief hadn't been protecting her at all. It was armor that was rusted and too small. More like a cage that kept her bruised and bleeding and deprived of oxygen.

She didn't know what to do about that. Cage or not, she had been convinced it made her safe. She didn't know how to leave it behind.

"How long have you been sitting on this, Bee?" Joyce asked, perching on the bed next to her. She stayed far enough away that they didn't touch, probably wary from the last couple times Beatrice had jerked away from her.

"Pretty much since I figured it out," Beatrice hiccuped, wiping her eyes with her sleeve. "Maybe before. Everyone always used to get so angry when Frank came up in conversation. And no one would talk about why he left, it was just . . . he was awful and he treated you badly, and it . . . it seemed like everyone wanted to forget he even existed. And I thought—since he was my dad—maybe you wanted to forget me, too."

Joyce bit her lips together like she was struggling not to cry. She wrapped her arms around Beatrice and held her tight. "No, baby. No, no, no. I'm so sorry. I should have made sure we talked about Frank a long time ago. But you stopped asking about him, and I guess I thought it didn't bother you anymore." She pulled back and smoothed Beatrice's hair. "Wishful thinking on my part, I guess."

"What do you mean?" Beatrice hugged her knees tighter, trying to resist the temptation to retreat back into the painful familiarity of her cage by assuring her mom there was no need to talk about him at all. She didn't know how else to protect herself from whatever horrible story she was about to hear. "Talk about him how?"

Joyce took a long breath. "Frank was . . . a troubled man. He had some mental health issues that he didn't cope with very well. He tended to self-medicate. Mostly alcohol. And then it was marijuana. And then he started getting into harder stuff. I didn't even notice it at first. I thought his mood swings were a reaction to stress. We'd gotten married less than a year before, and I was pregnant with you a few months after that . . ."

She stopped and pressed her lips together. "I should have left as soon as I realized he was shooting up. But I was scared of being a single parent, and I didn't know where to go. Part of me kept hoping that he'd get himself together once you were born.

"I think he tried," Joyce went on, meeting Beatrice's eyes. "I think he wanted to get clean and sober for you. He went to a few meetings. Seemed dedicated to getting it together. But it just . . . didn't take. He slipped. And I should have noticed. But I didn't. I didn't, and I still want to kick myself for not realizing in time."

"Why?" Beatrice asked. "What happened?"

Joyce swallowed, gripping her hands together in her lap. "You were about six months old. It was late, and we couldn't get you to go to sleep. So Frank took you out for a drive. The motion of the car usually got you to drift off.

"Only—he was gone too long. Over an hour went by and . . . nothing. Neither of us had a cell phone back then, so I couldn't call him. I was about to borrow a neighbor's car to go out and look for you when the police called and said you were both . . . both in the hospital. Frank had run the car off the road."

Beatrice's mind skipped back, trying to dig up some memory of the event. It seemed like the kind of thing she should remember, even if she was only a baby. Traumatic car accidents weren't things people just *forgot*, right? But all she could come up with was dead air.

"You were fine except for some bruising where your car seat got you," Joyce said, smoothing down Beatrice's hair like she wanted to assure herself that no lasting harm had been done. "That was a blessing. Frank got the worst of it. Whiplash, a broken wrist . . . plus a .17 blood alcohol level, and heroin in his system. The police found more heroin in the glove compartment, and a bottle of vodka under the driver's seat. Frank never admitted to it, but they were pretty sure he'd taken you with him to meet his dealer. And then the son of a bitch got high before driving you home."

Joyce's nostrils flared, her mouth set in a hard line. "I was livid. I would've killed him if he hadn't already been arrested by the time they told me what he'd done. If he was going to risk your life because he couldn't stay clean, I wanted nothing to do with him. I didn't want either of us to have anything to do with him. He could have killed you, and I just wanted to put him behind us. So I filed a restraining order on your behalf that night, and I filed for divorce, and I packed us up and moved us in with my sister."

"Is that why he never called? Because of the restraining order?"

"Well . . ." Joyce exchanged a guilty look with Mike.

"He did call a few times," Mike said. "Right around the time your mom and I got married. Kept saying he had a right to see his daughter. I wasn't too happy about it, but we took you to a park to meet him once. You probably don't remember. You'd only just turned two. It . . . ah . . ." He huffed out a breath, tapping one finger harder against his knee. "It didn't go well."

"Frank was still an addict," Joyce said. "He was twitchy. Kept hinting he was strapped for cash. Then he bumped into you by accident and you scraped your knee and started crying."

A dusty memory came to Beatrice as she spoke, of blinding sun and a stinging knee, and Mike arguing with someone while her mom whisked her back to the car.

"That was the last straw," Joyce went on. "We cut him off for good after that."

"Because we loved you and we wanted to protect you," Mike put in, scrubbing Beatrice's arm. "Never because we blamed you in any way for Frank's behavior."

"You were the bright spot in my life when I was with Frank," Joyce said, gathering Beatrice into her arms. "You were the reason I found the strength to get out of there. I have never, for a single second, regretted having you. Okay?"

Beatrice managed a small nod. She needed time to process all this new information before she could accept it. She'd been wearing that old armor for so long that she'd grown into the shape of it. She didn't know how long it would take to rid herself of the imprints and scars it had left on her.

"I'm so sorry I didn't notice you were suffering," Joyce said. "You've always been so responsible and independent. I guess we let you fall by the wayside, didn't we?"

"It's okay," Beatrice said, feeling guilty for how she'd shouted at everyone.

"No, it isn't. I should've paid better attention. I don't know what any of us would do without you."

"Probably kill each other," Nath said. He was still only half inside the room, his arms crossed. "Because of sadness," he added when both Mike and Joyce shot him reproving looks. "What? You think we'd all three magically start dealing with our feelings like emotionally mature adults? Not a chance."

"Nath," Mike scolded.

But Beatrice laughed wetly. "Come here," she said, beckoning Nath over.

Nath dragged his feet across the room and then jumped on the bed behind Beatrice. He wrapped his arms around her shoulders and squeezed.

"Are we okay?" Mike asked. "Do you want to keep talking?"

Beatrice shook her head. "We're okay. I'm sorry."

"Don't be sorry," Mike said.

"You're allowed to fly off the handle sometimes," Nath said, dropping his chin on her shoulder. "If you can't scream at your family, who can you scream at?"

"I love you, Honeybee," Joyce said, joining the hug. "You know that, right?"

Beatrice still felt raw and bruised, but for the first time in years, she didn't let herself listen to the knee-jerk reaction in her head that heard *I love you* and thought *lie*. She set that thought aside and cautiously, experimentally, accepted the words without question.

Nothing bad happened. The world didn't end. Her heart didn't break. She felt like someone had opened a window and let in a warm breeze.

Beatrice took a deep breath, put an arm around her mom, and pulled her dad into the hug, as well. "I love you, too."

TWENTY-SIX

The morning after Beatrice was released from the hospital, Kinsey drove her back down to the city. The police had asked Beatrice to go over her original statement at the station when she was feeling up to it. She probably should have put it off another few days, but she welcomed an excuse to steal a few hours away from her little band of helicopters. Even if she wasn't perpetually frustrated with them anymore.

Beatrice spent much of the drive sleeping. She was still doing a lot of that, even though she was trying to only take her pain meds before she went to bed. She woke up halfway over the Harlem River to Selena Gomez and a white mocha latte, which Kinsey must have stopped for while Beatrice was asleep.

"Are you sure you don't want me to take you straight to Sasha's?" Kinsey asked as she edged the car onto FDR Drive.

"I'm okay," Beatrice croaked, rubbing her eyes. She pulled her seat up and took a sip of coffee. It was warm and felt nice in her hands. "I think I can manage sitting in a chair for twenty minutes without dropping dead."

"I could come in with you," Kinsey offered. Again. "Take you straight home once you're done."

"You can't skip class," Beatrice said. "Finals are next week."

"So? What's so great about finals?" Kinsey asked, a grumpy frown drawing her eyebrows together. "Suddenly they're more important than best friends? That's dumb."

Beatrice felt the corner of her mouth twitch. She set her hand on Kinsey's arm and assumed her most tragic Victorian consumptive face. "It is my dying wish that you take these finals. For both of us, as I am surely not long for this world."

Kinsey made a face. "Your *dying wish* is for me to take my finals? Seriously? I'm not even being charged with avenging your death?"

"Nope. I'd say my dying wish is for you to *ace* all your finals, but I don't want to put any undue pressure on you. So I'll settle for you taking them."

Kinsey glared at Beatrice sideways. "Why am I friends with you?" she said, in an affectionate grumble. "You're so weird."

Beatrice dropped her eyes to the lid of her coffee, her smile fading.

Talking to her family yesterday had cleared the air some, but she still felt emotionally raw. She had to fight hard for the occasional reprieve from the gloom hanging over her. Stupid things kept making her cry. Last night, her mom had turned on a baking competition—probably thinking it was a safe bet, since there was no violence or substantial conflict—but it just reminded Beatrice of Julian's bit about the gravy-themed cooking show, and she dissolved into tears two minutes in. This morning she walked out the door feeling content and light for a split second—before she remembered she wasn't meeting Julian at the train station, she was going to meet Kinsey downstairs. The unexpected drop forced her to stop for thirty seconds, right outside her own door, to pull herself together. And here she was about to cry because she missed Julian calling her *weird*.

She hated that she couldn't stop thinking about him. Her mind kept turning over random memories, studying them from every angle, trying to reconcile them with what he'd told her in that hospital room. What drug runner got hearts in his eyes whenever he talked about the artistic efforts of little kids? Or encouraged acquaintances to change majors because he noticed they weren't happy with their career paths? Or persisted in days-long dad-joke battles over text?

But then . . . what contributing member of society got chased into libraries and dragged into alleys by vengeful drug dealers?

Beatrice couldn't get the pieces to fit together in a way that made sense, and she was furious at herself for even trying. For missing Julian at all, after everything he said. It was just another way to blindly believe the best instead of accepting the truth.

But she couldn't help it. She missed him so much it hurt. He had been such an important part of her life, and she didn't want to believe he wasn't the person she thought she knew.

"I was joking," Kinsey said, finding Beatrice's wrist and shaking it gently. "You know I was joking, right? You're the *good* kind of weird."

Beatrice shoved all her confused thoughts about Julian into the flimsy box in her mind that wouldn't stay shut. She turned her palm over and squeezed Kinsey's hand, forcing a small smile. "I know. It's okay."

Kinsey's eyes darted to Beatrice's face for a moment before they returned to the road. "I won't skip class if it's going to make you *sad*."

"Kins. It's okay. Really. I'm just . . . still not quite myself. I know you were joking."

"Okay." Kinsey gave Beatrice's hand a final squeeze and released her to navigate a rush hour merging situation.

Nursing her coffee, Beatrice gazed out the window at the buildings creeping by. The sky was heavy and gray, desaturating even the most vibrant colors the city had to offer. Normally bright reds and yellows looked anemic and grim, as though they'd lost the will to fight against the color-leeching dictates of the sky.

A flock of pigeons burst out of a bare-branched tree as Kinsey drove past a small park, and the world blurred into bright smears of brown and gray.

Dammit. Was there anything that didn't make her cry today?

Beatrice sucked in a breath, surreptitiously wiping her eyes.

"Are you *sure* you're feeling up to this?" Kinsey asked. Even with both hands on the wheel, and her attention on the taxi edging into her lane, she hadn't missed Beatrice's soft sniffle. "I could turn around and take you home."

"I'm sure," Beatrice said, turning her gaze to the taxi's license plate—she fortunately couldn't remember any taxi-related jokes or experiences she and Julian had shared, so at least that was safe. She took a fortifying breath of heater-warmed air. "I want to get this over with. And it's not like I'm trying to run a marathon, here."

Kinsey pursed her lips in disapproval.

"Pretty sure the cops will call an ambulance if I pass out," Beatrice added, smiling softly at Kinsey's stubborn protectiveness.

"Hilarious," Kinsey grumbled, but she let the subject drop.

It was bustling inside the police station, but not as forbidding as Beatrice expected. The room where Detective Flores took her to talk was surprisingly devoid of harsh metal tables or two-way mirrors. It was almost cozy. A well-stuffed couch against one wall faced two padded chairs. A low table stood between them, a couple of magazines and a collection of comic strips stacked to one side. There was a window, and the walls even had vintage drawings of the Chrysler Building and Brooklyn Bridge breaking up the monotony of plain white paint.

"Sit wherever you like," Detective Flores said, sweeping an arm across the small expanse of the room. She was around Beatrice's mom's age, with short black hair that was streaked with gray at the temples, and laugh lines etched into the corners of her eyes. She had an easy competency about her that made Beatrice feel less nervous about talking to her alone.

Beatrice sat on the couch, dropping her tote bag at her feet. The half-finished latte she kept in her hands, needing the reassurance of the warmth between her palms.

Detective Flores shut the door and settled in one of the chairs. She'd brought a legal pad and a folder with her, but she set these both on the table and turned a friendly smile on Beatrice. "Thanks for coming down. I know it's a long trip for you. Especially when you're still healing. Are you feeling okay?"

"No worse than usual," Beatrice said, wriggling against the armrest in an attempt to find a little bit of support for her back. The couch was too deep for her to reach the back cushions without her feet sticking out.

"Throw pillow there," Detective Flores said, pointing to the other end of the couch. "Feel free to lie down, if that's more comfortable. Or you can put your feet up."

Beatrice hesitated. "Isn't putting your feet on a police couch some kind of felony? Vandalism of public property or something?"

Detective Flores's smile widened. "Only the real sticklers in the Etiquette Unit care about making arrests on that one. I think I can let it slide."

"Okay . . ." Beatrice kicked off her shoes and tucked herself into the corner of the couch, coffee still gripped in her hands.

"Better?" Detective Flores asked.

"Better."

Beatrice had thought it would be easier, going over the events of that day a second time. And it was, in a way. Detective Flores had taken her first statement, too, so Beatrice didn't feel like she needed to prove she wasn't lying. But there was a lot more stopping and going over the same thing over and over this time. Detective Flores kept prodding for more details and a specific sequence of events, since Beatrice's initial statement had jumped all over the place.

By the time they got to the part where she'd passed out, Beatrice's small reserve of energy was drained. There had been other witnesses by then—a couple art center employees who came out when they heard the fight, plus the medics and police and hospital staff who took care of things after that—so Beatrice's first statement had concluded after she lost consciousness.

But this time, Detective Flores kept going. "Tell me," she said, making a mark on the legal pad with her pen before meeting Beatrice's eyes, "what do you think prompted the attack?"

Beatrice had already been calculating how many minutes it would take from the time she walked out of the interview room until she let herself into Sasha's dorm room to crash for a few hours. It took a second to bring herself back to the present conversation. "What do you mean?"

"We know Julian had a past connection with the men who assaulted you, but we have some evidence they may have been contacted by a third party."

"A—A third party? Like . . . someone told them where Julian worked?"

Detective Flores nodded. "Do you know of any reason someone might want to do that?"

Beatrice opened her mouth to deny it, but nothing came out. Her first thought, that day—before she recognized Vito, before Julian got so angry at her—had been that Greyson must have set it up. He'd gotten other people to hurt Julian before, and he had seemed set on believing Julian had manipulated Beatrice into wanting to break things off.

But then Julian started yelling at her, telling her he used to be a drug runner, and she figured she must've been wrong. After all, it had taken weeks for Greyson to arrange for Julian to get hurt the last time. And it wasn't like Vito hadn't gone after Julian before. Beatrice had *met* Julian because he was trying to escape from the man. It seemed more likely that Vito showing up at his work that day was just an awful coincidence.

Beatrice clutched her coffee cup to stop her hands shaking. It felt like she was trying to force the pieces of three different puzzles together. Nothing she did could make them into one coherent image. "But—But—No. That doesn't . . . No. Last I heard, everyone was talking like those men attacked Julian because he used to run drugs for them."

"Well—"

"He *told me* that's what happened," Beatrice said. "He said he flipped on them to escape prosecution, and that's why they wanted to kill him."

"That's . . . not incorrect," Detective Flores said, tilting her head to one side as though reluctant to concede the point. "It was the initial statement he made when we spoke to him at the hospital. Of course, when we followed up, his version turned out to be an . . . oversimplification." Detective Flores scratched her ear. "Julian hasn't spoken to you about this?"

"I haven't heard from him since last week," Beatrice said. "What do you mean he was oversimplifying?"

Detective Flores only looked at her at first, and Beatrice was sure she was going to tell her it was police business and change the subject. "Well," she began, seeming to choose her words carefully, "after Julian made his statement, I followed up with the Assistant US Attorney who prosecuted the case against Vito Cipriani two years ago. She told me Vito and his associates used to find young people in shelters and hostels and hire them for a 'messenger service' to take packages all over the city. Most of the 'messengers' probably didn't even realize they were running drugs. Or if they did, they were getting paid enough they didn't care.

"I don't know how Julian figured out what was going on, but one day he walked into a police station with a package containing a couple bricks of cocaine he was supposed to deliver, and told them everything he knew about the operation. They passed him on to the Feds, who had been trying to bring Vito down for months, and the Feds offered him a deal in exchange for his testimony. The AUSA I spoke to seemed convinced Julian was a good kid in a bad situation. Didn't even think he'd been using. Thought he deserved a chance to get back on his feet."

"But—" Beatrice closed her eyes, shaking her head. Her mind skipped back to the last time she'd seen him—*Some of us have lives that are already so chaotic and riddled with stupid mistakes that no amount of bullshit planning could pull us out of it.* "But he made it sound like he knew what he was doing the whole time," she said, sounding more argumentative than she intended. "Like he only stopped because he got caught."

"That was the story I got, too," Detective Flores said, tapping her pen on the legal pad.

"Why would he lie about that?" Beatrice asked, more to herself—or the universe—than because she expected an answer.

Detective Flores lifted a shoulder. "Guilt? That happens sometimes. People feel guilty for things that happen outside of their control and try to take responsibility for it. Even if they had nothing to do with it."

Beatrice rubbed her forehead, trying to sort all this new information into what she already knew. What she *thought* she knew. Pieces of memories fought for her attention—The defeat in Julian's eyes when she first tried to get him out of the alley. The fear when he saw she'd been hurt. His head bent over her hand in the hospital.

And then, strangely, that day after Thanksgiving weekend when she tracked him down on the late train home. The way he flinched when she reached for his hand. His knuckles white as he told her he wanted to cut ties.

She had been sure—absolutely *convinced*—it was because he was angry at her. It was because of her he'd run into Greyson again. She was supposed to be his friend, and instead she'd put him in danger. He had every reason to be upset.

But then he turned up at her apartment claiming he wasn't angry at her at all. He'd wanted to cut her off, he said, because . . . because he wanted to protect her. He said he was afraid she was going to get hurt.

And the next day she ended up in the hospital.

Beatrice felt lightheaded. She'd spent so much time in the past week trying to convince herself that Julian was some kind of villain. That way, if he'd been using her, if he'd been lying to her since the day they met, then maybe it wouldn't hurt so much to know he didn't want her. It might mean she was gullible— naïve—to have believed him, but it should make it easier to put him behind her.

But how was she supposed to do that now? When she couldn't dismiss him as a criminal anymore? When it looked like she had been right about his good heart all along?

"Can I get you some water, Beatrice?" Detective Flores asked, her brow furrowed.

"No, I'm—I'm fine."

"We can finish this later if you're not up to it now. Though . . . I did want to let you know we made another arrest this morning. We picked up Greyson Sayer-Crewe on conspiracy charges."

Beatrice's heels hit the floor, her stomach clenching. "What?"

"I don't want you to worry," Detective Flores went on, holding up a hand as though to calm Beatrice. "As far as we can determine from the recording, Julian was the only intended target."

That was supposed to make her feel better? "Recording? What recording?"

Detective Flores hesitated. "Julian went to speak to Greyson yesterday afternoon. Without my knowledge—I'd advised him to stay away. But I think he was frustrated we weren't turning up any evidence that supported his theory that Greyson had organized the assault. So Julian went to his apartment and tried to get him to confess."

Beatrice let out a puff of air. "What happened?"

"He confessed," Detective Flores said, looking mildly impressed. "And made a few threats for good measure. There's nothing to worry about, though. We're taking care of this. Julian wasn't hurt, and we got him and his sister into a motel for a few days to make sure it stays that way. None of the threats appeared to extend to you, though it wouldn't hurt to stay with a friend or relative for a while if it would make you feel safer." Her frown deepened. "You sure I can't get you anything? You look pale."

"I'm okay," Beatrice said. She wasn't. She couldn't breathe.

She wanted to go home. She was overloaded with information and needed somewhere quiet and familiar where she could sort it out.

Pushing her cup on the table, she bent to yank her shoes on. "I'm sorry, I—Can we finish this later? I'm not feeling well."

"Do you need to go to the hospital?"

"No, I'm okay. I just—I just need some air." She tugged the last clumsy bow tight and fumbled for her bag as she stood. "I'm okay."

Detective Flores got to her feet as well. "Do you want a ride?"

"No, I can—I'm okay." Beatrice backed towards the door, stammered out a quick goodbye, and fled.

TWENTY-SEVEN

Julian knew Beatrice probably didn't wear her yellow peacoat anymore. Even if it had escaped confiscation to a forensic lab, he doubted the bloodstains would ever come out of the wool. So Beatrice must have started wearing a different coat.

But knowing it didn't stop his eye being drawn by every scrap of yellow worn by passing strangers. And it didn't stop the heart-clenching disappointment every time he realized it wasn't her.

There was no reason to expect her to be in the city anyway. She should be home, recovering under the care of her family.

Julian probably shouldn't have been in the city today, either. After he left Greyson's apartment yesterday, he'd gone straight to Detective Flores with the recording he'd made on his phone, and everything had snowballed again. He had to make more statements while fielding lectures from several detectives and the prosecutor handling the mugging case—all of them peeved at Julian for not trusting the system to handle it. And then there was a scramble to figure out what to do with Julian and Fabiana, since Greyson had threatened to pass Julian's address along to Vito's gang. Finally, Julian and his sister were deposited in a mo-tel outside White Plains for a few days—courtesy of some victim's services program—where Julian had to put up with another round of lectures from Fabiana regarding his monumental stupidity in performing a sting operation on his own.

But Julian still had a few things he'd needed to take care of in the city. He had a GED exam to sit for early that morning which had been scheduled for weeks, and he'd wanted to turn in his resignation to Mr. Fisk in person. He'd technically been on a leave of absence since the attack, and explaining things to Mr. Fisk face-to-face seemed like the least Julian could do, after everything he'd done for him.

Since he was in the city, Julian figured he might as well check with Detective Flores to see if they'd arrested Greyson. Then he could go home. It wasn't even noon, and he was already exhausted—an issue compounded by his heart's insistence on looking for Beatrice in places his head knew she wouldn't be.

By the time he mounted the precinct steps, he'd trained his eyes to the ground in front of him so he wouldn't keep looking for her. Which was probably why he didn't notice the person barreling out the front doors. They rammed into each other, the momentum spinning them around.

"Shit." Julian barely kept his feet, his hand going out to the shorter person's elbow to keep them from taking a swan dive into the sidewalk. "Sorry."

Accusatory gray eyes flicked up to meet his and pierced him straight through. Beatrice.

Julian's heart threw itself hard against his ribs like it was trying to leap the space between them. It was a leap it couldn't make, though. The chasm he'd created was too wide.

Beatrice looked strangely subdued in the dull grays and browns she wore. Her new coat was a bland, charcoal parka, the hood lined in faux fur. She wasn't even wearing her floral hiking boots. She had on a pair of perfectly normal, perfectly boring black hightops. Only her bag—canvas with a rainbow of psychedelic florals printed all over—nodded to the usual riot of color she presented to the world.

"I'm sorry," Julian said again, releasing her elbow. It was a grossly inadequate thing to say, but he didn't know how to make things right. He'd gone over it in his head dozens of times, trying to come up with something that didn't sound like petty, meaningless excuses. But if he'd ever landed on anything even remotely acceptable, he couldn't remember it now.

Beatrice fell back a step, a puff of air leaving her lungs and blowing away in the chilly breeze. She seemed about to say something, but then her gaze snapped to the ground, and she pressed a hand to her mouth.

"Bee?" He reached for her, an instinct to comfort briefly overriding his knowledge that he was the reason she needed comforting. He checked himself before he made contact, curling his hands into loose fists at his sides.

She shook her head, the toe of her shoe finding the edge of the stair. "I don't—You—" With a frustrated growl, she turned and marched down the last few steps, head down, arms folded around her middle.

For a split second, Julian froze. She clearly didn't want to talk to him. He should let her walk away, and take it as a sign to stop agonizing over whether there was any way to fix what he'd broken. He couldn't take back what he said, and he didn't have any right to expect her to forgive him.

But dammit, he couldn't let her slip away from him without even *trying* to hold on. He couldn't bail on her again. Not without a fight.

"Bee," he called, jogging after her until he caught up.

She didn't slow down. She wouldn't even look at him. Her gaze remained fixed stubbornly on the sidewalk.

"What are you doing in the city all by yourself?" he tried, because he didn't know how else to get her to talk to him. "What if something happened and you had to go to the hospital? Isn't anyone taking care of you?"

"Well, you know," Beatrice said, a surprising amount of venom in her voice. "When you've got a wholesome little organized life to keep up with, sometimes your bullshit planning overrides your common sense."

Julian stopped short, the blow hitting him right in the gut. "I . . . That was a shitty thing to say. I shouldn't've—"

"No, I get it," Beatrice snipped, spinning on her heel to face him. Her eyes were too bright, and her cheeks and nose were flushed pink. "I do. I know I'm weird. I know I get so hyper-focused on checking all the boxes that I forget to make sure that all those boxes are taking me somewhere worth going. I know all my stupid problems seem insignificant compared with some of the stuff you've had to deal with—"

"Bee—" Julian began, moving to touch her arm.

She flinched back, a tear cutting a track down her cheek. "You didn't have to kiss me," she said in a choked voice, hugging herself tighter. "I know you think I'm this . . . sheltered, naïve little petal, but you could have just said you weren't attracted to me. I would have understood. You didn't have to—You didn't—"

Julian couldn't take it anymore. He closed the last gap of space between them and cupped her face in his hands, trapping her gaze. "Anyone who thinks you're a sheltered petal isn't paying attention. You're the toughest person I know."

She let out a breathy sob, squeezing her eyes shut. "No, I'm not."

"Of course you are," Julian insisted, bending his head to see her face better. "Are you kidding? You're smart, and beautiful, and compassionate, and brave. You shine daylight over the whole world when you laugh. You're—You're the most wonderful, precious little gem of a person I've ever known in my life."

Beatrice pressed both hands over her face as another sob shook her shoulders.

Julian wrapped his arms around her, at a loss for what else to do. "Please don't cry," he said, his voice hoarse. Miraculously, she leaned into him, her forehead pressing against his collarbone through his sweatshirt. He bent his head, her thick, soft hair brushing his cheek. "I fucked up. I shouldn't have said any of that, at the hospital. You've got every right to hate me."

Beatrice made a furious sound between her teeth, her fingers digging into the fabric of his coat. "What's wrong with you?"

A lot of things. Though he got the impression she wasn't looking for an actual list. "Bee—"

She pushed out of his embrace, her eyes flashing behind the sheen of tears. "Are you suicidal? Is that it?"

"What?"

"They said you went to talk to Greyson yesterday," Beatrice said, throwing an open hand out towards the precinct's entrance. "By yourself. And he threatened to kill you. *Again.*"

"Well," Julian said, fumbling for an explanation that would calm her down, "I mean . . . I—I didn't think he'd try to kill me in his apartment. He usually tries to shift responsibility to someone else, so—"

"And that's supposed to make it okay?" Beatrice demanded, her shoulders going up in a caustic shrug. "It's been less than a week since he arranged to have those assholes drag you into an alley to kill you, but it's fine to waltz on over to his house in pursuit of more death threats because, hey, he'll *probably* wait until you're out of the building before calling in the next round of hitmen. Yeah. *Great plan.*"

A cautious little seed of hope, which Julian thought was long dead, moved in his heart, its roots inching tentatively down. It didn't make a lot of sense—Beatrice was reaming him out, as she had every right to do. It didn't seem like ideal conditions for hope to grow. But she wasn't wishing him dead, or accusing him of lying to her. If a lifetime of sorting his sister's affectionate, protective rants from her angry, accusatory rants was anything to go by, Beatrice was upset because she cared about him. Maybe he hadn't fucked things up as badly as he feared. Maybe there was a chance he could make things right.

If he could just come up with the right thing to say.

"I'm sorry," he began.

"Don't apologize," Beatrice snapped. "Just—Just—" She balled her hands into fists at her sides with another frustrated sound in her throat. "You keep talking like everything bad that happens to you is your fault. But it's not. It's *not*. And I don't understand why you're so dead set on making everyone else think it is."

"I . . ." Julian pushed his hair back with one hand, trying to find the right words. Years of questionable relationships and bad luck had put him out of the habit of being open about this kind of thing. He couldn't hope for eloquence. But maybe honesty mattered more anyway.

Julian sucked in a lungful of damp, chilly air, his hand falling to his side. "I was in such a bad place when I met you. It seemed like my whole life was made up of a series of disasters, and I never had a chance to recover before the next one came along. If it wasn't losing people I loved, it was dealing with Greyson. Or breaking my hand. Or getting mixed up with gangs because I was too stupid to question what was going on. Or not being able to hold down a job because everywhere I worked went out of business, or downsized, or—or who knows what else. I couldn't get on my feet. Every time I tried, I got knocked back down.

"And then you came along. And it was like . . . like you put out your hand and said there was a way out from under all the cave-ins and debris that I'd been trapped under. You made me think maybe the disasters didn't have to go on forever. That I could . . . rebuild. And maybe I could be okay." He swallowed the hard lump in his throat that was making it hard to speak. "How could I not love you for that?"

Beatrice's mouth twisted, and she dropped her gaze to the pavement. "Julian—"

"I love you, Bee." He touched her cheek, and she turned her face into his palm, her eyes tight shut. "I think I loved you from the second you started sassing me in that library. Your optimism, and your kindness, and your humor. Everything about you. And it scared the shit out of me. I was terrified that someday another disaster would hit, and you'd end up right in its path. And I didn't know how to protect you."

"You don't—" Beatrice set her jaw and slid her arms inside his coat, hugging him tight. "Dammit, Julian."

Julian held her close and pressed a kiss against her hair before he could think better of it. "I was so scared I was going to lose you."

"But you didn't," Beatrice said, her voice muffled in the fabric of his sweatshirt. "I'm right here. I'm fine."

"I know. I fucked up. Just tell me how to make it up to you, and I'll do it. Anything."

Beatrice shook her head. "That's . . . God. I'm sorry you've had to deal with so much crap. I'm sorry you lost your parents, and you got stranded with a terrible step-family. I'm sorry no one was around to help you when you needed it most." She tipped her head up to look at him, her eyes stubborn and about as far from delicate as anyone could get. "But you can't just take yourself out of the picture because you have some stupid, misplaced guilt about how you're going to ruin my life. Like you don't make me laugh, or make me feel safe. Like you don't remind me how to breathe. Like you don't even matter. You can't do that to me, Julian. You can't. I love you too, you colossal moron."

The cautious seed of hope in Julian's chest shot its roots deep and wide, sprouts poking up everywhere like wildflowers in a wide, sunny field. He was afraid to breathe, in case he heard her wrong. But there was no hate in her eyes. No resentment. Just that unfathomable compassion he'd never done anything to earn. "You do?"

"Well, yeah," Beatrice said, her cheeks coloring as she tugged lightly on one of his hoodie strings. "What, you think I'd leap headlong into a knife fight for just anybody?"

Julian felt himself smile. "I wouldn't put it past you. You did save me from getting knifed the first time I met you."

She wrinkled her nose, the corner of her mouth twitching. "Yeah, but . . . that was still you."

He didn't know what to say to that. His heart was too full to translate what he felt into words. He pressed his lips against her temple, her cheek. She smelled like flowers, and coffee, and coming home.

"I love you, Bee," he murmured. "So much."

She made a tiny sound on an exhale and turned her mouth up to his.

Julian sank his fingers into her wild, beautiful hair, pouring all his hope and love into the kiss. He wanted to show her how much he missed her. How sorry he was that he'd hurt her.

Her hands moved over his back, to his shoulders, her body melding to his. She responded to his touch as though he'd never let her down. As though she trusted him. As though she loved him.

With one last kiss, Julian pulled back, his fingers trapped in Beatrice's hair. There was still one small problem. "I can't buy a house."

Beatrice's eyes, which had been half-lidded and unfocused a moment before, snapped open, her eyebrows pinching together. "What?"

"I can't buy a house. Not anytime soon. I had to quit at the art center, so I'm back to looking for work again. And I think I want to look into art school—I was talking to my boss about it when I turned in my resignation, and he says he can help me work out the portfolio stuff." Julian slung his backpack off his shoulders to hang from one elbow and dug around inside until he found the spiral notebook that held all his notes from the last few days. Handwritten lists and charts, and printouts of applications and portfolio requirements for several colleges. They were disorganized, and he really needed a better place to store them than between the pages of a spiral notebook, because they kept falling out. Somewhere in all that mess was the paper he wanted. "There's a college up in Syracuse that seems to have really good teachers, and I could do an art education program there, so I could get into teaching once I was done. But that's at least four years of the starving artist track, which means I'll probably be stuck renting crappy apartments or living with crappy housemates. And that's without factoring in grad school, which is a whole other beast—"

"What are these?" Beatrice asked, pulling the papers down so she could see them better. "You wrote up plans? To . . . to figure out when you can buy a house?"

"Not very good ones." Julian found a page where he'd scrawled some math. Even his most optimistic reckonings of future savings looked bleak. "There's no way I'm buying real estate of any kind for at least a decade. I'll be lucky if I can swing for a shitty car in the next two years."

"Julian. Stop a second. I have no idea what you're talking about."

"You said you wanted a house and a steady paycheck," Julian

said, meeting her eyes. "I can't guarantee either one right now. I just want you to know what you're getting into here."

Beatrice blinked, her gaze flicking to the notebook and then back to him. Her expression was blank, her mouth slack, as though he'd started speaking gibberish sometime in the last thirty seconds.

"I'm not even sure I could get a gig teaching art after I graduated," Julian said. He was rambling, but he couldn't stand the silence. "Art funding is so patchy. I could end up either splitting time between multiple schools or moonlighting as a dishwasher or something. Or only being a dishwasher, and questioning all my life choices while I pay off student loans on a minimum wage salary for the next thousand years—"

Beatrice huffed out a breath that was almost a laugh, her smile sparking life into the dull, gray world. She grabbed his coat and pushed up on her toes, her mouth pressing against his.

The papers in Julian's hand rustled as he grasped her waist to steady her. He could taste the smile on her lips as she kissed him again and again.

"You don't have to buy me a house, you ridiculous person," she said, bouncing onto her heels again. "The house was symbolic."

"But you said—"

"—that I wanted a place where I can breathe. And you already gave me that. All that other stuff doesn't matter, as long as I've got you."

Julian touched her chin with his thumb, brushing an off-center cluster of freckles. He waited for some new anxiety to overtake him. Some new reason this couldn't work. Could never work.

But the only thing overtaking him was a warm glow of joy. He didn't know what he'd ever done to deserve the love of someone as beautiful and good as Beatrice. He just knew he was going to do everything in his power to make her happy, for as long as she let him.

"You really should be resting." He found her hand and threaded their fingers together. "Come on. Let's get you home."

TWENTY-EIGHT

Beatrice stood in her favorite hole-in-the-wall cafe in Syracuse, listening for her order to be called over the din of students and nine-to-fivers getting their mid-afternoon fix. She was paying less attention to the textbook in her hands than she should have been, but she couldn't quite get herself to focus.

It was a gorgeous summer day, and the cafe's doors were propped wide open to let the lazy breeze diffuse the scent of sun-warmed air into the earthy aroma of fresh coffee grounds.

It felt like a new start, after all the stress of the past few months. For a while, it had seemed like Beatrice's life had turned into a courtroom drama. Vito and the other two men who had attacked Julian took plea deals—putting Vito behind bars for six years, and each of his cronies for at least four—so that part was over with quickly. But Greyson's trial had dragged on for weeks. Beatrice ended up dropping the two online courses she'd enrolled in for the spring semester because the trial was taking up so much of her energy.

Looking back on it, she was surprised she and Julian had made it through in one piece. He'd been under as much stress as Beatrice. Probably more, since he had a longer history with Greyson, and very little faith in the system. And very little support, besides his sister, whose support was like that of an angry Rottweiler. And Beatrice, who was never sure if her presence was actually helping. Especially since there was an angry bulldog in her gut that wanted to join in whenever Fabiana's inner Rottweiler started growling at threats.

Beatrice had all but forced her family to act as backup support for Julian. It was easy enough to get Nath on board—he'd practically adopted Julian into the family already. Beatrice's parents took more work. They both seemed stuck in over-protective mode, after Beatrice's stay in the hospital, and after some of the nastier details about Beatrice's relationship with Greyson came out. Joyce felt guilty for not realizing things were so toxic, and Mike seemed to think the best way to keep Beatrice safe was some kind of Rapunzel situation. Unfortunately for Julian, that meant his reputation was taking the brunt of their leftover panic.

It took more than one long, hard conversation where Beatrice flat-out refused to back down before her parents started coming around to Julian. To their credit—once Mike gave Julian the most mortifying obligatory if-you-hurt-my-daughter speech Beatrice had ever heard—both Mike and Joyce seemed willing to see the good in him. Within a few weeks, they even seemed to like him.

Which was good, because Greyson's defense team seemed to be taking a 'they deserved it' defense. They did their best to shred Beatrice's character, making her out to be some kind of femme fatal. And Julian got it even worse. They painted him as a jealous, lowlife gangbanger, no better than Vito or his thugs.

But the recording Julian had made of Greyson's confession was impossible for the jury to discard. And it was backed up by dozens of pieces of evidence. Vito had identified Greyson's voice in a lineup as the person who'd called to inform him of Julian's work address. Greyson was on camera buying the burner phone that call had come from. The prosecution had even acquired receipts and documentation from a private investigator Greyson had hired to determine Julian's whereabouts, including an email Greyson had sent the night before the attack asking for Julian's work address.

It took the jury only half a day to convict. Julian had slumped forward in his seat next to Beatrice, his face blank, like he couldn't quite believe it. Greyson seemed shocked that the jury wouldn't take his side, and furious to be taken out in handcuffs. He snarled at his attorneys under his breath, but didn't so much as glance at the gallery, though Beatrice, holding Julian's hand tightly, had one hell of a glare ready for him if he'd tried.

Julian operated in a stunned sort of haze for the next day or two, as though at any moment he expected to get news that the verdict had been overturned, or Greyson's lawyers had found a last-minute loophole. But no such calls ever came. Greyson was sentenced to ten years in jail, at least seven of which had to be served before he could qualify for parole. And that was it. It was over. They could move on.

"Iced mocha for Bee?"

Beatrice stowed her neglected textbook in her bag and thanked the barista as she swiped her coffee from the counter. A moment later, she was on the sidewalk, the breeze playing with her hair, sun warming her shoulders, canary yellow canvas sneakers slapping against the pavement.

The day was warm, but her classrooms were always chilly, so she'd compromised by donning high-waisted jeans with a huge, messy slash in one knee which she'd scored at a thrift store last week, and a plain gray tank topped with an oversized, black-and-yellow plaid shirt she kept open, but tied at the waist.

It had taken a while for Beatrice to work up the nerve to tell her parents she was planning on transferring to the same college in Syracuse where Julian would be starting his art degree in the summer. She wanted to tell them she was changing majors first. They were somewhat confused by that, but took the news in stride. Beatrice hadn't wanted to press her luck, so for a few weeks—while Julian was waiting for applications to come back and deciding between programs, and the two of them were working through the details—she'd let her parents believe she was going to keep commuting into the city for another two or three years.

When she finally broke the news of her transfer, their stunned silence at least gave her time to lay out all her reasoning, and get out in front of the *you can't change colleges as an excuse to be with your boyfriend, Beatrice Bauer, and I don't care if you* are *twenty-one* lectures. Syracuse had lower housing costs than New York City, cheaper tuition, and Beatrice could do away with the dead weight of long commutes every day. She'd miss taking classes with Kinsey and Sasha, but they were set to graduate at the end of the following spring semester anyway. Even if Julian hadn't been a significant factor in her decision, there were plenty of good reasons to transfer.

"Beatrice!"

She spun around at the sound of that voice, a grin spreading across her face. Julian ran up to her and scooped her up, startling a happy squawk out of her.

"Hi, there, Simba," Julian said, his eyes scrunched up under the force of his smile.

"Hey, handsome," Beatrice said, locking her ankles around his hips. She pinched the brim of his ball cap and lifted it off his head, dropping it back on the wrong way around a moment later. One of his black curls stuck out adorably from the opening in the back. "There. Much better."

"Why, because now I match the '90s grunge thing you're doing today?"

Beatrice snorted. He'd come straight from his shift at the burrito place near their apartment and was still wearing the teeshirt with their logo on the back. The only thing remotely grunge about him was the tattoo climbing up his arm and under his sleeve to touch his neck. "I don't think backward baseball caps were ever grunge, dear," she informed him, tracing one of the swirling lines of ink creeping from his collar with the tip of her finger.

"But they were very '90s," Julian said.

"True." Beatrice raised her eyebrows. "Though I don't care so much about our clothes matching decades. I was thinking more along the lines of how I'd rather not get a visor to the forehead when I kiss you."

"Mmm," Julian said, managing a sage expression for about half a second before the smile she loved so much crept back. "Sounds dangerous. You might put out an eye." He cocked his head to one side. "An eye patch might be a cute look for you, though. Maybe in lime green?"

Beatrice wrinkled her nose. "You gonna shut up and kiss me or what?"

"Anything for you, Bee," he said, the words brushing her skin.

His kiss was sweet and unhurried, and it filled her up with sunshine. She rested her forehead against his when their lips parted, basking in the steady rhythm of his breath.

"I love you," Julian said.

Beatrice grinned, a blush warming her cheeks. No matter how many times he said it, her heart leapt in recognition. "I love you, too."

Planting a light kiss on the end of her nose, Julian set her down. Hand in hand, they strolled down the warm, breezy street.

It was a new semester and a new start. Beatrice didn't know what that would bring with it—what obstacles would crop up, or what unexpected joy. But whatever happened, she had the man she loved beside her, holding her hand and reminding her to breathe.

And she knew they would figure it out. Together.

ACKNOWLEDGMENTS

First, thanks to my family, who are not only ridiculously supportive, but give excellent advice. My awesome dad let me ask him strange medical questions about the logistics of getting stabbed and gave me detailed answers and some knife-fight tips to boot. Any errors remaining in either the medical details or the alley fight are my own. Sorry I couldn't use that idea about driving Vito and Greyson off a cliff to their watery doom, Dad. It was a good one.

My amazing mom lets me run random plot problems by her when I'm stuck, and is proof-reader extraordinaire. She's also been the number-one encourager in my sudden re-direction from pursuing traditional publishing to throwing myself headlong into self-publishing. Thanks for believing I can do this (even when I don't) and cheering me on. I love you. And sorry about making you cry with that one scene.

My rad little sister lets me run even more plot problems by her and asks all the right questions to get me back on track. She also regularly tells me, "you said that about the last book, too," whenever I start wailing about my inability to write, for which I am incredibly thankful, since I always seem to forget about that part a month later. *AN: U rok!*

Thanks to all the Scrib folks who read all or part of this book and made helpful suggestions. In particular, Shannon Murphy, who stayed with me from start to finish, even though she had to wait a crazy long time for me to finish the last section, and encouraged me with her comments; and Regenia Pillitteri, who marathoned the whole thing in record time, gave me lots of good notes to work with, and said lovely things about the book when she finished. Thank you both so much.

Extra-super-mega-thanks to Christa Bakker and Melinda Perzy, who never let me get away with anything, whether it was goofy typos or misplaced character beats, and who both gave me pep talks and virtual snacks when I needed them most. You're two of the most nicest, encouragingest, bad-assest writers I've ever had the pleasure to know.

For my lovely proof readers, Brae, Kymberly, and Karen, I've composed a special poem:

Thank you, dear proofers,
for the help! Your hair looks great
and you are the best!

And last but not least, thank you, dear reader, for coming along for the ride. I hope you enjoyed spending time with Beatrice and Julian. I certainly enjoyed writing about them, even when it was a battle to get the words out. I hope to see some of you back for the next book!

ABOUT THE AUTHOR

Rachel Stockbridge is an indie romance author based in central California. She's a lifelong accidental nomad with a music degree in Electronic and Acoustic Composition (yes, really) and an ever-growing collection of books, Post-its, and art supplies. She believes everyone deserves a happy ending and a healthy dose of humor in their lives, and tries to write stories that provide both.

When she's not writing, you can usually find her crafting, making art, dabbling in hand lettering, playing music, or running D&D campaigns.

If you enjoyed this novel, please consider writing a short review at your favorite retailer's website. Honest reviews help other readers find me. Even a sentence or two helps me out immensely!

If you're interested in finding out when my next book is released (and getting a few sneak peaks!) you can sign up for my newsletter by visiting my website, rachelstockbridge.com

Made in the USA
Middletown, DE
25 September 2020

20559751R00175